Best Wishes

Not Quite A Judas

Philip Baker

'He that hath a secret to hide should not only hide it, but hide that he hath it to hide.'
Thomas Carlisle. C 1850

AuthorHouse™ UK Ltd.
500 Avebury Boulevard
Central Milton Keynes, MK9 2BE
www.authorhouse.co.uk
Phone: 08001974150

First published by AuthorHouse 4/12/2011

ISBN: 978-1-4520-9101-3 (sc)

This book is printed on acid-free paper.

Author's Note.

I wish to acknowledge the information and assistance
so willingly given to me by some of those fortunate to
live in that part of Devon known as 'The South Hams'.
The sad story of the boy footballer, as told by John,
is the version known to him then.

In writings, and on current maps of Dartmoor, spellings
of place names, and even the location of those named
places, can – and do – vary considerably. Eg:-
Three Barrows/Three Burrows. Stall Moor/Stahl Moor.

I also wish to acknowledge help with my researches, from:-
U-boot Archiv, Cuxhaven-Alterbruch, Germany. David Carter
and Robert Henderson, Canada. Jak Mallman-Showell, UK.
And my many friends and acquaintances in both Germany
and the U.S.A.

Illustrations are copied from:-
Das junge Reich. (1935) H.J. Im Dienst. (1940)
Thanks also to Jeff Hammond.

Prologue. A Time To Tell ?

I woke with a pounding heart, and it was a little time before I could get my breath back. This was the first time in years I'd had that nightmare. Nevertheless, the crash landing at Nuremberg, and the subsequent fire, was every bit as vivid – and just as terrifying – as it had been in reality, that night I first arrived in Hitler's Germany – almost sixty years ago.

But on this occasion, for the first time, and for some quite inexplicable reason, my Grandson – Young Bill – had been there too, as a shadowy but clearly recognisable onlooker. Whilst I lay back recovering from the shock, it came to me that this must surely mean the time had come to share my story, and my secret, with the lad.

When one gets to my time in life, secrets can become a burden, and Grand-children can either be a pleasure – or a pain in the neck, and sometimes a bit of both. But I've been very lucky, especially with the trio I see most often. After Anna died, I decided to make over the big house to my son Eric and his family. Maureen said she wanted me to stay on there with them, but I knew I'd get no peace with her running the place. (Every time anyone gets out of a chair, my dear Daughter-in-Law rushes to plump up the cushions and to straighten the rug.) My son finally suggested building on a Grandpa Flat; but I felt even that would be too close. So, early in 1995, I moved about half a mile, taking the ground floor of a small terraced house backing onto the Park. There Mrs Wilson 'does' for me five mornings a week. She leaves after I've started my lunch, and that suits us both very nicely.

Maureen is a caring soul – in an overbearing way – and she has made it a rule that at least one of the children must look in on me as they walk home from school – 'Just to see if you're still alive' – as Eric so charmingly puts it. The nice thing is that the kids don't seem to find it an imposition, and often two or all three of them come, and they usually stay quite a while too. Both the girls are good company, and they are always welcome; but its Bill who somehow finds the time to stay the longest. He's the youngest, and I have to admit it – my favourite. I try to excuse this by telling myself that with two older sisters, and a mother like Maureen, he needs masculine support; the more so because he's the only boy amongst my ten Grand-children. But – if I'm really honest – its because he's all the things I had hoped his father might be.

My son was lively enough as a little boy, but even before leaving school Eric had begun to take life too seriously – and rather too cautiously. Of course I never say as much, but he was over-cautious when it came to girls, and his pals snapped up all the best ones. So that's how he got left with Maureen, for whom he works damned hard, trying to keep her in the style she wants to rise above. Maureen has always insisted that her boy should be addressed as 'William', but I well remember him as a determined toddler, screaming at her through his tears, 'I'm not a William-boy – I'm a Bill-boy – I won't be William!' And because of that I usually call him 'Young Bill', which helped to strengthen the bond between us – though his mother took it as yet another slight on my part.

It pleases me that Young Bill is quite an athlete. He goes to my old School and usually gets into the teams. I often toddle along to support them, and the youngster seems to appreciate that; perhaps all the more because his father is always 'too busy' to go near the place – even though he's an Old Boy himself. This Saturday, Bill was due to play his first match for the Second XV – which is quite something when a boy is only just past his fifteenth birthday. Maureen had long-standing plans, to take the girls up to Wembley, for the Hockey International, and then on to the Royal Ballet for a touch of culture afterwards. Eric would be working as usual, so it was decided that Bill should come to me for his lunch, and we'd go on to the match together afterwards.

The lad hadn't visited me for a couple of days, but he arrived unexpectedly early – saying the match was off because of frozen ground. Nobody could have missed the black-eye he was sporting – it really was quite a shiner. However, he chose not to mention it, so I didn't either. In his first year at the school, Bill had won his Weight. Immediately after the presentation of the trophies, the newly-appointed Headmaster announced that 'In keeping with modern thinking, Boxing is to be dropped from the school's list of Activities'.

Bill was disappointed by this and, acting on the moment, he then asked if he could take the cup home with him – because it would never be presented again. Everybody but the Sports Master was horrified by this audacious suggestion. But I was well pleased; remembering how Jock Cochrane and I fought for that cup, which had just been presented by some relative of his. We had a terrific battle. The judges making us equal, and the Referee asking for 'One more minute's boxing.' After which he gave me his casting vote, and so mine was the first name engraved on that cup. Nevertheless Jock and I remained good friends. When he rose to dizzy heights in the Royal Navy, the school decided to honour him – and to cash in on his rank and title – by appointing him to the Board of Governors.

The boy doesn't know about this, but I have asked Jock to raise the matter of the boxing trophies, and nobody pulls the wool over the eyes of Admiral Sir Jock Cochrane. There should be the names of three generations of Hardwicke's engraved on that cup – so who could have a better claim?

But, there being no Boxing, I knew there had to be some other explanation for that eye; one which Bill would most probably tell me in his own good time.

"It's a pity about the match." The boy sounded disappointed. "But at least I'll not have to go dashing about in boots that are killing me!" I'd heard that tale before. The lad was growing fast, and the last time he'd needed new boots his mother had declared she didn't understand Rugby, and so his father must get them. As always, Eric was 'too busy' and the resulting delay had done the boy's feet – and his performance on the field – no good at all. Knowing that, I marched him off, there and then, to the shop where we settled the matter in just five minutes. I took care to keep the receipt for his parents, in case they should be foolish enough to raise objections, to my having paid for something they well knew they ought to have bought themselves.

Young Bill is always hungry, so we ate before starting back, arriving just as a blizzard began – which meant he had to wait before trying out those 'Ace' new boots. Instead we built up a roaring fire and watched sport on television together, but when the Woman's Hockey came on he wasn't interested, so I switched to a Video, of Wrestling, which I'd recorded earlier. We both knew it was mostly 'fixed' but he enjoyed it thoroughly, for he was never allowed to watch it at home, because Maureen considered it to be 'uncouth'. Then we got our own early tea, with hot buttered toast – made at the fire – from the fresh crusty loaf I'd bought that morning. We agreed it was a great improvement on the electrically scorched pre-sliced 'plastic' bread we had to put up with at his house.

After helping me clear away the tea things, Young Bill picked up my old photograph album, which had come to light whilst I was searching for something else the previous evening. He started asking questions about those fading snaps – giving me the opening I'd been seeking for quite some time.

"Put it down," I told him firmly, "whilst I tell you a story. You can look at the pictures of it afterwards." Reluctantly he laid it aside. "If you have a secret," I began, "you need to be very careful about whom you share it with. It's not enough to be careful – you must be very very careful, about whom you decide to tell ... Years ago Bill, I shared a secret with a good friend – and I'm still not sure how much I ought to regret doing it ... but I suppose I'd better begin at the beginning – or you'll get all mixed up."

I found it a relief – to be telling that tale again – for the first time in many years. But this time I was determined to tell everything, in a belated attempt to clear my own conscience – by using the boy as my Confessor. Hoping that he, in his youthful innocence, would be able to justify my act of betrayal – with all its tragic consequences.

At first Bill showed little enough enthusiasm, probably considering himself too old for 'stories'; but his interest was soon aroused when I told him it was a true story, and one that I'd not be telling his sisters. A story about myself – which he was now man enough to understand. Then he settled himself on the floor, into his favourite listening position, leaning back against the sofa, with both arms clasped around his knees – and I knew I would have a good audience. Rufus, my old Red Setter knew it too, and he wriggled across and lovingly laid his head on the boy's stockinged feet.

"It all began before the war, Bill, when I was perhaps a year older than you are now."

Junkers 52

1. Nürnberg. 1936.

Darkness was already falling as we came in to land at what I must now think of as *Nürnberg* – in Adolf Hitler's Germany. So, even though my companion had nobly given me the best seat, there would be almost nothing for me to see. But, in spite of that, it was an experience that I shall not forget in a hurry.

From the very moment our three engined *Junkers* 52 touches down, it begins lurching drunkenly from one side of the runway to the grass on the other – and back again. Luggage falls onto us from the overhead nets whilst the pilot fights to regain control. A tyre has burst, then the wheel collapses, and showers of vivid sparks are flying past my window as it drags along the tarmac.

It must be the undercarriage leg has given way completely, because the wing drops, sending the still spinning port propeller into the ground, causing the juddering engine to shriek its dying protest. The plane staggers on, swinging off to the left, bouncing onwards until the wing collides with something very solid – slewing us round even more violently before coming to a sudden stop. Then – for a fleeting moment only – there is an eerie stillness.

I have only confused memories after that – of a fire starting outside the aircraft. Of moans and cries for help ... screams of terror. Of seeing Erich slumped forward, his head at an un-natural and worrying angle against the back of the seat in front. Of a small explosion, when all the lights went out. There followed a strange rushing sound as a swirling wall of orange flame swept through the cabin towards us. I ducked down to avoid it.

Next, I was bending over Erich, who had somehow slipped sideways and was doubled up over his seatbelt. I had the devil of a job getting him upright enough for me to reach the buckle, and all the while, I was frantically looking for a way out. Then I saw light through a jagged hole, where the wing had partly torn away from the fuselage.

My next clear memory is of being out in the open, strangely aware of the night air cold on my thigh – although I was wearing long trousers. I was running over grass towards on-coming headlamps, but – try as I would – I could not go fast enough, because I'd lost a shoe – and had Erich's lifeless body in my arms. I well remember how bright the stars were that night – how the flames behind us lit up the blood on Erich's face. They told me afterwards, that when the first Ambulance man came to help me, I just bowled him over – running on as if he hadn't existed.

Erich was showing the first signs of returning consciousness as we got him onto a stretcher. In fact the pair of us had been extraordinarily fortunate. Although we both had singed hair, scorched hands and faces, and even holes charred through our clothes, neither of us had any real burns, not ones that mattered anyway. I had a big lump coming up on my forehead, two long rips in my trousers, with matching ugly parallel grazes across my thigh; but they were as nothing to the nasty gash above Erich's temple.

After these injuries had been treated it appeared my friend was recovering, but I have no recollection of how I got to the hospital; only of lying in a bed, repeatedly re-living the horrors of the crash, seeing it – as though in slow motion – again and again. But I ended up knowing no more about how I'd got myself out of the plane, nor how I managed to take my new friend with me.

I found myself wondering. *Can it really be that only a month – perhaps five weeks – have passed since I first met Erich Falkenberg, at Al Kahla'ab, on the Persian Gulf?* I'd gone there to join my parents for the summer holidays. So much happened in that time, and by now it seemed as though we had known each other for years. Al Kahla'ab was only a tiny place in 1936 – on the edge of the desert, well down the Gulf, in the middle of nowhere – but they've found a lot of oil since, and its part of a big port today. Of course I didn't speak any Arabic at first, and I quickly learned that the only youngster of anything like my own age I could talk to was Erich, the son of *Herr Doktor* Falkenberg, who was German – and the only Doctor in a hundred miles or more.

It was lucky that Erich Falkenberg and I took to each other at once, and we very soon became close friends, even though I didn't understand any German before we met. Erich knew only a little English, and although we were both learning French we did have some unfortunate misunderstandings over language. The first problem was our respective Christian names. It seemed natural for me to call him 'Eric', but he insisted I must call him '*Eearich*', and he too struggled with my 'John' – the hard 'J' being almost unknown in German – and it was some time before I could get him not to use the German form '*Johann*', which he pronounced as '*Yohaan*'. Because of the language difficulty we tried to spend our time together doing things, rather than getting bogged down in long tiresome tri-lingual conversations that too often left us both utterly confused and frustrated.

Fortunately, the Olympic Games were being held in Berlin that year. The Nazis had made them into a huge event, and Erich – like most Germans – was suffering from 'Olympic Fever'. As a result our lives became one long *Sportfest*. Whenever it was cool enough, we practised many of the scheduled events on the wide sandy beach, using palm ribs for Hurdles and High Jump, with another as a Javelin, and a brick as a Shot. In competition we often showed more enthusiasm than skill, but the honours were about evenly divided.

My new friend was just sixteen, and so almost two months older than me, and just a little taller. A slim, fair haired, good looking boy, with an infectious – though sometimes rash – enthusiasm, for whatever business we had in hand. He was a fine swimmer, and could always win in the water, but on land I was usually the faster, especially over the longer distances. In spite of this, Erich was determined we should run a 'Marathon'. (He had a theory that with his 'second wind' he'd be able to beat me.)

However there was at first nothing we could pick out as a distant finishing post, nor anything we could turn around before heading back to the start. Then Erich pointed to the top of a palm tree just showing above the dunes away to the East.

"How far that *Johann?*" He asked eagerly. "For sure big adventure to race into unknown!" (At times like that – whenever he was challenging me, or asking a really serious question – his ice blue eyes seemed to look right inside me, as if to be certain I was giving him a truthful answer.) So far as I could judge, it would be something over a mile and a half, possibly two miles tops, and that would be much shorter than the Cross-Country I was used to at school – but plenty long enough in that climate.

"Four or five kilometres." I replied. (His maths wasn't too good, so I always had to do the conversions – and I thought a little exaggeration wouldn't hurt.) "But we'll have to start really early – just as the sun comes up – before it gets too hot."

We each left word we would be going for an early morning swim, and possibly having breakfast at the other's home, which left us free – though probably hungry – for the whole morning. The air was pleasantly cool, and almost fresh, as we strolled towards the beach. The light had that blue-pink quality, typical of dawn over a tropical sea. Erich wrapped our shirts around his water bottle and hid it under a thorn bush. The Palm tree was out of sight, hidden behind a small headland, so we agreed to run on damp sand, close to the sea – where the going was better. When the trunk of the tree came in sight, each of us would be free to choose his own route – first to touch tree to be the winner. Then we were ready to start.

"Fertig?" he asked eagerly. *"Los!"* We set off at a steady trot, side by side. It was my reputation at stake, so I lengthened my stride and moved ahead. Erich dropped in behind, matching me step for step. The tops of the distant mountains were now turning pink as the sunlight caught them; before very long the sun would strike down on them – and – on us. So I knew it was important to cover as much distance as possible before then.

There was a full mile to go, as far as I could judge, for the tree was not yet in sight. Again I increased my pace in the hope that Erich would crack. He should have been well back, but our slow speed must have suited him, because there were still only a few yards between us. At the bend in the coast I was alarmed to see the sand giving way to bare rock, which rose in a gentle slope before us, but dropped sheer into the sea on my left. We pelted on across the headland as the sun leapt over the eastern mountains, and immediately I felt its warmth on my heaving chest. Then I saw the trees. There were in fact three of them – and in that light it was difficult to judge the distance – though they looked barely half a mile away, standing further back from the sea than I had expected. The rock surface became rougher, and it dropped quite steeply down towards a small sandy bay. I slowed a little, looking for the best route to the trees – and that was when Erich passed me. He was panting hard, but making the most of the downhill, by running far faster than was really safe, and I wondered what we'd do if he fell and injured himself there. Although he was taking the most direct line, I bore away right, towards the higher ground on which the three trees stood.

In the growing heat we pounded on – and still he did not see it. I was heading for a deep dry Wadi, that would give me an easy way to the higher ground. Stretching from it, towards the sea, lay a streak of wind blow powdery sand, in a drift that was narrow at the mouth of the Wadi, but further out – in Erich's path – it was wider, and piled much deeper too. He was plugging on gamely, but his head was lolling – that famous 'second wind' either hadn't come, or else it had already gone.

I turned into the mouth of the Wadi, treading the pale sand which was soft but not deep enough to check my speed. I glanced across at Erich, and at that moment he spotted the drift in front of him. He faltered, looking desperately to left and right, before plunging on again ankle deep, and kicking sand high before him – until he pitched forward onto his chest. He got up and fought his way on, falling to his knees again before he was clear of it.

I ran on for the last hundred yards and finished. Thankful for its shade, I leaned against the hairy brown trunk of the nearest Date Palm, struggling to get my wind – until I remembered my opponent. Wearily I made my way back to the top of the dune. Erich was running still, though achieving little more than a walking pace – his front caked in sand that was darkened with his sweat. Heaven knows where his energy sprang from, perhaps he was dreaming that Adolf Hitler, his beloved *Führer,* was watching; but for the last twenty yards he ran on up the slope – head up and chest out – throwing his arms up as he breasted an imaginary tape. Slowly he sank to the ground and rolled over onto to his back, white teeth shining through a mask of sand as he fought for breath. When I sat down beside him, Erich raised himself on one elbow, rubbed the sand from his face, and grinned at me.

"Tell me – *Engländer,*" he demanded aggressively, "who was the *Dummkopf* who want Marathon in first place?" I let that pass, because he already knew the answer, but before long he's d recovered enough to suggest a swim.

Leaving our shorts hanging on a tree, we refreshed ourselves in the warm water. We had no need for towels either, because the sun was so powerful we were near enough dry before we reached the trees again. It was at Erich's suggestion we agreed to swim back to avoid getting burned by the sun. That made good sense but there was no hurry, and we were both pretty well drained by our long run in the growing heat. Erich appeared somewhat disheartened by his defeat, and our efforts to make intelligible conversation gradually flagged and died. I was happy enough just to lie there, re-living my success, but – as usual – Erich's mind was more on the future.

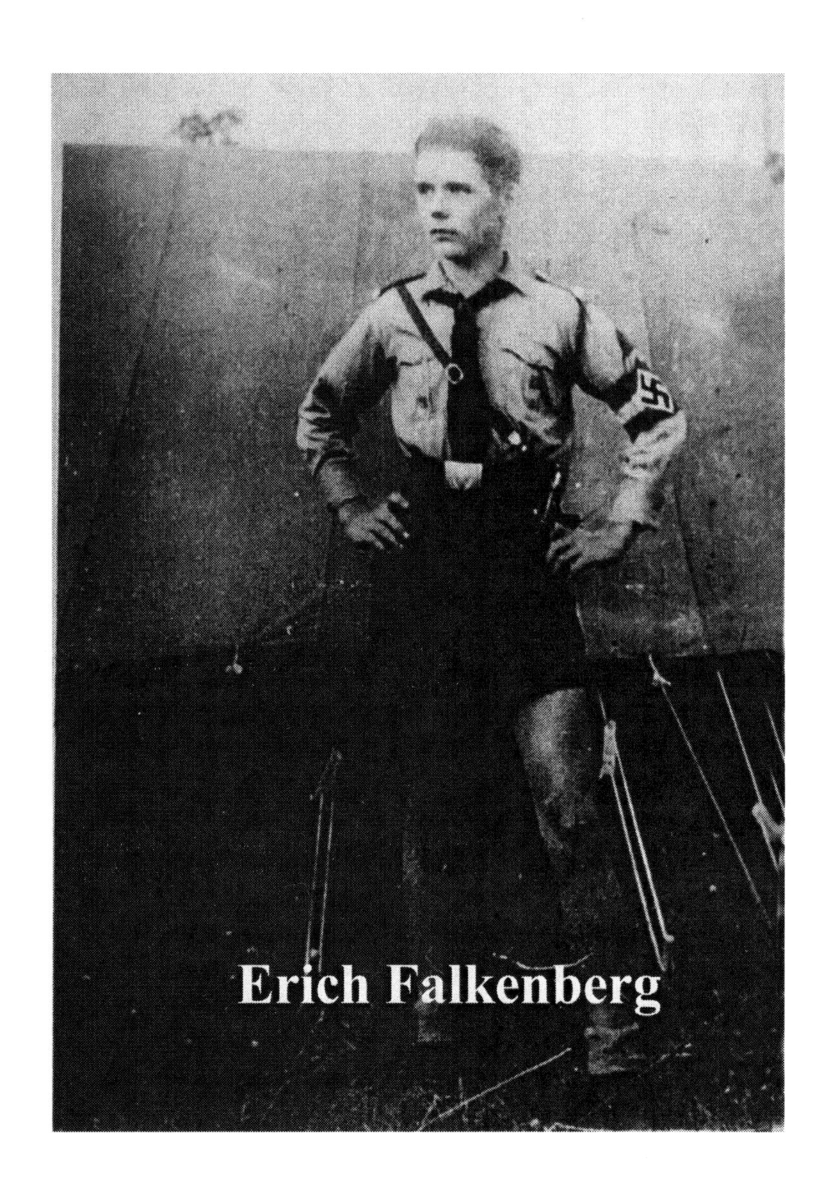

Erich Falkenberg

2. Erich, and an Emergency.

So we lay – in moody silence – grateful for what little shade there was. The three date palms stood at the edge of a depression, which was encircled by low dunes that completely hid it from all directions. I was idly staring up at the delicate palm fronds arching gracefully above us, smugly congratulating myself on being both faster and a little bit smarter than Erich. And I'd almost fallen asleep when something brushed against my thigh. I glanced down in time to see another pinch of sand arrive – from Erich's direction. I chose to ignore that, and the next – and the next. But the large handful that thudded down on my belly was rather more than I could be expected to take. I leapt on top of Erich – which was exactly what he'd been hoping for.

I suppose if I'd stopped to think that we were both still naked, I might perhaps have hesitated. Not that it would have made any difference with Erich in his state of mind then; he was always freer in that, usually being the first to strip right off. It wasn't that I minded, but I was conscious of what I'd been brought up to at home; and what was expected at school ... where every boy was made to go under the shower with the others after games, but the slightest suggestion of nakedness at any other time had all the Staff in a panic.

It was the first time we'd come to grips, but that didn't worry me, for I rather fancied myself then – and I'd always considered Erich was a bit on the skinny side. However he proved to be surprisingly strong – and a good tough wrestler too. My small weight advantage was fully matched by his longer reach and greater skill. Neither of us could keep the upper hand long enough to gain a submission, and so we rolled each other to and fro around the little arena, fighting on until we were both so exhausted we had to settle for a draw. But it was typical of Erich that he wouldn't even agree to that until he'd got my firm promise to face him again, in the morning, when we'd both be fresh, and we agreed to meet on the beach as usual.

"Erich." I asked, "Where did you learn to wrestle so well?"

"In *der Hitler Jugend*, that's Hitler Youth, that's like Boy Scouts, only more. We make physical fitness, *Kampfsport* and 'fighting spirit." As he went on it sounded to be a lot of fun. Plenty of games, camping, and public service, with marching, rifle shooting and other military style training thrown in for good measure. (Although Erich did not mention it at the time – there was a quite different, and very political side to the story. One which I was to learn for myself – and that came about rather sooner than I could have expected.)

I'd thoroughly enjoyed that scrap, which was more of a test of stamina than a proper contest, though Erich liked to refer to it as *Eine Mutprobe*, a test of courage. And rightly so, because neither of us had known the other's strength or skill, nor – much more importantly – whether he could, or would, keep his temper under control, or if he might have turned it into a real fight. Whatever it was, that tussle left me with a new respect for Erich.

We'd been resting for less than a quarter of an hour when – and without any warning – Erich suddenly leapt to his feet, slipped on his shorts, and set off sprinting towards the water. He was showing off as usual, and calling me to follow him. So, of course, it was up to me to try to catch him – although I'd much rather have saved my breath by walking. I dashed after him through the shallows, but stubbed my toe on something, and fell – full length, with an enormous splash. Only then did my friend stop, to shout insults about my clumsiness.

The sun was beating down as we swam out around the headland, and I kept dipping my head and shoulders, regretting I'd not got a shirt to swim in – uncomfortable though that was. We ploughed steadily on, and twice I felt a twinge of cramp that came to nothing, but my right leg was definitely getting tired. Before long Erich was looking back. Then slowing, and waiting for me – and my leg had become almost useless.

"It's no good." I shouted to him. "We must go ashore!" Seated at the water's edge I looked with horror at my foot, now badly swollen and discoloured, as was my ankle. With some difficulty I got up and tried my weight on it – and thought I was standing on razor blades. My head swam with the pain – until the sand came up and hit me. Whatever had grazed my toe had been poisonous, far more poisonous than Fire Coral, so what had ... *God! What if it was a Stonefish I kicked? Only hours without the correct treatment and I could be dead!*

In the distance, the village floated shimmering in the heat, raised high above the ground in a mirage, and beyond that – two miles or more from where I was – lay the little hospital. I could only pray that *Doktor* Falkenberg would know what to do, and had the necessary medicines on hand. By now his son was kneeling beside me, anxiously examining my leg.

"Erich." I mumbled, "Perhaps – maybe – I think – a Stonefish. Is it two hours I've got?"

"Are you sure? Not sit there John!" He was almost shouting now.*"Auf! Auf Stehen!* On You Feet! *Schnell!! Schnell!!"* He helped me up, and then took my arm about his shoulders, but every time I hopped the pain shot through my leg, and we made very little progress before I was close to fainting. Next he carried me piggy-back, making good speed although he was staggering under my weight.

"Iss not good. I not get you there like this." He gasped. "I pull you instead." The cool water soothed my leg as he towed me by the arms, striding ahead and going faster than he had done on land. But each time my face went under, I choked and struggled. So he twisted his fingers into my hair and hurried on. Towing like that hurt, but it didn't begin to match the pain at my other end. My eyes were closed against the sun, and ... the water ... gently rippling past my ears ... made soft sweet music ... like a sort of ... lullaby ...

* * *

The sun was scorching my back, and sand was moving, moving erratically – *Sand, moving above my head?* No. It was I who was upside down – across Erich's shoulder. He stumbled, almost falling, banging my leg in the process ... and a wave of nausea swept over me.

* * *

It was cool again, and darker too. A white figure came and went. Something stabbed my arm. *Doktor* Falkenberg loomed over me.

"You will sleep now John. All is well. My boy got you here – by himself – but only just in time." I tried to focus on the wavering shape at the foot of the bed.

"Dummkopf Engländer!" Erich's voice came from miles away. I wanted to reply – but he had already dissolved into the blue mist that now engulfed me.

* * *

My recovery was quick, thanks to the combined efforts of my good friends, the Falkenbergs. Then, when I was almost fit again, *Herr Doktor* brought some extra good news for me. He had managed to pull strings so that I could travel home cheaply, and with Erich too. Better still, we'd be able to spend a few more days together at his Grandparent's home in Fürth, close to the city of Nuremberg. And that before I had to be back in England for the start of the Christmas Term.

Two days later *Herr Doktor* decreed that I was fully healthy again. Only then did Erich cautiously remind me of his challenge. I could only accept, knowing he'd not look too kindly on my genuine excuse, that I'd be weaker after my time in bed, and the consequent lack of exercise. No sooner had I agreed, than Erich proved himself to be a real sportsman.

"*Gut Mann, Johann.* But I give you time to be more *kampffahig.* We not fight until last day here at Al Kahala'ab." He had solved one problem, but I had another in that direction, because I was more than a little envious of Erich's new style swim trunks. They were jet black, with a chromed buckle on the white belt; but I – like most Englishmen at that time – had to wear a hideous full length scratchy woollen costume. I couldn't be sure of winning, but I badly wanted to look as smart as him when we met for our final contest, so I cut away the top half of my old maroon coloured school costume to make my own 'trunks'.

Erich made a big thing of it that morning, setting out a lot of rules – a few of which I managed to understand – but I knew he'd fight really hard to avoid losing the all-important single round. It was a fine, hard, but fairly fought scrap, and he nearly had me three times, but I ended on top with him pinned face down in a Full Nelson. His face was in the sand, but I'd no hesitation about that, because he'd already had me the same way twice. When I was sure he was close to submitting I allowed him to turn his head sideways, so he could breathe better, but at the same time I put on all the pressure I could. He had me worried before he did finally submit. Although he said nothing at the time, I did notice him working his shoulder for a couple of days afterwards. Erich took his defeat like the sportsman I knew him to be, offering me his hand whilst murmuring "I'll do better next time *Engländer.*"

As it happened my crude stitching just wasn't good enough and – to Erich's un-disguised amusement – I'd very nearly lost my 'trunks' before that scrap was over. I said nothing at the time, although I had my suspicions, that Erich might have been doing his subtle best to help that happen. But I am quite certain that he did nothing to avoid it.

Although trunks were just beginning to be 'respectable' by then, Mum created quite a fuss when she found out what I'd done. But – for once – Dad took my side, and he persuaded her to sew them up properly for me before I set off for Germany next day.

My Father drove Erich and myself some forty miles north to a rickety jetty where we were dismayed to find the modern once-a-week coastal steamer was out of service, and we had to board its rusty replacement instead. Whilst exploring her I found the maker's plate and, believing that Erich hadn't spotted it, I decided to show off my knowledge.

"She was built in Britain, on the river Clyde, in 1855." I told him.

"*Ja!* And she only have one painting after that I think!"

We were soon feeling hungry, but one look into the galley was quite enough to persuade us to stay that way, because neither of us wanted to risk a dose of the Gulf's special version of the dreaded Gyppy-tummy.

"Erich, you always say your Arabic is better than mine. So, at the next stop, you go ashore to find something for us that's safe to eat." He was obviously unwilling. "Don't worry." I told him. "I'll stand on the gangplank, to make sure we don't sail until you're safely back on board." Erich was gone a long time, and a jabbering seaman was trying to drag me out of the way when he returned with something a bit more wholesome. We had been allocated bunks in a tiny airless four-berth cabin, but the blankets and mattresses looked so disgusting – and probably verminous – that we settled for a bench out on deck.

At long last we made our way up the *Shatt al Arab*, and went ashore at Basra. Taken all in all, it had been an unpropitious second leg of our three thousand mile journey. And it was with some relief we changed to the doubtful comfort of the train to Baghdad, but at least we did both manage a little fitful sleep.

I had been greatly looking forward to the fourth leg, when we would be leap-frogging from one country to another – in a German airliner – en route to Nuremberg. Standing on the ground, the three engined *Junkers* 52 looked very impressive, both safe and powerful, even though – at first glance – it did appear to have been built from corrugated iron sheeting. I was a little scared and very excited, because this was to be my first flight, and my first visit to Germany, which many people then spoke of as 'Hitler's Germany'. Shortly after take-off, Erich produced a letter of introduction to the Pilot, but the plane was full, and for long enough we were thinking it would not work. After landing and eating at Damascus, Rhodes, and then Athens, clouds closed in around us as we flew above the mountains of Yugoslavia.

At Belgrade we learned there was no plane to Nuremberg that day, and we had to continue on to Berlin.

Soon after take-off, the Air Steward brought an invitation for us to go forward to the cockpit. The young Pilot explained the many gauges and controls to us, and he even allowed Erich to hold the joystick for a few minutes. We had a wonderful view of the seemingly endless plains of Hungary, but about halfway to Berlin the plane began to buck again, and we were immediately asked to go back to our seats, with a firm reminder to fasten our seat belts.

There were three hours to kill before our flight to *Nürnberg* was due to leave Berlin, but that gave Erich time to telephone his Grandparents, advising them of our time of arrival. They decided it would be too late for them, and we were to take a taxi to Fürth. With that sorted out, we boarded another, older looking, *Junkers 52,* for what turned out to be a thoroughly bumpy trip. The Steward was insistent that we kept our seat belts tight at all times, and he would not risk serving hot drinks. By this time I was wearying of Air Travel, and thinking the greater part of the adventure was over, and how welcome a real bed would be.

* * *

My Grandson looked up at me, as though wondering whether he ought to ask questions.

"Yes Bill?"

"Gramps. How big was your airliner, and you said it had three engines – with propellers? I've never seen a plane like that."

"There were seats for twenty passengers, one behind the other, ten on each side of the gangway. Of course there were also two Pilots, and a Steward. Very different from the giants of today. And, Yes ... three engines with propellers, one on each wing, and one in front of the pilot. I think some passengers liked to see several engines – it probably made them feel safer. Rather like the biggest Trans-Atlantic liners, which often had an extra funnel – a dummy one, just for show – which made them look even more powerful, and therefore likely to be safer, and go faster too. And later on, during the war, the Germans used a lot of these Junkers 52 aircraft as transport planes, and for dropping paratroopers too."

Young Bill seemed satisfied with that, and I went on with my story.

3. Fürth, and a Surprise.

I awoke to find two elderly persons bending over my hospital bed. In very fast excited German, the woman explained that they were Erich's Grandparents. From then on, and with tears running down her cheeks, she spoke so quickly that I could only recognise occasional words – repeatedly it was *'Danke! Danke!'* Finally she bent down and kissed me. The man then gently moved her aside and started speaking slowly.

"My boy, maybe you do not yet know, there are only five survivors from the twenty on board the aircraft, and none of the others say they helped you get our Erich out of the wreckage. So it must be that you did it alone. And for that we cannot, ever, ever thank you enough. Erich is a tough boy, a real Falkenberg, and he is recovering – but only thanks to your bravery. From now on John, you will always address *Grossmutter*, and myself, as *'Du'*."

Fortunately I already knew enough to greatly appreciate his allowing me that degree of familiarity – which is something of an honour – signifying close and lasting friendship; for which we have no equivalent in England.

They left me, moving back to Erich's bed on the other side of the ward. He was lying there – head heavily bandaged – but he gave me a cheery wave. I replied, but then lay back, trying to take in what I had just learned. Fifteen souls had perished, but I and my friend had lived – surely that called for a silent prayer. (*Grossvater* had said I got Erich out on my own, but to this day, I still wonder whether some unknown German lost his life helping us to escape.) We were allowed out of bed for lunch, and then the Press arrived. Of course they wanted photographs, and I soon noticed that whilst Erich could speak freely to others about the crash, he just would not talk to me about it at all.

The hospital authorities seemed unwilling to let us go, and it was not until late afternoon that our clothes arrived, still damp from the laundry. Even so Erich and I looked like a couple of young tramps as we all climbed into the taxi that would take us to Fürth. Only then did it occur to me how fortunate it was that the Grandparents did not come to meet us. Because, had they seen the fire, they would probably have believed us dead; and at their age, one or both could have had a fatal heart attack.

The old couple made me very welcome in their home, and they both danced attendance on us until *Grossmutter* insisted we went off to bed very early in the evening. Only then, when we were alone for the first time since it happened, did Erich say anything about our escape. As I sat on the edge of my bed undressing, he came and stood in front of me, then clicked his heels and bowed, before beginning a very formal little speech.

"John, my good friend. I am deeply grateful for your bravery in saving my life. I say – for myself – and for my parents, *Vielen, Vielen Danke!* We are good friends now, and we will always be good friends. You and I, for the rest of our lives, no matter how far apart we be, nor whatever may happen to us, we shall always be friends." I found it all most embarrassing, and if he had been less sincere, or less serious, I might well have told him not to make such a drama of it. But when he bent down, taking my hand in both of his – I just had to look away. Because there were tears welling in his eyes – and it would never have done for me to see him crying.

We just stayed like that, saying nothing. Never before had anything remotely emotional crept into our friendship – and neither of us knew how to deal with it. That was a moment I shall certainly never forget, neither the uncomfortable silence that followed. Nor my feeling of shame when I recalled the all-too-English understated thanks with which I'd acknowledged what Erich and his father had done for me – in my hour of greatest need.

It came as quite a relief when he finally turned off the light and settled down to sleep. But sleep would not come for me. At first I tried not to, but I could not avoid re-living all the horrors of the crash. Seeing them, over and over again – in slow motion – as in the hospital. But I ended up knowing no more about how the pair of us got out of that burning plane. In the short time we'd known each other, we had become close, and to know each other well. Yet – as I'd learned only a few minutes previously – Erich could still surprise me with his German manners and thoughts.

However, by next day we were almost back to normal, so far as one can be following an experience like ours. *Grossvater* was a fine old man, a sterner version of my own Grandfather and, like him, a retired Army Officer. In spite of this he showed – by a frown, and a barely audible snort – that he clearly disapproved when Erich came down to breakfast in his *Hitler Jugend* uniform. But I thought he looked fine in the brown shirt with its be-swastika'd scarlet armband and black neckerchief. With the black shorts he wore a broad black leather belt, its shoulder strap supporting his *Fahrtenmesser*, and the bright square buckle bore the *H.J.* Emblem and *Blut und Ehre* motto. White stockings, worn with black shoes emphasised the deep tan of his skin. All in all, I was more than a little envious of his appearance – with the possible exception of the bandage around his head.

My clothes had all been ruined and I'd lost everything else in the plane, so *Grossmutter* took the two of us on a grand shopping expedition – and nothing was too good for me. She spoiled us both and we enjoyed that – which is more than I can say for the rest of the day, when we were shown off to her many friends and relations. I very quickly learned that it's not all fun being a hero, and Erich too was finding it hard work carrying his self-imposed burden of obligation. Indeed it was easier, for both of us, after he forgot himself enough to drag me out of bed the following morning.

And that morning's post brought an unexpected package addressed to Erich. He unwrapped it immediately, and found a long blue presentation case which looked as if it might contain a really good wrist watch. My friend opened it eagerly enough, but then his face fell.

"From my Uncle, in Solingen." He said sadly. "*Onkel* Wolfgang is an important Nazi, but he can never remember when my birthday is – and he's probably forgotten he gave me one of these when I first joined the *Deutsches Jungvolk*." Erich turned the case so that I could see the sheathed *Fahrtenmesser* inside – which was identical to the one that already hung from his belt. Whilst he read his Uncle's letter I began to examine the new knife. It was certainly a high quality piece, of the standard pattern, with the Hitler Youth's diamond shaped badge set into the black chequered grip. The usual blackened *Blut und Ehre* motto was deeply worked into the highly polished single-edged blade. However, the other side was something of a surprise. Erich's initials were beautifully etched across the top, and below them, stood a bare headed boy in what I was to learn was a typical *H.J.* pose – hands on hips and legs apart – his uniform complete in every detail; and below his feet, a graceful curving scroll carried a brief legend, in a most ornate Gothic script.

By now Erich was reading aloud from his Uncle's letter, translating into English for my benefit.

" ... a most unusual order. Twenty Extra Quality *Fahrtenmessers* for the sons and grandsons of managers in the Krupp Works ... a bar of superb quality steel sent especially from Essen ... it was meant to be just enough for the twenty blades – but we just managed to squeeze one more out of it, especially for you. Take good care of it Erich. It has an edge like a razor – and it is the only one we'll make with a design like this. See that you live up to its message." He reached for the knife and then pointed at the blade.

"Look John, its me standing there! So that's why *Onkel* Wolf insisted that I wore my summer uniform – for the photograph he took last *Weihnachten* ... but I think you'd say 'Christmas'."

"Its a superb knife." I said enviously. "But what is that message Erich – its too difficult for me to make out?" He read it slowly.

Eine Junge so hart so Krupps Stahl. That is from *Der Führer's* speech at Potsdam; Hitler was saying he wants the Youth of Germany '... to be a cruel unflinching Youth, as hard as steel – Krupp's steel'. But my Uncle has made it read 'A boy as hard as this Krupp Steel' – meaning me – and that's going to take some living up to!" Erich only needed a moment to slip the old knife off his belt, and to replace it with the new one. And from that day on, I hardly ever knew him to be without it, although he should not have been wearing it when he was out of uniform.

Erich's friends in the Hitler Youth were all wildly excited about a visit Adolf Hitler was due to make in two days time. They were to help line the route, but there was disappointment, and even jealousy, because some other units would actually be marching in the procession to the *Rathaus*, where *Der Führer* was to make his speech from the balcony. (Erich found it difficult to understand why I laughed every time he used the word – which seemed so inappropriate for the Town Hall.) In spite of his evident eagerness, G*rossmutter* did not want Erich to take part – saying he was not fit enough – suggesting that he would not be allowed to parade with a bandaged head. However, over the telephone, the *Gefolgschaftführer* was most insistent that Erich would be needed, lest there be too few boys present for their allotted section of pavement.

Almost two hours before *Der Führer's* train was due to arrive, we set off to the Station. The whole town had an air of expectation about it, and scarlet be-swastika'd flags or banners were hanging from every building. Erich formed up with his *Schar* and marched to the main street, where the boys lined the curb in hot sunshine. I stood behind him, and a crowd soon gathered around me. Loud-speakers on lamp-posts began to blare martial music. At intervals this was interrupted, and the crowd were urged to show the loyalty of their town, by giving a great welcome to *Der Führer* – the man who alone, had brought work and prosperity back to their town after its years of depression – and the one who would lead their nation on to future greatness.

As time for the procession grew nearer, the growing crowd began to press forward, and the *Gesfu* ordered the lads to take hold of each other's belts. Then he stood in front of them, angrily grumbling to the *Scharführer* about absentees, and doubting whether the boys would be able to hold the crowd back when the great moment came. Now Erich intervened, very respectfully.

"*Herr Gefolgschaftführer.* My friend is here, behind me. Could not he help us?" Irritably the *Gefolgschaftführer* snapped back that it would be quite impossible for anyone not in uniform. But then he stopped, looking very hard at me.

"Have I not seen you – your photograph – in *Die Zeitung?* You are the English boy – from *der Bruchlandung!*" I nodded. "Please help us now, *Der Führer* has need of men like you. Stand here, in our line, beside your *Kamerad* Erich."

When the loudspeakers announced that *Der Führer's* train was entering the Station, everyone surged forward, forcing us into the gutter. Away to our left, a band struck up, followed by the sound of marching feet. The air of anticipation grew noticeably, and again the crowd were pushing forward, straining to see. Storm Troopers and Policemen strutted up and down, ordering them to stand still, and us to stand firm. All eyes were on the corner around which the head of the procession must surely come at any minute.

A Hitler Youth Leader suddenly appeared, flanked by the flags of the *Jungvolk* and the *H.J.* The drums of the combined bands were painted in the distinctive flame pattern, whilst the *Fanfare* trumpet banners bore either the

Sieg Rune or the square and swastika, according to the age of the musician. Next came long columns of uniformed boys and girls, all staring rigidly ahead. After them, portly be-medalled veterans of the 1914-18 and earlier wars, followed by a large contingent from the Labour Corps, marching with polished shovels on their shoulders. Storm Troopers pounded past us – then soldiers with rifles and fixed bayonets. And all the time a growing roar of approval from the crowd and – finally – the cry *'Der Führer – DER FÜHRER – DER FÜHRER KOMMTT!'*

We could no longer hold them back, and the open space was barely wide enough for the marching troops. The noise became deafening. *'Unser Führer! Sieg Heil! HEIL HITLER!'* They had seen the big three axle Mercedes – and now the Police were pushing us back, trying to keep the roadway clear. A forest of arms shot out over our heads – in *Deutsche Gruss;* the 'German Greeting', which was accompanied by the cry *'Heil Hitler!'* on all sides. Then, directly before me, stood the object of their adulation, upright in the car, arm raised in *Gruss.* He turned from left to right – acknowledging the cheers – a slightly ridiculous figure in a too large military cap, that looked as if it might drop down over his ears at any minute. But his personality was magnetic – and because of that I can recall absolutely nothing of those who were riding in the car with him.

Immediately beyond us the Storm Trooper's line broke, and the crowd surged forward bringing the car to a halt. A girl of about eleven, dressed in the white blouse and blue-black skirt of the *Jungmädels,* was forced forward against Hitler's car. Instinctively she stepped up onto its running board, to avoid cutting or bruising her knees. I could see the sudden look of horror on her face when she realised what she had done. But Adolf took it in his stride. He bent down, gently took her cheeks between his hands, turned her face up to his – and said something reassuring. Then he quietly asked the crowd to stand back, so that the girl could get down without being hurt. They of course obeyed – and the car drove on – leaving one bemused *Jungmädel,* with a story she would surely tell to her grandchildren.

More cars passed, then the pressure of the crowd eased, and a few went away. However, we had to stay on, to listen to the speech – a long ranting impassioned speech that was so distorted by the loudspeakers that I could not understand any of it. In all we had to stand for something like three and a half hours before being dismissed – without a word of thanks – or even an acknowledgement that we boys had held firm whilst men of the *S.A.* had broken. Perhaps the honour of seeing and serving Adolf Hitler was considered to be reward enough in itself.

After that parade, *Grossmutter* decided that I must see something of what she discreetly described as 'The Old Germany'. So, early the next morning, we were whisked off for a day's sight-seeing in nearby *Nürnberg*. We started with a visit to *Grossmutter's* youngest sister. *Tante Elfriede* was a maiden lady, who proudly wore the uniform of an officer in the *Frauenschaft* – the principal Nazi Women's Organisation. She immediately took charge, insisting that I must see everything. First the ancient castle on its mount, which I enjoyed, especially racing Erich to the top of the great tower – from which we had a magnificent view over the whole city. Then on to Albrecht Dürer's House, which I found boring. Next we had to see the *Deutschen Hof* Hotel, from the balcony of which Hitler took the salute – as boys of the *Adolf Hitler Marsche* passed with their standards, en route to the huge stadium for *Reichsparteitag*. The *Deutschen Hof* was just a big hotel, though Elfriede spoke of it reverentially, as though it was an ancient cathedral. Later on she was most insistent that we must stay overnight so we could all enjoy the new floodlighting.

Despite *Grossvater's* vocal objections, we spent the night crowded into her tiny flat, which over-looked the vast *Adolf Hitler Platz*, with the ugly but historic, and now skilfully lit *Frauenkirche*, at its centre. Elfriede spoke in glowing terms of how – if she was not on duty – she would watch the big parades which frequently made their way through the city.

"When he comes himself, I always use binoculars, so as to bring *Unser geliebte Führer* closer to myself." This was greeted with a clearly audible snort from *Grossvater*. It had already become quite clear to me that neither of the Grandparents even began to share her enthusiasm for everything National Socialist; and as soon as we were clear of her flat next morning *Grossvater* very quietly expressed doubts as to whether Elfriede even knew what *National Socialismus* was, let alone understood where it was leading Germany. Not until we were back at Fürth – and on our own – did Erich tell me, very firmly.

"You must not repeat what *Grossvater* said John – about *Tante Elfriede* – just in case the wrong people might be listening to you." By then I was beginning to understand the significance of these repeated warnings.

* * *

After the crash, the airline had offered to fly me home – for free – obviously thinking it would be good publicity if they could show I still had faith in their planes; and I certainly enjoyed being treated as a very important passenger.

Back at school I started a great battle with my Form Master, and eventually the Head, but in the end I won; being allowed to drop Latin – which I hated – and to take up German instead. Spurred on by my wish to communicate properly with Erich, I made progress, and actually surprised the authorities with my grasp of the living language – something I'd never even begun to have with Latin.

Oddly enough, it turned out that Erich was to be the one who would have the greater need to speak my language, and not vice versa.

John Hardwicke at *Nürnberg* Castle.

4. Noss Mayo. Devon.

At the start of 1937 *Doktor* Falkenberg took a post at the London School of Hygiene and Tropical Medicine, and I saw something of his family during a short visit to their flat at Easter. My parents then wrote saying they would soon be on leave and back in England, probably by mid- August, so arrangements had been made for me to remain in Devon, with Granny, until they arrived.

Once again the Old Lady suggested a friend should come and stay with me at her cottage in Noss Mayo. Knowing as I did, how much Erich hated living in London, and what good company he would be, my new chum was the obvious choice. Whilst I waited for Erich's train to arrive at Plymouth Station, I found myself regretting that he hadn't come two years earlier; for then I'd have been able to tell him, 'We'll take a train, change to a paddle-steamer, and that will drop us off right at our front door!' In actual fact, Pope's Landing where the ferry tied up in Noss Mayo, was perhaps a hundred yards from Granny's cottage – even so it would have been a nice bit of 'One-up-manship' on my part. But, sadly, the ferry no longer ran, having been unable to compete with the much less exciting motor bus which we now had to take.

It was dusk by the time we reached Noss Mayo. Even so, Erich was clearly delighted with the village, and intrigued by the old whitewashed cottage with its rose-grown wrought iron porch, and the one tall twisted stone stack topped by a single drunkenly leaning chimney pot. Fortunately my Grandmother took to Erich at once. although I did notice her frown of disapproval when she spotted spotted the *Fahrtenmesser* on his belt. (It must have been the swastika in the badge she objected to, for she never complained when I wore my own sheath knife.)

Erich shared my room. And on that first night he lay on his bed, gazing across at the mysterious mass of Coombe Down, then no more than a tree-topped silhouette against the western sky. The single window was set unusually low in the wall, almost at floor level, so we could also see the dark sparkling waters of Noss Creek, reflecting the lights of the Globe Inn, and the straggle of houses that lined the road at the foot of the Down.

"*Besser ist* ... is so much better than street lamps and neon signs." Sighed Erich.

"Wait until you see it in daylight!" I told him. "Its really beautiful country round here. Just wait till I take you to see the sea."

* * *

Knowing it would be nicely past High Water, I roused Erich for an early dip next morning. We only needed to cross the road and run down three stone steps before diving into the water. We swam down our creek, and then across the bigger one to land on the Newton Ferrers side, where we rested, giving Erich the chance to get the lie of the land around his new home. Whilst we sat there, a couple of Oyster Dredgers drifted past on the ebb tide.

"They'll make their way to the mouth of the River Yam," I told him – using the local pronunciation of Yealm. "Then across Wembury Bay to the open sea, and I'll take you to that a bit later on." By the time we returned, eager for breakfast, two more of the stone steps were showing. But in a few hours, all the water would have gone, allowing the villagers to walk – on stepping stones – so they could arrive, dry shod, at the steps leading up to the road on the opposite side of the creek.

Granny packed us a generous picnic lunch and we set off for the cliffs, and what I liked to think of as the 'Real' Sea. I led the way past the old Fishermen's cottages at the head of the creek, then on by the little school and up the rough track, heading South towards The Warren; leaving the two tidal creeks – like Noss Mayo itself – half-hidden in the trees far below us. At first Erich just couldn't understand why we had to climb so high to find the sea, but, at the brow of the hill, we crossed the Worswell Lane, and had our first view of the English Channel, calm and blue – and empty. Our route continued between stone-walled fields which soon gave way to scatterings of gorse and bramble, beside a rough roadway.

"This is the Nine Mile Drive," I told Erich, "at the turn of the Century, Lord Revelstoke had had his men digging here for weeks, cutting into the sloping green downland, creating a superb scenic carriage drive for his Royal Guests to enjoy whilst they were staying at the nearby Great House of Membland."

From the top of Blackstone Point we had a clear view westwards, beyond Great Mewstone, to the mouth of Plymouth Sound. To my joy a couple of battleships, together with their escorts, were leaving the Sound and coming our way. My friend had talked so often about the growing might of Germany, and I was glad he should now see such a show of Britain's strength. Erich watched as the ships came nearer.

"They are fine looking, John, but old and out of date. Our German Pocket Battleships, will all be new, better armed, and better armoured – and much faster too."

I knew he was right, but of course I didn't want to discuss that – so we scrambled down to the little beach at East Hollowcombes – for another swim. After the white tropical beaches we had shared, he wasn't too thrilled with the dark sand and sharp shingle there, but it was too soon for me to tell of the treat that lay in store for him later in the week. This was the first time Erich had swum in a northern sea and I could tell that he found the water chilly, though he was too tough to admit it. But he certainly enjoyed the challenge of swimming in waves and amidst the jagged rocks – in my Real Sea – far from the safer, but over-crowded holiday beaches, and their swarms of noisy tourists.

The weather stayed glorious and we took full advantage of that to explore the district together, though our greatest pleasure came from swimming, mostly on the rocky unvisited shore below the Nine Mile Drive. Each day the tides were later, until the times were right for me to share my great secret with Erich.

"Today," I challenged, as we left Granny's. "Will you swim with me, Erich – and ask no questions – wherever I go?" Of course he had to agree, as I'd always known he would. At Hollowcombes, I hid our clothes behind a boulder and then sent him to wait for me at the water's edge. He was bursting to ask why, but my steely glare kept him silent. A moment later, my preparations being completed, I followed him into the sea.

As soon as we were well clear of the cove, the tide took hold, sweeping us rapidly away. Erich realised this at once, and he turned appealingly to me.

"No Questions!" I shouted. "Just follow me – exactly. If you don't, you'll probably drown!" (There was more than a little truth in that too.) We hardly needed to swim, except to keep clear of the waves that surged dangerously against the sharp rocks – making a landing almost impossible. Soon the two Great Rocks came in sight.

"Keep with me Erich, very closely now!" I gave the order firmly, knowing he'd doubt my sanity for leading him towards those wave-swept barren rocks, with only sheer cliffs visible beyond them. Even so he followed me across the tide, into calmer water between the two huge upright slabs. And then onwards – sometimes wading, sometimes clambering – through a deep winding crevice. By now he was looking at me in utter disbelief.

"Close your eyes Erich." I told him. It was childish of course, but I did want to make the most of my surprise. "Only six more paces." I took his arm and guided him on round the last bend. "Now, my friend, what do you reckon to that?"

Before him lay a tiny steeply sloping beach, perhaps eight yards long and rather more than half as wide. The smooth un-trodden sand, carried by some quirk of the tide, was already drying out to a silvery whiteness. Facing due South, and set beneath a huge alcove that Nature had carved out of the rugged cliff, it formed a perfect sun-trap.

"See those high rocks." I pointed seawards. "They will hide us completely from any passing boats." Then I pointed upwards, at the overhang, some forty or fifty feet above us, and at the gorse thicket at its edge. "Nobody walking the cliff path, up there, would ever suspect that this little beach even exists. We have to stay here until the tide turns, Erich. Isn't it a super place?"

"*Wunderbar!* Is even better than Three Palm Trees." He looked about him appreciatively, then spread his trunks over a rock to dry, before stretching himself luxuriously on the sand. "Much, much better John!" Moments later I was beside him, basking in the hot sun – dressed as nature intended – relaxing after the long swim, and sharing my chocolate with him. The paper wrapper had turned to pulp but the silver paper was still intact. Although we couldn't wash away the salt, our rations were no less welcome because of the unusual flavour.

"Do other people come here?" Erich asked quietly.

"I don't know of a single person who's even heard of this place. Two years ago, the tide really caught me, and I was lucky to get ashore here – but I couldn't get away for hours. There was an awful fuss because I was so late and wouldn't explain where I'd been. You are the only one to share my secret Erich. No one else must ever know. I call it Porthyn Pryva. Granny was born in Cornwall, where many place names are in the old dead language. She told me what some of them mean, and this would be Porthyn Pryva – a secret beach. A bit later I'll show you the cave – but that's even more of a secret."

Typically, Erich did not want to wait, but I was enjoying my rest.

"You go look for it by yourself." I told him. "You should be able to see it from where you are now." And in actual fact that was partly true. After spending almost ten minutes scrambling among the rocks, he came back to me for more directions. I teased him, saying "You'll only be able to see it after I've spoken the magic words." He ignored that and went back to his searching, becoming quite angry when it still eluded him. To avoid a row I led him to the alcove, where the cliff rose sheer from the white sand. Raising my arms – in a dramatic gesture – I paused, before solemnly intoning,

"Sim Sala Bim ... Dummkopf Deutschländer ... Dig Down In!" and stamping my heel deep into the sand, in a forceful finale. To my amazement, Erich immediately began to dig – and without any argument – though he did threaten what would happen to me if he found nothing. Just a few inches down, where the rock turned inwards, I joined him in scraping away the sand with my hands.

Only minutes later he was squeezing his body through into the cave that was now ringing with his shouts.

"Oh Prima! However did you find this?" He demanded – from the darkness inside. I dug away a few more handfuls of sand and then joined him.

"Just once, after a terrific storm had washed away most of the sand, it was partly open when I came here – but its always been completely hidden since."

In the days that followed we made several visits to Porthyn Pryva; Erich even taking his torch so we could see the interior of the cave, and that did allow me to learn just how extensive my cave really was. Its sandy floor was almost twenty feet square, and to the landward side a broad rock shelf stood four feet higher. The jagged ceiling peaked at something approaching forty feet – which was not much less than the height of the cliff itself.

We both valued the total privacy of our little beach where – so far as the rest of the world was concerned – we might have been on another planet. Being unfettered by ingrained inhibitions, we became our real selves, and whilst we were there no topic was taboo. We could, and we did, exchange intimate confidences – discussing our fears, uncertainties, beliefs, hopes and ambitions – with a frankness that would have been impossible elsewhere. Only there did I ever hear Erich express any doubts about the way Hitler was leading Germany – and stamping so ruthlessly on anybody who stood in his path. My friend told me of his two great fears – that it might become known his mother had a Jewish ancestor not so very far back. And, worse still, that his father privately disagreed with *Der Führer* in many ways.

"Do you know, John, they would say I was disloyal to the State, and the Party – because I, a *Hitler Junge*, have not denounce them both ... My

Own Two Parents! *Ja, in der Hitler Jugend,* John, we are told, so often, it is our duty to listen what people say, even in our home, in school or in street. And if they say wrong bad things, perhaps you say 'disloyal' things, we must report them – what they say – to our *H.J.* or *Jungvolk Führer.* But I too must be careful what I say – *der Steifendienst* is always listening too. They have duty to Hear everything, to See everything, and to Know everything – and to report accord." It was then I remembered being warned by Kurt, to watch out for the Hitler Youth's equivalent to the Military Police – the unpopular 'Patrol Service' – who could easily be recognised by the embroidered *'H.J. Streifendienst'* band they wore around their left cuffs.

We always spoke softly at Porthyn Pryva, partly for fear that others might become aware of its existence, but more in keeping with the peaceful atmosphere there. I remember Erich speaking very quietly as he told me more about the *'Hi Yacht'* as he always pronounced *'H.J.'*

"It was before we lived in Fürth, and I was twelve – near thirteen – when I had Jürgen as my *Fahnleinführer.* He was a pleasant enough young man but he did very much want go up in *Hitlerjugend.* So he always look after the 'Pheasant Chicks', and they got Promotion, or Proficiency Badge, even when they not able to qualify for by themselves. These 'Chicks' are over-fed sons of important Nazi Party Officials; who often known as 'Golden Pheasants' from colour of very important looking uniforms they love to wear." Then his voice dropped lower. "And there were Jürgen's 'Special Boys' too. They were often useful lads, who like myself – were in last year in *der Jungvolk.* But they had to be *Puppengesicht* ... I think perhaps you say 'Pretty Boys'? Jürgen, he look after them too, but he always expect something in return, if you understand my mean." I think Erich expected a question from me, but I said nothing.

"One evening Jürgen tell me I must go to office after closing parade because he need me help with some paperwork. There he offer me promotion to be *Jungenschaftführer* which I hoping for. But then came more than hint what he want – in return. As you see John, I don't mind be naked with lads my own age, but not with the likes of Jürgen – even though he say he only want to photograph me. But I already know of his wandering fingers, and I hear talk of worse. So I ignore it all and ask him *direkte.* 'What about all this paperwork you want me do?' Of course there was not any papers, and he make excuse that he tired, and it must wait to other day, and anyway it time we both going home." Erich rolled onto his back, and lay looking upwards, almost as if waiting for some approving comment from me. But I wondered where this conversation was leading us, and waited for him to continue.

"I think that end of my chance of Promotion, John – but I lucky. My father had been *Pfadfinder* – that's Boy Scouts – with Claus-Dieter, and they stay close friend to this day, and he like a Uncle to me. Claus's father was Civil Servant who's boss keep asking 'Why your son not with the *H.J.*? Are you not loyal to the Party?' So Claus had to join *Hitlerjugend*, and at first he were suspect as a ex-Scout leader. Then they find he had many good parts – good leadership – good musician – and they send him to *Jungvolk*, where they soon made him *Oberstammführer* – and that put him two rank above Jürgen." Erich was very emphatic about that, and turned so he was looking at me again.

"One day when Claus-Dieter come to visit, I am in uniform. He ask 'When are you going be promoted?' Quite without thinking I say ' Jürgen did offer it, but he wanted ...' And then I not knowing what to say. Claus look hard at me.

'He wanted ....?' And having ask, Claus wait until he see I do not want to answer him. 'And you said ... No?' I just nod. Then *Vati* arrive, and our talk change – how you say, abrupt?" Erich looked to make sure I was still paying attention. "But at very next parade Jürgen he call me forward and he promote me *Jungenschaftführer*, but everybody there must see how much he hate doing it. Three week later Jürgen is moved to other side of town, and we get really good *Fahnleinführer Helmut* in his place. You must remember this John, in our New Germany, rank is everything, and – just this once– it be on my side!"

Such was the influence of that peaceful spot that I believe Erich would have flatly denied having told me anything of the sort – had I ever been tactless enough to repeat his words away from Porthyn Pryva.

Little did we know then, that the secrets we shared at Porthyn Pryva, were but the forerunners of much greater ones to come.

Granny Hardwicke's Cottage.

5. Erich Takes Charge.

After a few days in Devon, Erich was beginning to find his feet, and it showed.

"John. You do all planning, and you say what to do, and where we go. It must be right I now do some saying what we do. Yes?" That was surely fair, although I cannot recall the reverse ever being suggested when we were in Germany. It soon became clear Erich was determined that we should go hiking.

"We make *Eine kleine Fahrt* – sleep two nights in the tent I bring. I say everything, and you must do. We will have *Eine Mutprobe,* courage test – for you, and me also – to see how brave you are, John." I had heard of these tests, examples of the Hitler Youth's ethos, known to have hilarious – and occasionally truly tragic endings. Erich had been asking a lot of questions about Dartmoor, so it was fairly obvious what he was planning, and I was willing enough. Granny's only concern was that we should enjoy ourselves, and not go hungry – so there was no difficulty in that quarter.

After a good breakfast we set off inland, following the creek to Bridgend and up the hill to Yealmpton, where Erich made me sit outside the shop whilst he went in alone. Afterwards he checked the map, then pointed East along the main road, and I guessed he was heading for the Southern edge of the Moor. However he ignored all the minor roads that might have taken us there and, to my surprise, just short of the Ermington fork, we turned right, down a muddy bridle track. He held the map, so I wasn't too sure where it went, though judging by the position of the sun, it was taking us about South-west – back where we had just come from!

"Erich. Do you have any idea where you are going?" My question had been firm, and his reply was very much more so.

"John. Today I am Leader. In *der Hitler Jugend* nobody question a Leader his decision, or if he right either!" Soon afterwards we passed through Holbeton – heading South – towards the sea. I hinted that he was lost, but he just strode on ahead without replying. Having accepted him as my Leader, there was nothing I could do but follow, and if he was making a muck of it – that was just my bad luck.

In sullen silence we climbed the hill into Mothecombe where – without any hesitation – he turned left towards the mouth of the River Erme. It was a crazy move because the lane comes to an end at the high-water mark – and there is no longer a Ferry across to the other side. In spite of knowing this I kept quiet, to avoid giving him the satisfaction of snubbing me again.

When the beach came in sight, my chum calmly said we would take a swim, and have our lunch afterwards. At least I had no hesitation in obeying those orders, for they seemed to me to be the first sensible decisions he'd taken in a long time. Whilst we were eating, Erich kept glancing at me and, although he must have known that I was far from happy about the route he was taking, he offered no word of explanation. Every step seemed to be taking us back to Noss Mayo again.

But, as we neared Stoke House, Erich said he wanted to leave the road and go down to the shore. *Can that be the site for our camp, and perhaps for the Mutprobe?* I asked myself that because Erich had shown quite a lot of interest when I told him about the long abandoned 15th century church of 'St Peter the Poor Fisherman'. *But No!* I told myself. *Not there, not with his little weakness ... Once he's seen all those gravestones ... especially the one with the big skull and cross bones ... he most certainly wouldn't want to spend a night anywhere near them!*

And so it proved. After a too hurried examination of the over-grown ruin, he moved us on, fighting our way through the tangled scrub until we came out on the open downland – far below the Nine Mile Drive. (Although he always tried hard to hide it, and nothing on earth would have made him admit it, I had noticed – particularly after dark – that Erich could be very uncomfortable, or even scared, in any surroundings that were in the least bit 'spooky'). With growing irritation I trailed after him. There could be no doubt he now knew where we were, although I could see no possible reason for our being there. We passed Netton Island and Dunny Cove, pausing only to fill Erich's water-bottle and the tin kettle, at one of the springs.

When Blackstone Point came in view he began to search for a site where our camp could be hidden amongst the gorse and bracken. I helped him pitch the tent, which was even smaller than I had expected. With the two of us inside we'd be very cramped – and that wasn't at all a good idea when relations were so strained.

"Erich. This is madness!" I told him, heatedly. "You make us trek fourteen miles on a hot summer's day, just so we can sleep on hard ground, barely a mile from our own comfortable beds." Erich only grinned.

"You put our blankets in tent John, ready for sleep." In a growing sulk I did so. Meanwhile he made coffee on the spirit stove. Not until we were drinking it would he tell me what was in his mind. "You and I are going to swim to Porthyn Pryva, John. And in just a few minutes."

"You can't do that Erich!" I retorted angrily, almost shouting at him. "You know the tide is wrong! We'd never get back – not until after dark – and I am not going to swim amongst those sharp rocks when I can't see them!"

"That is why we go now. It will be a real test of your courage John, and mine also, to spend the night in cave, cut off by tide – and not able to get back until morning. Surely, *Engländer*, you are not afraid to come with me?" And of course that settled it. I knew full well that refusal to take part in such a *Mutprobe* – foolish though it was – would leave me shamed, for ever, in Erich's eyes.

So, and much against my better judgement, I was forced to agree it would indeed be a fine adventure. My Leader emptied the sugar out of the screw-topped jar Granny had given us, and then told me to fill it with biscuits, as our rations for the night. (Water-tight plastic containers were not then available as they are today.) By the time my task was done, he had the tent bag hanging heavily around his neck, but I chose to carry the jar at my waist. We closed up the tent and set off barefoot, gingerly making our way down to the beach. I found the water wonderfully refreshing, and soon felt that perhaps his idea wasn't quite such a bad one after all.

With the tide as it was, we faced a hard swim, but I enjoyed that challenge too. Even so, both of us were pretty tired by the time we got ashore, because Erich's mysterious load was obviously much heavier than mine.

The evening was windless and the sun stayed hot, though as dusk approached I began to feel chilly – and had nothing to put on for warmth. By then the tide was rising fast; half the sand was already covered and there would soon be water in the hole we had dug at the cave mouth. The time had come to go inside whilst we could do so without getting wet again. Some minutes later the first wavelets swept across that hole and into the cave, reflecting ripples of silver-blue light onto the damp rock above our heads. Each succeeding wave washed more sand into the hole, and the light grew rapidly dimmer. Following my suggestion, we settled ourselves, and our rations, up on the cold high rock shelf that ran along the Northern, landward, side of our cave. Quite suddenly we were left in total darkness – and the sound of the sea was silenced.

Only then did I realise that Erich had chosen to maroon us at a Spring Tide, one of the highest of the year and – never having been at Porthyn Pryva for High Water before – I had absolutely no idea how far up the water would come, whilst we were trapped inside the cave.

For a moment I felt very alone, and was relieved when my companion spoke – but his voice now produced a ringing echo, far louder than it had been only minutes before.

"John, now to make time go, we tell stories, like we was sitting round camp fire." His mention of a fire made me all the more aware of the cold – and how much colder it would be before we could leave our prison again. Erich was a good story-teller, and I enjoyed his version of Siegfried and Brunhilde. Then we munched biscuits whilst I told him what I could remember of King Arthur and the Round Table. I was glad enough when more food was suggested.

Moments after Erich opened his bag there was a metallic hammering – which was repeated.

"Here, John. Suck this." He handed me a round tin can, that was oozing something thick and sticky. Condensed Milk – the sweetened sort – and my favourite. In the dark it wasn't easy to find the holes he'd punched in the top, and I was soon left wondering why he hadn't brought a thicker nail – a thought that was to be often repeated before the night was much older. We sat for a while, huddling together, partly for warmth but largely for companionship. I found the cave a frightening place, the echo made it seem immense, and yet the darkness was somehow claustrophobic. I believe there were times during that night when each of us felt deeply grateful for the presence of the other – because it was a truly unnerving experience.

Later on – we had of course no way of knowing the time – Erich said he would open the main rations, which was good news indeed. There followed a faint clicking, a gentle splash – and a loud German curse. Erich slid off the shelf, landing up to his knees in water, where he began to feel, for the key he had dropped – the key without which we could not open the can of corned beef he had bought so secretly. It seemed ages before he found it. Again I heard him fiddling with the tin – and I offered to help. But instead of accepting my offer, he burst into a long and fluent stream of what I took to be profanity, from which – with some difficulty – I discovered that he had broken the opening tag off the tin, and he'd gashed his thumb in the process. Tactfully, I enquired if it might be possible to get into the tin by punching a row of holes with the nail. He tried this, but the nail soon became too bent, and so was useless – leaving us with nothing but a hunger provoking-smell.

Time passed slowly, and we grew steadily colder. I was again sure that my friend's idea was not a good one – and my bad temper was rapidly returning. When I started shivering, he insisted we should stand up on the shelf and do the 'Wood-sawing' exercise. That certainly got my circulation going, but inevitably he had to turn it into a trial of strength, and finally overbalanced me, throwing me right off the shelf – full length into the icy water – and the cave rang with his laughter. That made me absolutely furious. Indeed I'd gladly have hit him – if only I'd known where he was. Erich had taken an unfair advantage, and as a result I was going to be colder than ever. But worst of all, neither of us had known where the edge of the shelf was, and a drop like that could have left me with a broken bone; and what would he have done then? I gave him a piece of my mind – but then had to ask him to guide me back to the shelf, and that did rather spoil the effect.

At first I wanted to sulk alone, but it was far too cold for that, and before long I had moved right beside him – for warmth. He put an arm around my shoulder.

"Come closer John, *mir ausserden ist kalt ... eiskalt!*" It was something that he'd weakened enough to admit that much, and at least it gave me a small degree of satisfaction. Of course we both knew who's fault it was, but I felt there was nothing to be gained by my reminding him then. Half-reluctantly I put my arms around him, and it was good to feel his bodily warmth, even if the warmth of our friendship was somewhat lacking. Eventually I fell into a fitful sleep. Each time I awoke, Erich seemed to be asleep, and I dared not move for fear of waking him. Although – in my discomfort – I did wonder whether he deserved to be treated with such consideration.

Finally, I woke, so chilled, stiff and hungry, that I broke free from Erich, and began to pace the floor of the cave, so learning that all the water had gone. I tried to dig my way out, but could not find the exit. Then Erich joined me. But only after some moments of panic, and a lot of frantic scrabbling, did he find the right spot, and we had soon dug through to daylight, although the sun was not yet fully up. Only a little strip of sand was uncovered but – for warmth – we dashed about like a couple of puppies let off the leash. Suddenly I stopped, and listened. Waves were now breaking heavily on the shore. There was no doubt ... overnight the sea had built up into an angry swell.

"Erich. Do you hear that?" I asked, pointing at the rocks and the sea beyond. "We must leave at once. Come on, follow me – Now – before it gets any worse!" That swim back was a desperate struggle – and definitely one I prefer to forget. Erich ignored my warnings, getting himself thrown against the rocks whilst trying to take what he believed was a short cut. He was lucky to escape with nothing worse than a scraped thigh, and a skinned elbow. I'm doubtful which of us was the most exhausted as we dragged ourselves ashore at Hollowcombes.

Then came the long steep haul up from the beach, to the rough track that led to our tent. For hours I had been dreaming of steaming hot coffee – but instead I just crawled into my blanket, and was instantly asleep.

Some four hours later I woke up, sweating and gasping for breath. Our little tent had caught the full strength of the sun, and it was like an oven. Erich agreed that more sleep was impossible and, over a belated breakfast, he unbent enough to seek my advice on how we could reach Dartmoor. Then, after breaking camp, and carefully avoiding Noss Mayo village, we took the bus to Bittaford.

6. On Dartmoor.

Noon found us a thousand feet up, and striding northwards from the Western Beacon, following the track of the Dismantled Tramway which used to serve the China Clay workings at Red Lake Mire. It was a perfect day for walking the Moor, clear and sunny, with larks singing overhead and a gentle breeze to keep the temperature just right. Nevertheless Erich was volubly disappointed at finding so much close-cropped grass and smooth rounded hills.

"Here is 'Soft Country' John. Not rough wild country like you tell me." And worse still he felt cheated by the realisation that, on maps of Dartmoor, *'Lake'* marks a little stream, not a decent expanse of water.

"Erich. Do they not teach you how to read a map – in the H.J.? Look, there is nothing big and blue there. Anybody can see that's not a lake – or even a little pond!" And he didn't take kindly to that remark.

"But, John. You look out and see. This Moor, Soft Country. It can not be dangerous as you tell me!"

To prove him wrong I repeated what I'd been told was a true story.

"Not so many years ago – barely a mile ahead of us now – a schoolboy ran down the slope from this very Tramway. He disappeared into thickening mist. He was chasing after a football, kicked by his own father. Not until two days later was the lad found, lying dead beside the River Erme, almost two miles away. The body was discovered there by the local Foxhounds – called out especially to help in the search." By his response Erich made it quite clear that he didn't believe me – but even so I continued to point out all the Cairns, Stone Rows and the many other Antiquities that we could see. From the jagged rocks of Sharp Tor – which were surely 'Rough' enough for anybody – we had a fine view over the Erme Valley and the canopy of primaeval oaks at Piles Copse, down by the river. Then, back to the track, and on past the distant hill known as Three Barrows, with its trio of burial mounds showing boldly on the skyline.

Where possible the builders of the Tramway had followed the contours of the land, which made for easy walking, and we soon reached the old workings at Leftlake Mires. Erich wanted to explore the abandoned buildings, but then he spotted the flooded china-clay pit.

"Now, John. We swim." He seemed delighted by the discovery of that disused pit, with its jade green water. And he simply would not be persuaded that – however tempting it might appear, especially on so hot a day – such a pit is never a good place for swimming. But of course I went in too ... which was just as well with the way things turned out.

For a while we thoroughly enjoyed ourselves in the water, and stirred up a lot of silt in the process. Then – quite suddenly – Erich just wasn't there any more ... and I hadn't seen him go under! I spun round and round, but with ripples coming and going in all directions, there was no way of telling where I should try to find him. *And if I do go down, mightn't I meet the same fate?* I wondered, becoming really alarmed before he shot to the surface – gasping for air, and bleeding too. I went to him, but had tact enough not to grab hold, so allowing him to get himself ashore unaided, although it was a very near thing.

"I dived down to see how deep it is. I swam into what must be coil of old wire rope!" Erich told me this whilst we tried to get the slimy white clay off ourselves. He was obviously feeling pretty shaken, so he wanted to stay there. "Let have our food now, John." He was almost begging, but I too had been badly scared by his antics, and because of that I showed him no sympathy.

"Of course not Erich! Far too early. And we must carry on until we can sit down on proper seats, to eat like civilised folk." Not knowing what I meant, Erich sulked about that, but surprisingly he had made no objection to my taking over the lead; though he did grumble when I left the easy walking on the Tramway, and headed down the uneven grassy slope to Stony Bottom, where he showed little interest in the remains of the Tinner's Blowing House.

"John. I'm empty. All I can think is food – please!" So, to keep the peace, I hurried on to Erme Pound where my companion was quite impressed with the ancient hut at the entrance. In no time we'd settled ourselves inside the Bothy – as it is generally known – sitting on the stone benches that line three sides of its low roofless walls.

Erich sliced everything with his new *Fahrtenmesser* – but in his haste – he had forgotten to wipe the protective oil off its brightly polished blade.

That oil did nothing for the flavour of the first sandwich, which he had given to me, and likewise, it did not improve my temper either. Up to then conditions had been quite perfect for walking, but when the sun went behind a solid bank of dark clouds, everything changed abruptly. The skylarks disappeared in an instant. The normally muted moorland colours darkened by several shades, the temperature dropped noticeably and, although the gentle breeze seemed to blow twice as hard, an almost eerie brooding silence settled over the Moor.

At the prospect of food Erich had cheered up considerably, but now his mood changed as suddenly as our surroundings had done; and the meal continued with hardly a word spoken between us. Whilst we were packing up, I took a wicked pleasure making a 'helpful' suggestion – even though I knew it was much too early in the day.

"Erich, shouldn't we pitch camp here, now? Its a really good spot." Before replying he had a quick, almost furtive look around the hillside.

"No. Not here, John." He'd said that clearly enough, but I most certainly was not meant to hear his softly murmured afterthought of *"Zuveiel Menschen!"* It was quite ridiculous to say *'Too many people!'* because we hadn't seen a single person since climbing up to the Beacon almost three hours ago, but in spite of that I knew exactly what he meant. So many men, and their families too, had lived up on the Moor, labouring through the centuries – and many of them still lay close by, in long forgotten graves, or beneath the cairns and barrows we had already visited. And of course, with his weakness – I suppose I could call it his Achilles Heel – Erich was only too well aware of that. So – without giving me the chance to argue – he set off, striding out purposefully, hurrying to put some distance between himself and all those frightening *'Menschen.'*

Following the westward curve of the River Erme, we turned away from the strangely beautiful white eyesore of the Red Lake spoil heaps. After consulting the map for the umpteenth time, Erich looked around us and began to complain about there being still more 'Soft' country ahead. However, he became quite excited at the change of terrain as we neared the foot of the Wollake Valley. There he discovered the remains of tin workings beneath the rocky outcrop; and further up the boulder-strewn glen – between the almost vertical cliff and the brook – lay a tiny ruined Tinner's hut.

"Härte Landes – endlich!" This it the sort of place for men like us John." At long last he was feeling happier, and he was getting cocky again. But I had an answer ready for that. About a hundred yards beyond the hut stood

a massive boulder, which aeons of frosts had split, first horizontally, and then vertically In the following centuries the two upright halves have moved far apart, and with the third slab still forming a natural capstone, they now look something like the *Trilithon* or *Kistvaen* graves found elsewhere on the Moor. And I couldn't resist the temptation to offer Erich some more *Menchen*.

"See this, its the burial place of an early Warrior Chieftain." I spoke knowledgeably. "His followers knew this was a proper place for real men. They laid him to rest under the stones and then covered them with earth, but that has washed away in time. Look at that roof stone, how low it is, that means it is almost certain the body still lies buried between the uprights." (As it stands now, there is just enough space in the cleft to shelter a crouching man.) My friend examined the stones closely – and probably knew I was pulling his leg; though – out of bravado – he pretended to believe me.

"We camp now," he announced confidently, "in *Herrlich Gessellschaft* John – here beside our Royal Host." In fact we had to cross the brook, onto the right bank, where the ground sloped less steeply, in order to find a suitably level space. There we pitched our tent – amidst the boulders – but reasonably free from ghostly neighbours.

Now that our camp was established, Erich wanted to continue exploring the little valley, leading me further upstream than I had been before. Where the valley opened out my eye was caught by three enormous flat rocks, lying close together on the gently rising hillside. As we moved nearer it became apparent that large stones and turf had been jammed in to fill a gap beneath one of the slabs.

Then I began to recall the long story an elderly walker had told me on an earlier visit to the Moor. *What did he call it – Pitt's Cave? No. Phillpotts' Cave, after Eden Phillpotts – the popular author – who'd had it turned into a shelter – provided with a stock of tinned food, and even whisky, for Moormen and walkers caught up there in bad weather.* Skirting around North of the rocks we came to the mouth of the cave – which wasn't a cave at all; but a vastly enlarged version of my 'Warrior's Grave', formed in much the same fashion, but with space for several men to stretch out under cover, not in any degree of comfort, but protected from the worst of the weather. We clambered inside and whilst we crouched there I told Erich about Eden Phillpotts, and the food supplies. He didn't say as much but I doubt if he accepted this truth any more than my earlier nonsense about the Warrior.

By evening a thick fog had come down, and we were blanketed in silence. Erich soon noticed this.

"Now so quiet here. All I hear is water in stream, three metres away."

After we'd eaten I was glad to have my blanket to wrap around me, and whilst we sat chatting, I answered his questions about the early days on the Moor, when Bronze Age folk worked the streams for tin. Then I told him of the 16th and 17th century Tinners who began to mine deeper for the precious metal.

As it turned dark Erich changed the subject, to the mountains where we planned to walk when we were next in Germany together. He chattered on but I stopped him twice, signing for silence, whilst I listened intently – before urging him to continue – without offering any explanation.

"Didn't you hear it?" I asked, after my third interruption. "A soft moaning and a sort of shuffling sound?" But Erich had heard nothing at all. "That was Thomas the Tinner," I whispered, "surely you must have heard him?" Erich shook his head emphatically. "No? Well ... one foggy night like this, many years ago, when they were mining hereabouts, a party of Tinners left the Inn at Hexworthy after an evening of heavy drinking. By the time they got back to the huts, they were all too fuddled to do more than fall into bed. In the morning they realised Thomas was missing, and he never did turn up – not alive that is! However, it soon became clear he'd strayed from the path, and perished in one of the many quags, maybe the terrible Foxtor Mire. For, on nights such as this, Thomas can still be seen – and heard too – crawling on all fours, covered in slime, and moaning softly, as he endlessly searches for his hut, and his bed." I waited for this to sink in. "Erich. As *Eine Mutprobe*, why don't you go outside now – so that you too – can see the ghost." (And by saying that I was implying, very clearly, that I had already seen it.) Erich paused rather too long before making a hesitant reply.

"Better not," he mumbled. "I think I – I could ... I might get lost in the fog also." He was right enough about that, but from his uncertainty and tone of voice, I was sure his answer was much more of an excuse than a considered judgement. What's more, I was secretly very well pleased to learn that my friend was far too afraid to go out in pursuit of a spectre. The one which I had only that very minute invented – just to scare him.

There was an awkward silence, as though Erich was gathering enough courage to re-assert himself after such a show of what we both knew was weakness – if not actual cowardice.

"I am still the Leader of this *kleine Fahrt?* It came from the darkness, more as a question than a statement of fact. I agreed, quietly – and hesitantly. "So you John will obey my orders." That was more of a statement than a question, and I agreed even more hesitantly – not from any real reluctance, but to maintain the advantage Thomas had given me. "Tomorrow John, we have a long march. We need our sleep, and you did not tell me it would be so cold high up here on your Dartmoor. I think we must now share our blankets – or we get no sleep." Having scored off him so well with my brand new 'Legend', I found it unnecessary to remind him that he had forgotten to take even one blanket for us to share in the cave at Porthyn Pryva.

Next morning I was first awake, and seeing that the fog was still down, felt there was no need to hurry over striking camp; believing as I did that the fog would soon start to clear. When he woke, Erich seemed to think the same, and so we just lay there. I was hoping he'd offer to get breakfast ready – but he had something very different on his mind.

"We go back as planned John. With the map and my compass I can easily find way to that Stone Circle." But I'd seen his compass, and thought it little better than a toy. I knew the danger of becoming lost amidst the quaking bogs and mires – which have been know to swallow men as well as cattle.

"No Erich. Not in this fog – far too dangerous. Do you want us both to end up down in a bog – like Thomas the Tinner? No, we use the river." And without too much difficulty I got him to accept that it would be safer – even if less adventurous – for us to follow the river Erme down to Ivybridge.

The fog was as thick as ever when we'd finished breakfast, so we packed the tent and set off regardless, walking beside the Wollack stream to its junction with the Erme. Then, with visibility down to ten feet, or sometimes less, we followed the river, which did – as I had predicted – indeed lead us to civilisation, and the bus back to Noss Mayo.

After he left us, Erich wrote a very nice 'thank you' letter to my Grandmother, also enclosing one to me, saying how much he was looking forward to next summer, when we planned to spend a few days in Devon, before travelling around Germany together.

7. Germany, 1938.

The spring of 1938 was one of widespread anxiety, caused by the German occupation of Austria. But the peaceful summer that followed was – for me at least – one to be remembered. Erich and I started our holiday at Noss Mayo, with seven gloriously sunny days, during which we made several visits to Porthyn Pryva, so we were both well tanned and thoroughly fit before we set off on the long overland journey to Southern Germany. The original plan was for me to stay with his Grandparents for ten days, but he would be there much longer. The old people again made me very welcome. Erich was much relieved to find they had made no definite commitments for us, because we already had tentative plans for our own two or three day camping expedition.

Immediately after our arrival in Fürth my friend telephoned the Hitler Youth Office, reporting his return and asking if I might be allowed to attend the next Duty Evening with him. When permission had been granted, Erich stressed that I would have to get my shoes as brightly polished as his – and to try to keep my hair tidy for once. This was to be Erich's first attendance at the new *Hitler-Jugend-Heim* which turned out to be a fine purpose-built meeting place, having ample space for all four groups – both boys and girls – of the local Hitler Youth. Outside the *Heim* we met up with Kurt, boy leader of Erich's *Kameradschaft,* who gave us a quick tour round part of the building. Afterwards I stood watching, whilst the boys paraded in the street – with much stamping and shouting of orders. Then they sang an *H.J.* Song – that told how Youth would continue their struggle to make Germany even greater. Finally the *Gefolgschaftführer* announced that Boxing would be their activity for the greater part of the evening. He went on at quite some length, telling the boys of the great importance that Adolf Hitler – their *Führer* – attached to this particular sport above all others.

When the lads were dismissed to change, Erich introduced himself and me, to the *Gesfu;* a rather pompous young schoolmaster who had only recently taken command of the unit. He welcomed me, and then asked if I would like to take part in the Boxing. Although much out of practice, I really did appreciate the invitation to join in, instead of being treated as a mere spectator. They quickly found some shorts for me, and a plain white vest – because the Leader said I should not wear the red-banded *Hitler-Jugend* sports singlet with the black swastika on the chest.

Kurt then proudly led us down to *Die Grosse Keller* which lay beneath the *Heim*. (The Great Cellar was all that remained of an early 18th century warehouse that had burned down only twelve months ago) It was a huge place, now used as a dramatic setting for sports activities, parades and other gatherings. The stone ceiling arched from the high wall on one side, to a row of massive pillars, beyond which lay a narrow space, newly walled off as a rifle range.) Some twenty boys – myself included – were called out, paired off around the floor, and set to box a three minute round

My opponent was thickset, with very close cropped hair – almost the cartoon German in fact. Otto spoke no English and he had no idea of skilful boxing either, but he made repeated purposeful rushes at me with arms flailing, lashing out wildly – and hard. While we boxed the Leader and a *Sportwart* moved amongst us, always giving encouragement and advice, but also demanding greater effort. By the end of the bout, I was beginning to hit Otto, bit it is very doubtful whether I won, and certainly the performance was no credit to either of us. Erich had his turn next, and he beat a lad of his own age and build quite easily.

Later they matched me against Kurt, who was much taller and perhaps eight to ten months older than me. Being a true Nordic Aryan, handsome, blond and blue-eyed, he ought to have been the Ideal German Youth – but he was built like a beanpole, and so probably matched me in weight. However, his height and longer reach gave him the advantage, and for a while he was able to keep me at a distance, punching me almost at will. (No wonder the others had nicknamed him *'Die Spinne'*. For there were times when I felt sure he had six arms and two legs.) But later on I did get in really close, landing a series of hard blows to the swastika on his vest that left him gasping, and by the end I'd near enough evened the score.

The *Gefolgschaftführer* and Erich had been standing together watching us in action, and the Leader now beckoned to me to him.

"Your friend tells me you two have never boxed each other, although you compete in many other sports together." Erich was grinning, and he seemed to know what was coming, as the *Gesfu* continued. "How would you like to box against your *Kamerad* – in a few minutes time? Up there in the big ring, for a proper contest – of three rounds?" Erich was obviously keen, and I was happy enough to accept. Even if I hadn't been so willing, a refusal in those circumstances would have been quite unthinkable.

The *Sportwart* made it into a big event, announcing it as 'An International Contest, with Erich Falkenberg, representing the Fatherland, versus Yon Hardwicke, our English Visitor.' As we prepared to climb into the ring Erich leaned over and whispered to me.

"I shall be fighting to win John – for My Country – afterwards we shall be friends again."

"O.K Stranger!" I replied, airily. "And I shall be fighting for England – and Saint George!" There was no sign of a smile at this, and it was clear he was taking the whole matter very seriously – though in front of the assembled *Jugend*, he could do no other.

From the first punch Erich showed he'd really meant what he said, and a bit after halfway through the round he almost put me down with a right to the jaw. I managed to stay on my feet, but my legs felt rubbery, and my brain was still spinning. The only thing to do was to hunch up against the ropes – keeping my head and body hidden behind my gloves and arms – until things improved. Of course Erich took full advantage of this, and the *Jugend* – sensing a quick victory over the foreigner – were loudly cheering him on. Somehow I succeeded in weathering the storm, but by the end of the round he was way ahead of me on points. My Second, a weedy bespectacled youth, wafted his towel aimlessly in front of me, and he offered not one single word of encouragement. Meanwhile my opponent sat on his stool, looking relaxed – and fresh. Then I remembered ... he'd fought only once that evening – whilst I'd already had two hard bouts.

Nevertheless, I did much better in the next round, getting fully into my stride, and coming to terms with Erich's awkward crouching style. Because of my earlier hard treatment I was now even more determined not to let him beat me, and for much of the round I had by far the best of it. For the last few seconds we both went at it hammer and tongs, but when the bell sounded he was sitting on the canvas, mouth hanging open, looking every bit as surprised as I felt. Nevertheless, in those circumstances, at least some of the applause had to be for me, and I reckoned we must now be about equal on the Judge's cards. Erich looked much less confident after his Second helped him back into his corner. My own *Junge* showed a little more enthusiasm, sponging me down and using the towel properly. Then he spoiled it all, by stooping down to murmur in my ear.

"Erich is a good German Fighter – you won't be able to beat him *Engländer!*"

The Referee called us together and we touched gloves as though we really were strangers. There was a cold single-minded look in my opponent's eyes. He was still grimly determined to win, but so was I. Halfway through this longer final round things were about even, though we'd each had the advantage for a short time – and made good use of it too. But my strength was ebbing; that second bout was really beginning to take its toll. I took a wild swing at Erich's jaw – and missed – but caught him full on the nose instead, putting him back on his heels. Then the blood began to flow. This clearly worried him, so I went in fast – repeatedly stabbing my left into his face. My glove – like a rubber stamp – was spreading the gore, and soon he looked an awful mess. The shouts of the *Jugend* now changed in tone. Earlier the lads had been cheering Erich's success, but now they were imploring him to fight back. From somewhere I clearly heard a couple of yells for *'Der Engländer!'* which I thought was pretty sporting. Perhaps I got careless, or maybe he was skilful – even just plain lucky ... it doesn't matter which ... for a fist came crashing down on the bridge of my nose – and I saw real stars! I shook my head clear, dragged in breath, and then tasted blood on my lips. The sight of this brought a roar of satisfaction from the spectators, which built up as we stood, toe-to-toe, slugging it out for what we both knew must be the final seconds of the match.

At last the bell rang and the Referee parted us. Erich's gory face split in a gruesome panting grin, then he threw his arms around my neck. We stood there, hanging on each other, gasping and waiting – waiting anxiously for the result to be declared. A hand gripped my wrist ... and raised it ... I had won! I'd managed to beat him after all. I stood back to take the applause – and then saw the referee was holding Erich's hand up too.

"The judges have scored them even. " He announced solemnly. "And I cannot say who did best. The result must be – a draw."

Erich led me over to his corner amidst a storm of clapping. The Second, who did know his job, immediately began to sponge my face, trying to stop the blood flowing. He looked at me closely.

"I thought you were cut *Engländer* – but I am glad to be wrong." Then he turned his attention to Erich. "Didn't you tell me he was your good friend?" Erich's reply was half-smothered by the sponge.

"He is now ... again. Aren't you ... John?"

"Nonsense, you great *blutig Dummkopf!* We were friends all the time."

When the Leader ordered everyone back into the changing room, Erich and I were swept along by a crowd of boys who were noisily disputing which of us had actually won. There was a general rush to get showered, but I suddenly found myself standing all alone, under the beautifully hot deluge, whilst an apparently hostile crowd gathered around Erich. A fierce argument developed, and angry glances kept coming in my direction. I couldn't make out what was being said, but only moments later Kurt and the others joined me under the shower and were chattering to me as though nothing had happened. Whilst we were drying afterwards, Kurt came to me.

"*Yon*. I want you must stand *mit die Kameradschaft*, between Erich *und* me, for *Endparade*." It was meant as an honour, and I took it as such. But the parade itself was a bore for everyone but the *Gesfu*. He droned on, amidst a growing shuffling of feet, about the need for Youth to develop fitness and strength – ready for the great struggles that lay ahead for Germany – and toughness too, such as had been shown in the ring only minutes before. The Beanpole nudged me hard, drawing a black look from the Leader. I glanced at Erich, but couldn't be sure whether he was glowing with pride, or just blushing with embarrassment – like myself. At last, after the Hitler Youth's own song 'Forward Forward!' had been sung, we were dismissed. But even then the *Gesfu* hadn't finished. He came over to Erich and myself.

"I am proud of you two boys. You boxed bravely. *Der Führer* himself would have approved. I am glad that you two are friends – for Germany and England are friends, and will remain so. Not like France. France is the sworn enemy of Germany, and will have to be dealt with before long." Fortunately at that point a *Scharführer* arrived with an urgent problem, and only then were we allowed to go.

Several of the older lads insisted in taking us to a nearby *Kaffehaus*, where it soon became clear they were trying very hard to give a good impression of their organisation to the foreigner in their midst. Nevertheless I liked their easy friendliness and – in spite of the constant talk of Adolf Hitler, and the many improvements he had brought about in Germany – I enjoyed their company too.

Just after we left the *Kaffehaus* Erich and I met a latecomer, whom I'd noticed earlier as a very useful boxer. He was at least a year older than me, and he wore two small stars on each shoulder-board. Erich introduced us.

"This is Gerhard Gotz, my *Scharführer*, and Kurt's immediate superior. He's just finished duty, seeing all is safe and tidy at the *Heim*, and he had to lock up too." They held a very rapid conversation, but because of Gerhard's difficult accent I was quite unable to follow most of it. Then he shook hands with me, formally, before tying out his limited English.

"Ve meet *Montag Johaan* – I hope ... you *und mich, in Nahkampf Engländer? Auf Wiedersehen! Heil Hitler!*" He raised his arm in *gruss*, and was gone, leaving me more than a little confused.

"Erich. Whatever was all that about, and what is *Nahkampf*?"

"Oh, I asked if we could borrow some extra camping gear from the *Heim* stores. He says we're not meant to, but if he can manage it, he'll come with us and that way we can take whatever we need. I think you'll like him John. He really likes the look of you, and likes the way you boxed. He thinks you're tough, and wants to test you in *Nahkampf* – that's wrestling. I told him you're not much good – so you can give him a surprise. But you will have to go at him hard – if not he despise you for it – because he hate any suggestion of cowardice. And one more thing – he is my *Scharführer* – so if he do come, you will have to do whatever he says. *'Oh Yes.'* I remembered, *'Here in Germany – Rank is everything!'*

On the way home I asked Erich what had happened whilst we were in the changing room. At first he pretended not to understand, then he was quite clearly embarrassed when I pressed for an answer.

"Well – when they saw you under the shower John – some of the lads thought perhaps you might be Jewish, and they say I should not have brought you. I nearly had to fight that *idiotisch* Heinrich before I could persuade him you're not."

"Dummkopfs!" I snapped disgustedly. "They knew damn well that I'd just fought a draw with a fine *Aryan* youth ... and you know how often they've been told that no Jewboy could possibly do as well as one of the *Herrenvolk!"* An uncomfortable silence followed whilst Erich tried to find a less delicate topic – without making it to obvious.

"Remember *Engländer,* you were only as good as me, not better, you bled a lot too."

"I was just as good as you – and after TWO fights *Deutschländer.* And you know *Sehr gut,* I didn't bleed nearly as much as you. Even so – *Mein Mutig Kamerad* – it was certainly *Blut und Ehre* for us tonight!" Bragging like that would always clear any tension that might build up between us, and with arms around each other's shoulders we strolled back to *Grossmutter's.*

In spite of our happiness, one major problem loomed ahead. During the evening we had been alarmed to learn that – quite unknown to Erich – a change of dates for the *Sommerlager* had brought it forward by a whole week – which was going to ruin our own plans. Erich had gone at once, to make a formal request that he be excused the first few days in camp, because I would still be staying with him. This was bluntly, even indignantly refused; and he was then reminded of how much training he had already lost by living outside the Fatherland, and the effect that was bound to have on his chances of being promoted. All of this meant I was faced with returning home early, or spending time on my own, whilst it would be so much more agreeable to be with my friend. Nevertheless we had to make the most of the time that was left to us. Erich decided we would visit a nearby lake where we could swim and then go canoeing.

Next morning Erich received a note from his *Gefolgschaftführer,* confirming that it would be impossible to excuse him from duty at camp; but, in view of our performance at *die Grosse Keller,* his English friend would also be welcome at that camp. He went on to say that I would have to submit to the usual discipline and to wear uniform. Though a foreigner who was not a member of the H.J. could not be allowed to wear the red armband with the H.J. Square and Swastika, nor the black *Halstuch* either. But, in spite of those minor details, our problem had been very neatly solved for us.

That night I found sleep a long time coming, and I eventually drifted off whilst wondering what new adventures or strange encounters lay in store for Erich – and now myself – at the long awaited *Sommerlager.* But first we were to have our own private *kleine Fahrt* – with or without *Scharführer Gotz* in charge.

Blut und Ehre!

8. Kleine Fahrt.

On Monday Gerhard met us at the *H.J. Heim*, and shortly afterwards we were heading for the Bus Station, laden down with all the camping equipment we could carry. Around midday we left the *Autobus* at a picturesque little village, but under threatening skies. Gerhard then led us on a long damp hike that was only enlivened by our encounter with a bunch of overall-clad motorcyclists. They came into sight – one after another, in a somewhat wobbly single file – around a sharp bend in the road just ahead of us.

"Ist der Motor H.J.!" Shouted our Leader. *"Jump!* For your lives *Meine Jungen – Sprung machen!"* Following the example of the other two, I leaped over the fence and stood watching the crash-helmeted newcomers chug past us. When the last boy turned his head to shout something rude at us he very nearly rammed the bike in front. For this he, and we, got a hearty cursing from the Instructor who was bringing up the rear on a much more powerful machine.

Our *Schafu* was somewhat taken aback by his arrival, and Erich told me afterwards that we were fortunate Gerhard hadn't got us into real trouble.

"Most of the *Motor H.J.* know why a sparking plug actually sparks." He explained. "And because of that, they all believe they're very much superior to the rest of the H.J. – especially the *Allgemeine H.J.* like us."

That first day our hike ended at an official H.J. Camp Site, where we were greeted by a very officious, and too delicately groomed *Ober-scharführer*, shouting that I ought to be in uniform. He demanded my membership card, and became most difficult when he realised I was a foreigner, and not even a member of the *Hitler-Jugend*. Only when Gerhard quoted some senior Leader's words about 'The International Brotherhood of Aryan Youth' were we allowed to stay. But the *Ober-schafu* did remind us, pompously, that we would be under his personal supervision – and that he would inspect our tent. (To see it was properly constructed, from the groundsheet, jointed poles, and pegs that every Hitler Youth – and I – carried in his pack.) Finally he gave us what seemed to me to be quite unnecessary camp duties to perform, and whilst we did these Erich said he and Gerhard were lucky not to have been given Sentry Duty as well.

As darkness fell we joined the other campers around a great log fire, happily singing to the accompaniment of Gerhard's mouth organ and an older boy's guitar. But, with the Camp Leader's arrival, the atmosphere changed abruptly. We had to sing the songs he chose – all from the official songbook, about marching behind trumpets, drums and the swastika flag. He was most obviously put out when several *Jungen* demanded a song from *der Engländer.* I was greatly tempted to give him 'Rule Britannia', but good manners forbade that, and 'On Ilkla' Moor baht' at' would have been incomprehensible – even to Erich. So they had to make do with 'Loch Lomond', because I just could not think of any truly English songs which would have been suitable for that gathering.

Whilst we were making our way back to the tent, Gerhard asked. "Who has got a torch?" His question, and our silence, made it clear we'd all forgotten to bring one.

"Better not advertise the fact." Erich suggested. "Best to get settled down and be 'asleep', then even that *nette Oberschafu* can't find fault with us." Fortunately we had already prepared our bed spaces so that wasn't too difficult. Later, the other two held a whispered conversation, remarking on something I'd already noticed myself – that despite his greater age – the camp's *Oberscharführer* did not have the large pin-on H.J. Silver Proficiency Badge worn by both my companions.

At some time after midnight we were awakened by a terrific clap of thunder, and halfway through the following downpour two strange *Jungen* burst in on us, demanding shelter. They were big noisy know-alls from the rough end of Essen, who had foolishly pitched their tent in a hollow – which had now become a pond. Even though they were dripping wet, and trampling mud all over our blankets and clothes, we could hardly throw them out; but their most unwelcome company meant nobody had much sleep for what was left of the night.

In the morning Gerhard got us out of the camp just as soon as he could.

"Now, *Jungs*, we go straight to the nearest railway station, and we take the first train that come – in any direction." I was most surprised by this decision.

"But Gerhard, I thought you Germans always planned everything so carefully in advance!" He gave me a wry smile.

"*Ja Johann*, last night I planned! Tonight cannot be worse. But we find own camp site, *und wir singen* the song you two want sing. *Johann*, not all our Camp Leaders are like that smooth *Schlappschwanz!*"

After only a short wait we took a train that stopped at a small market town, by which time the sun was shining brightly. Gerhard studied the map carefully before leading us under the railway-bridge, and setting off along the almost deserted main street, which he said would soon bring us to open countryside.

When we had left the shops behind, he stopped Erich and myself, whilst he ran across to a corpulent elderly man wearing the tightly stretched brown shirt and knee breeches of a Nazi Storm-trooper. They exchanged salutes, talked for a while, and then the trooper pointed along the road we were taking. Gerhard stepped smartly back, raised his arm to *gruss* yet again. He turned about, and was clearly taken aback by the sight of a tall and smartly uniformed much younger *S.A. Sturmmann* who was striding purposefully towards them. Gerhard threw him a hasty G*russ*, turned abruptly away, and stepped out into the road, shouting to us as he did so.

"Come on *Jungs!* Follow Me! Is not far." I said nothing then because I had already learned that Gerhard was keen to exercise the authority of his rank, and he tended to regard my questions as a challenge to that authority;

and quite contrary to the 'Blind Unquestioning Obedience' he could expect – even as a lowly Hitler Youth Leader. After about fifty yards I looked back, and saw the two *S.A.* Men were staring at us, and it was fairly clear the younger one was urgently demanding 'Who are those three – and where did you send them – and Why?'

Our route led us quickly out of the town into shady suburbs. Some five kilometres further on, in the midst of wooded hills, we came on a high stone wall beside the road.

"Here we are *Jungs*. This way!" Our Leader crossed over to an imposing entrance, and pushed open huge iron gates, beyond which a moss-grown drive curved its way through tall trees and dense silent shrubberies. It seemed odd to me that Gerhard should so confidently lead us into what was quite obviously private property. When the bushes thinned out, a garden came into view – with overgrown lawns and neglected flowerbeds. The big old house had a dejected appearance too, although it had clearly once been the very pleasant home of a wealthy family. Then I noticed the tell-tale signs ... broken windows ... a crudely painted swastika on the door ... the single word *'Jude'* ... and a black Star of David daubed on the white stucco wall. Then I understood why the place was so silent.

Gerhard appeared to take no account of this as he scanned the garden.

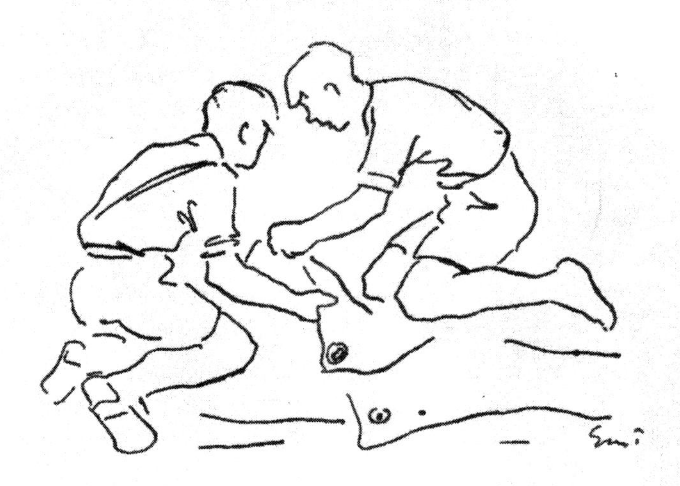

"Round here," he ordered briskly, "the sunny side for us. Erich, you get us water – from the house. Johann! *Kommen sie mit.* You come – now – with me, to build our camp." He pointed to a spot at the furthest corner of the lawn. "*Unter die grosse Lindenbaum.* Tree make ... how-you-say pole for tent?" I was beginning to sense that when I did what I was told, and didn't ask awkward questions, Gerhard could be more relaxed with me – especially if Erich wasn't around. "No inspection tonight Johann – so to make more bigger *und besser* – the tent."

Gerhard then helped me button our three *Zeltbahn* groundsheets to the spare ones we'd had to keep hidden the night before. Then he threw a rope over a branch of the big Lime tree, and hauled up the apex of our tent. The result – without a central pole – was that we had a lot more space, and headroom, inside.

Having found wood as well as water at the house, Erich now had a brisk fire under his mess tin – and that meant coffee in a matter of minutes. Last night's storm had cleared the sky, allowing the sun to beat down on us. Gerhard stripped right off, eager to make the most of it. He was envious of our all-over tans, and was determined to match us if he could. When the coffee had boiled, Erich and I joined him, lying lazing in the long grass – with only the buzzing of insects to disturb us. Gerhard's English was slowly becoming more fluent and I had grown accustomed to his thick Saxon accent, so we could converse well enough – and Erich even persuaded him to get my name right.

The other two were dozing, making up for lost sleep, but because the midges were eating me alive, I decided to start on the midday meal. When Gerhard had first sent Erich for water, it seemed to me that our *Schafu* was making sure that I didn't get near the house. But the need for more wood now gave me the perfect excuse to go and explore. I too found plenty of wood. Not only bits of old and worn-out furniture, such as Erich had selected, but the remains of fine and beautiful antiques, smashed beyond any possibility of repair ... and only utter barbarians could have done such a thing. I gathered up an armful of the better pieces, and took them back to show to Gerhard.

"*Mench,* they were only Jews." He sounded quite unmoved. "Just *verdammt Juden* John – and not they, not anyone else can make any use of those bits again – so we must have a good fire and enjoy it." I could see Erich was embarrassed by my discovery, and didn't want to get involved, especially when I started to complain, bitterly, about such wanton destruction and persecution. Nevertheless he did reluctantly intervene.

"But you both of you know we'll never ever find a camp site with such a super supply of wood ... ready chopped and waiting for you!" That was utterly indisputable, and it effectively closed the discussion.

"I reckon its about Gerhard's turn to do some cooking." I whispered, when Erich came across to help me.

"You can suggest it if you like John. But remember, *Schafus* are the ones who give the orders. I can't say anything – and perhaps its best if you don't either."

During that afternoon Gerhard demanded that I should meet him in *Freiringen*, the Hitler Youth's officially approved style of wrestling. Erich had never suggested that he and I should try this, in which a bout can only be won by a Fall. (He probably realised we'd be certain to have arguments without someone else to judge ' ... when any part of the opponent's body between knee and elbow – touches the ground'.)

Later on, after I'd taken several falls, Gerhard suggested it might be more fun if we abandoned the Official Rules and tried to win by 'Submissions' instead of 'Falls'. Only then did our contest develop into the *Mutprobe* he had promised me. He quickly showed that his idea of 'fair' ways to beat an opponent, were a good deal 'freer' than in *Freiringen*. Indeed they were a whole lot rougher, and tougher – but it was just a matter of trying to give as good one got. I could take it, and I was prepared to dish it out too – and we both enjoyed ourselves. I noticed later, when it was Erich's turn to tangle with Gerhard, that he was fully prepared to fight according to what we came to know as 'Gerhard's Rules'. In fact neither of us managed to beat the *Scharführer*, but even so we did achieve a sort of victory over him; because – having proved his physical superiority – he no longer felt the need to assert his rank. And for the rest of that trip Gerhard treated us much more as friends and equals, asking or suggesting – instead of ordering. Better still, he did his share of the work too, which made life more agreeable for everyone.

Nobody mentioned singing whilst we sat round our fire in the darkness, and that was a comfort – for solo performances were never my strong point. Our fire had died down, and the dew was settling, so we moved into the tent. Gerhard lit the single candle in his three sided *Gebirgsjäger* lantern, and then hung it up under the apex, telling us it would pose no fire risk to the tent, and it would be safe from damage too. (He was very proud of that battered folding lantern – with its two mica 'glasses' – which his father, a twice-wounded Iron Cross winner, had carried throughout his service in the elite Mountain Troops.

Knowing Gerhard's insistence on H.J. Camping Discipline, Erich had carefully instructed me how to fold all my clothes neatly, and to stuff them inside my shirt to form a pillow. Socks had to be placed inside boots, which were placed close to hand, so they could easily be found, and donned – in the dark – in the event of an emergency ... or an 'Enemy Attack' on the camp. Our Leader gave me an approving nod as I did this, and he positioned his own pile well clear of mine – something that had not been possible in the cramped space of the smaller tent. But with the enlarged version we were able to enjoy a degree of luxury that would probably have infuriated the 'smooth little *Schlappschwanz*' at the official site. All three of us got into our blankets and continued chatting. I began to wonder who would be given the privilege of performing 'Lights Out', and then getting back into his blanket in the dark.

The conversation was flagging, and it appeared that Gerhard, in his new 'Friendly Leader' role, was actually getting up to do the job himself. But – to my amazement – he blithely threw discipline to the winds, by stooping to drag my blanket away, before starting a rough-house there in the tent! Heaven only knows what he'd have said if Erich had so much as given me a shove or prod during the previous evening. But now it was very much rough-and-tumble *Rauferei* – purely for the fun of it – and with Gerhard even submitting, and laughing too, when he did so ... though I usually had to pay for it next time. We came up against the canvas several times, setting the lantern swinging wildly, and its a real wonder we didn't bring the whole tent down around us. For quite a while it was just the two of us, but after we'd rolled over Erich a couple of times, he joined in – though I'm not sure whether that had been Gerhard's original intention ... or what he really wanted either. By now we were all soaked in sweat and eventually we had to stop exhausted.

The shambles in our tent appeared all the worse in the gyrating light from above. An egg had been smashed, an open bag of sugar sent flying and the whole floor of the tent was a chaos of tangled boots, uniforms, packs and blankets.

'*What?*' I wondered wearily '*What would happen to Gerhard's so precious Scharführer rank if an 'Enemy' should chose this moment to attack our unguarded camp – or, even worse – if a senior H.J. Officer was to arrive for a surprise Midnight Inspection?*' It was quite a relief to realise that nobody in the whole *Hitler Jugend* could possibly know that the three of us had enjoyed ourselves so much, and in such a non-approved, and most definitely '*Verboten*' manner.

After some degree of order had been restored, it was back into our blankets again. Gerhard did indeed put out the candle, and then settled himself down beside me.

***Gebergsjäger* folding lantern.**

9. Kleine Fahrt, Pt. 2.

A half-heard shout awakened me. Drowsily I rolled over and saw that Erich was still sound asleep, but between us lay Gerhards's blanket – already neatly folded. "Erich! John!" It was an urgent shout – from a distance *"Raus RAUS! Kommen Sie HIER!!"* I kicked Erich awake and stumbled from the tent, bleary-eyed, out into the blinding sunlight.

"Coming, Gerhard – COMING!" I yelled, as a bewildered Erich joined me.

"Over here *Faulpelz!"* The voice came from behind a thick evergreen hedge. We started running towards it, feeling the grass dry beneath our feet, the dew already burned off by the sun. Following a concrete path through the hedge, we came upon Gerhard, hand on hip, proudly pointing – at an enormous swimming pool. We moved forward together, and stood in a row at the edge of the sparkling water.

"What a bit of luck," exclaimed Gerhard, "but I ought to have scouted around and found this last night."

"It's just what we need – on a super day like this." Erich was obviously delighted by this new discovery, and so was I. There were a few autumn leaves floating at the deep end, and a hint of green algae spreading over the blue walls of the pool, but apart from that it looked wholesome enough to me. So I pushed them both into the water. As they surfaced, spluttering and swearing, I leapt over their heads, tucking myself into a ball before landing in a great 'bomb-burst' beside them. In retaliation they grabbed me and held me under. For a long time afterwards we splashed and ducked one another, revelling in the cool warmth of the pool.

"Enough of this! We ought to be swimming properly, racing and competing – not playing like little kids." Our *Scharführer* had suddenly remembered his duty, and he lined us up at the shallow end. Slipping off his dripping shorts, he glared at me as though challenging us both to do the same – which we did. *"Ja! Besser ist Jungs* – and more manly too." He'd said that quietly enough, with obvious approval, but now he was almost shouting. *"Funf Lange* – for one hundred metres – *Actung –Fertig – LOS!"* Gerhard hit the water well before Erich and myself – so he must have been actually diving before he told us to start.

Half way down the pool I glanced across at Erich, who was drawing away as usual. Beyond him, at the far side, Gerhard was further ahead still – and not all of that distance could have been gained when he 'jumped the gun.' By the turn things hadn't changed, which proved my swimming was definitely getting better. Over the third and fourth lengths we both steadily gained on Gerhard. After the final turn Erich really pulled out the stops. He surged away from me and overtook Gerhard, who was beginning to tire. Realising that I too had a chance of beating our Leader, I put every thing I had into that last half length. Erich finished as I caught up with Gerhard – and with only four or five metres to go. A moment later there was a muffled yell, but I ploughed right on, and eagerly grabbed the rail.

"Did he ..." I gasped, peering up at Erich. "Did I beat ...?"

"EINE KATZE ... a stinking cat!" Gerhard's near scream cut me short. He was now seated on the pool edge, several metres from the finish, spitting and frantically flicking fingers over his face and chest. "A filthy dead cat," he shouted. "I swam right into it! *Verdammt* thing – it – its been there for weeks!" He jumped to his feet, sprinted to the shallow end, dived in again – and began to wash himself vigorously.

Erich and I looked down into the clutter of leaves and twigs. It had indeed been a cat, but that was a long time ago. Then, with all interest in swimming gone, we walked back to our tent. In spite of his misfortune, our Leader received neither respect nor sympathy from Erich.

"So you couldn't beat us Gerhard. Not even with a flying start! And even if you hadn't met your furry friend – John would have beaten you to the touch. There's no possible doubt about that!" Then I had my turn.

"I'd have thought a good leader would have made sure the water was safe and pure before he allowed his *Jungen* to swim it it." Poor Gerhard; he was too dis-spirited to even give me the scragging I deserved for that.

After breakfast we idled in the long grass, luxuriating in the late summer sunshine, determined to build up our tans for the coming winter. Then I heard a noise; a motorcycle had arrived – its engine running badly until it stopped with a half-hearted backfire. Moments later we heard footsteps. Someone was coming towards us. We all lay low, trying to hide ourselves, but I knew our tent would give us away. The footsteps came nearer and nearer.

"Heil Hitler! I thought you lads might still be here." It was a Storm Trooper, not the fat one Gerhard had spoken to the day before, but a much younger and taller man. "Old Hans told me about you three ... " Then, realising that this might mean nothing to us, the man continued rather lamely, in his high pitched voice. "He told you about this place – yesterday ... so I've come to join you. I ride here to sunbathe sometimes – when I'm not on duty." Only then did I recognise him, as the one with some authority, that Gerhard had moved so swiftly to avoid. I left it to our Leader to respond to that, and he must have decided silence best expressed our degree of welcome. The *S.A. Mann* didn't seem to have noticed and, when he began to strip off his uniform, it became apparent he must have been a frequent visitor to the garden. I had an uneasy feeling he was paying rather too much attention to our naked bodies as he stood there – showing off his own very ordinary physique, as though it was something to be proud of.

"I'm Jochen, and I have just finished my time with the *R.A.D.*" He declared – flexing what few muscles he had. Later, when I got a too close look at his delicate hands, I found myself doubting whether they had ever seriously used a pick or a shovel – let alone worked long hours with either – during his time of compulsory service with the Labour Corps. Quite uninvited, he settled down beside Gerhard. Although he had chosen to join us, the *S.S. Mann* made little conversation at first – and that almost entirely with Gerhard, whom he probably recognised as our Leader – rank being everything in the New Germany.

Getting little response in that quarter, he began to talk across Gerhard to Erich and myself, and he seemed to think we'd be impressed by his having a motorcycle. But I was not the least bit interested; not after a narrow escape when riding pillion behind my older cousin Peter who had just got his licence.

Whilst Jochen was talking I had the feeling Erich and I were being carefully scrutinised, but all his attention switched to me when he learned I was English. At first I'd kept quiet, then said a little – though for some unknown reason – none of it in German, and Erich had started, unwillingly, to translate.

"The English make very good motorcycles, but mine is a B.M.W. .... I show you." The *S.A. Mann* got up, walked to his clothes, took out a photograph, and came and lay down beside me – rather too close for my liking. *"My name is Jochen. What is your name?"* He spoke slowly and much too loud for one so close, looking across at Erich, expecting him to translate if I failed to understand his new method of communication.

"John," said Erich, with great emphasis on the hard 'J' which is almost unknown in German. Jochen held the photo in front of my face, bringing the other hand around the back of my neck to point out the details as he told me – at great length – all about it. So eager was he, that he hardly waited for a translation. I could understand most of what he said, not that I wanted to know any of it. Even so, I thought the photograph itself was rather odd. It showed Jochen astride the bike, in what I took to be proper *R.A.D.* Uniform, and wearing a crash helmet with goggles around it.

"Erich, will you please ask Jochen if he was a *R.A.D.* Despatch Rider?" Although Erich translated this, Jochen merely pointed out where the gear change was, and how many gears there were. Then he passed the photo to Erich, repeating much of what he'd told me, meanwhile bringing his own hand and arm back onto my shoulder. I'd soon had enough of that, so I slapped myself several times.

"*Verdammt Deutschen* midges!" I muttered. There were in fact very few, but I got up from under his arm, and went to our tent. I came out, stinking of Insect Repellent Oil, and lay down beside our Leader. "Do you want some Gerhard?" I offered him the little bottle.

"You rub some on my back *bitte*." I obliged – with Jochen watching closely whilst I did so.

"Erich. *Auffangen!*" He caught the bottle I'd thrown.

"But there's hardly any left!" He grumbled as he tipped out the remaining few drops. In fact that oil did very little good when midges were around, but at least it had got me away from Jochen. Even so, I wondered what Erich would say when he went into the tent, where it would be only to apparent that I'd poured away a quantity of his expensive oil, to make certain there would be none left for our uninvited guest.

Gerhard began to tell us his plans for the rest of the day, even to the train we'd be catching later in the afternoon. Our conversation pointedly ignored Jochen, and I slowly began to speak more German. At that the *S.A. Mann* started talking to me again. I'm not really sure what I had in mind when I began to enquire about the former occupiers of the house.

"*Juden!*" He fairly spat out the word. "They were filthy Jews, enemies of *Führer und Reich*. They brought this country down in 1918 – and they've kept us down ever since, filling their pockets so they can live in a place like this – whilst others starve ... " He continued with a long tirade, repeatedly quoting what Hitler had said on the subject. "But we came along one

Saturday – and we threw them out whilst we smashed the place up. You should see the inside, there's not a door left on its hinges. We did a fine job! I found their candlestick – with the Jewish star and many candles – and I smashed that as well. Two nights afterwards the whole family ran away. They all left the *Reich* – and good riddance too. *Jude Verreke!"*

This was the first time I had met such blind and bitter hatred, and it appalled me. Propping my head on my hand, I stared straight at him.

"And the cat? I asked defiantly. "Their cat – was it an Aryan cat – or a Jewish cat?" The Storm Trooper couldn't meet my gaze. He made no reply but turned onto his back, and lay looking up into the cloudless sky. Time passed, and the uneasy silence continued until I spoke again, softly and in my best German – as though thinking aloud. "Now if only I had been born a true Aryan, and one of the *Herrenvolk* – perhaps I too would be brave enough – to drown a little pussy-cat!" I saw the Storm Trooper's muscles contract – and I prepared to run for it, knowing that if he should start trouble, I might have to deal with it alone. Certainly Erich had the physical courage to stand by me, though I couldn't be sure he would do so in those circumstances – and Gerhard was much too loyal to the Party to help me out.

"Its funny to think how wet and cold yesterday morning was ..." Erich butted in, desperately trying to change the subject. " ... and now its as hot as this."

"Yes." I retorted peevishly. "It certainly is hot today – which makes it all the worse that superb swimming pool isn't fit to swim in!"

"But Johann, it was more hotter in Arabia." Gerhard spoke quickly. "I do envy you two – flying and travel world. *ich selbst* – I do not ever even see the sea!" He was trying to silence me, but his authority had vanished. He looked pleadingly at me, giving the slightest backwards nod at the still motionless Storm Trooper. Having won a considerable moral victory, I decided the time had come to drop the matter – before things got completely out of hand.

For a while we all lay silent. Then at last Jochen got up slowly. "Duty Calls." he murmured. After he'd finished dressing he snapped to attention, raised his arm stiffly. *"Wiedersehen. Heil Hitler!"* Somehow he managed to make it clear that I was not included in his parting gesture. Fortunately not even the most ardent Nazi can *gruss* properly whilst lying on his belly, so we just gave him an offhand wave – and started our own conversation. Gerhard spoke softly to Erich for a few moments, and then turned to me. "Did you understand that John!" I'd picked up on what sounded like *'Warne Bruer'* which meant nothing to me then, but there were times when I felt it best to appear able to keep up with our Leader – whilst hoping I'd be able to sort it out later – or I could always ask Erich for an explanation – so I nodded firmly. Then, as an abrupt change of subject, Gerhard decided we must all set about preparing our midday meal.

Afterwards, when we'd finished cleaning our mess tins, he suddenly took command again, announcing that we were to go on a long hike. Although this was a complete change of plan, our Leader offered no explanation, and Erich showed no surprise either. We struck camp immediately and set off heading across fields, and away from the road back to town – the one the Storm Trooper would have taken. Map in hand, Gerhard led us along kilometres of country lanes, right round the little town – until we finally reached the Station, but only just in time to catch our train.

As it moved off, we caught a glimpse of four brown-shirted figures lurking behind a wall, apparently lying in ambush, eagerly watching the road we had marched up the previous day. Gerhard ducked back from the window. Instead of bragging about his cleverness in avoiding trouble, he began talking to me, saying anything to stop me asking questions about what I had just seen ... and avoided.

Back at Grossmutter's, and in the privacy of our bedroom that evening, I seized the opportunity to catch up on a few matters.

"Erich, what was it Gerhard meant about that *nette Oberscharführer* at the camp?" This resulted in an embarrassed silence.

"You weren't meant to have heard that John. Gerd said he thought he'd probably won at least one of his stars in bed. That's because a boy can't normally expect promotion if he's too feeble to qualify fairly for a Proficiency Badge like this." He pointed proudly to the large round arrow-backed metal *Leistungsabzeichen* pinned to his shirt pocket. "But, John. You must never again behave – to anyone in a Party Uniform – as you did today with the young Storm Trooper, not however much you dislike him. He was an *Ober-sturmführer* and probably the top *S.A.* Man in that little town. He's the type that always wants to show how powerful he is, and so get promoted. And anyway he's too much like that *O'Schafu* – certainly a *Warmer Bruder*, definitely 'Like That' – and not at all the sort you and I would want to get mixed up with.

"Erich, just remember I'm British, so an *S.A. Mann* – even with a little bit of rank – means nothing to me." There followed a long pause before he replied.

"John. You MUST listen to what I say ... this is NOT England." He had spoken softly, but now his voice dropped to a near whisper – although we were quite alone. "Surely you wouldn't want to put your friends in

DANGER – would you John?" That was the first time I had ever detected real fear in his normally confident voice ... and I was shocked to hear it. Then I recalled that before we parted, Gerhard had been most insistent that we must not mention our 'private' camp at the Jew's house to any of the other boys. And he'd been even more emphatic that we should not let slip that he'd been with us – not even at the official camp site. It seemed there were an awful lot of secrets to be kept, and things that must not be said out loud, in Hitler's Germany.

Even so, and taken all in all, they'd been an exciting three days, full of incident and new experiences; and meeting strangers – some with even stranger attitudes. Having so much to savour, I found sleep a long time coming, but I eventually drifted off whilst wondering what new adventures, or strange encounters, lay in store for me, and Erich, at the long awaited *Sommerlager*, in just four days time.

10. Sommerlager.

The summer camps of the Hitler Youth were often very big affairs, and it was most unusual for a single *Schar* to be allowed a long camp on its own. Everyone had been told, repeatedly, that in our case it was a very special privilege, and that Gerhard's temporary promotion to *Oberscharführer* would not be confirmed unless the experiment turned out to be a complete success.

The *Schar's* little camp was well organised, except for the food supply, and that was certainly not Gerhards's fault. Rations arrived daily, from the Main Camp, some five kilometres away. But they seemed to be exactly the same every time, which made it even more fortunate we had a good and very popular cook – known to one and all as *Mops*. He was a cheeky pug-nosed freckle-faced lad; a trainee-chef, who proudly wore a large badge showing he had come first in the local finals for the National Trade Competition that year.

However, not even *Maps'* skills could disguise the endless beans and pretty awful sausages. My remark ' ... these are the very worst *Würste* I've ever tasted ...' was received with great delight by the best English speakers. Nevertheless, by the time Erich had translated and then carefully explained it to the others, my joke was beginning to sound a bit feeble.

Our days in camp varied between normal H.J. Training, and work on the land. That first morning we marched several kilometres before spending an hour throwing wooden clubs, competing for distance and accuracy. (These 'clubs' had an iron band around the head, and my suspicion that this was practice for throwing the German 'potato-masher' hand grenades was confirmed when – after throwing whilst standing – we had to throw them from kneeling and lying positions too.)

Then back to camp by a short cut through woodland; under the watchful and unwelcoming eye of a uniformed and armed State Forester, who shouted a warning at us not to start any fires. The afternoon was taken up with a variety of sports, and ended up with us swimming in a nearby lake.

As if that wasn't enough, *Rottenführer* Franz – our acting *Sportwart* – organised an evening of *Freiringen*. He and Gerhard had a terrific scrap – to show us all how it should be done – but I'm not sure whether Franz won, or if Gerhard deliberately took a fall to make him look good. After that I felt more than a little insulted when Franz matched me against Theodore – an overweight *Muttikind*. But in the event I had a job to even catch up with Theo, who went down almost as soon as I touched him – which left me feeling pretty silly. Erich had a spectacular win over *Rottenführer* Hugo, grabbing his neck before turning, dropping to his knees and throwing the heavier lad over his shoulder, to a crashing fall. Erich was loudly cheered, because the newly promoted Hugo was over-keen in exercising his very limited authority.

That evening Gerhard showed the others he trusted me – with two hours of Sentry Duty. I was called at midnight, and although one of us should have been patrolling the camp perimeter, I spent most of the first hour beside the fire with Rolf Schrulle – better known as *'Der Yank'*. His family had spent more than two years in the United States, mostly in New York. They then decided to leave, in the belief that with Hitler firmly in charge, things would be better for them back in Germany. In his strange mixture of German and Bronx-American slang – which he believed was English – Rolf told how the whole family had become very active in the pro-nazi German-American Bund.

"The top *Bund* guys know I *Hitlerjunge* from *Deutschland*, so make me *Kameradschaftführer* over kids in *Jungvolk*. We have many goddam *gut Wochenende* out at Yaphank on Long Island, at *Bund's* own swell *Camp Siegfried*. I sad to leave God's Own Country." Shortly after telling me all that, he went to call his relief, whom he warned was a 'Super Nazi.'

Axel immediately took charge of the old boar spear, the symbol of our *Wachtdienst*. He declared it was a great honour for me, to be allowed to stand guard over his sleeping Comrades – but he pretended not to understand when I asked who our attackers might be. Instead, for almost the next hour, he went on and on about his family, and how loyal they all were in serving their beloved *Führer.* Both his parents were Party Officials, two older brothers had joined the *Leibstandarte* – Hitler's elite Bodyguard – and his sister was Leader of a *B.D.M* girls unit. But Axel seemed most proud of their 'Baby Brother', a *Jungvolk* boy, who had been promoted – at an exceptionally early age – and was also awarded the Golden Honour Badge of the Hitler Youth. Although Axel would not tell me the reason for this, he did hint darkly that the kid had done something secret and heroic – and he had been told by High-ups that because of it, he could expect a good career in the *Hitler Jugend.* Axel then told me to do a hurried round of the perimeter, whilst he went to awaken Hans. It was a relief – in more senses than one – when the time came for me to crawl back into my blanket.

After the Flag-raising Ceremony next morning, Gerhard led the *Schar* out of camp and onto a main road. Soon we heard the sound of marching feet. Around the corner ahead of us came a squad of some forty *B.D.M.* Girls, with a pennant flying bravely at their head. Gerhard hissed at us to march smartly, before he gave their Leader a terrific *Gruss,* and a very loud *'Heil Hitler!'* The lanky horse-faced *Führerin* had blonde plaits coiled about her ears. She returned our *Schafu's* greeting, but looked at the rest of us as if we had crawled out of a drain. Her girls were mostly about our age and many of them were either smiling at us, or giggling amongst themselves. But one single word from the Dragon stopped all that – and she promptly began to call the step, as though hurrying her charges away from the likes of us. (Everywhere in Germany one met uniformed groups marching – marching – just for the sake of marching.)

But we had been marching with a purpose, and the rest of the day was spent working in a vineyard. The grapes were small and bitter, the sun beat down fiercely, and there wasn't a breath of wind. But at least I could enjoy good company, and the farmer let us take our time on the job. When we'd finished Kurt asked where we could get a wash. He was only offered a hose-pipe, but we had a lot of fun with that – and we got rid of some of the dust too. Whilst we were doing that, several of the older lads suggested it was only fitting we should end the day sampling the local vintage. Gerhard ignored this.

"Tonight you have *Weltanschaulisch-schulung,*" he announced, and many loud groans greeted that most unwelcome news.

After the evening meal, Gerhard called us to parade, and then handed over. "*Kafu* Kurt, you can take charge, because I have important things to see to." Kurt began by asking individuals very easy questions about *Der Führer*, the National Socialist Workers Party, and recent German history. Even I could earn approval by knowing Hitler's birthday. (Its the day after my own, so it wasn't too difficult – but I didn't tell them that.) When questions got harder the *Kafu* threw them open to the whole group, and one of our two '150% Super Nazi' would always come up with the correct answer. Axel could even list every bit of territory Germany had lost under the Treaty of Versailles, and Heinrich – without being asked – proudly gave their individual populations too. After perhaps ten minutes of this dreary stuff, Gerhard returned and Kurt jumped to his feet, klicked his heels, *grüssed* very smartly, and confidently reported.

"*Oberscharführer. Schar Eine* has a very full and thorough knowledge. Every one of my questions has been correctly answered, even by *Der Engländer.*" Kurt stayed rigidly at attention, looking expectantly at Gerhard.

"Excellent *Kafu*. In that case, those who wish to support the *Autarkie* of the Third Reich may do so by visiting the inn. But do remember *Jungs* – tomorrow will be another long day, so don't over do it." As we made our way back to the tent, Kurt gave me a big wink, and then reminded me what I'd need to do if I hoped to pass inspection before being allowed to leave camp.. "Have your hair tidy, a clean shirt, shoes well polished. And you must be able to produce a clean handkerchief, and a comb free of hairs. Otherwise you stay in camp!"

* * *

First thing next morning, despite the rain, Franz led us – shirtless – on a long run, up-hill and down-dale, cheerfully saying it would give us a good appetite for a delayed *Frühstück*. After we had eaten, Gerhard decided we should try out our military skills. The *Schar* was split into two groups. One to defend the camp, the other was to attack and try to get possession of the flag. Gerhard appointed himself as Referee. Erich and I were in the attackers, with Kurt as our Commander. At first our attack showed more enthusiasm than subtlety. *Kameradschaftführer* Hans led us out from the wood, in a yelling charge – as though we would just sweep into the camp and take the flag. But, as soon as battle was joined, our enthusiasm faded, and then some of our number began to fall back, and despite our loud cries of 'Cowards!' they did little to help us, so we too were driven back, and for two hundred metres or more it was a rout, with the Camp group triumphant in hot pursuit. Then, at the blast of a whistle, we all turned – as planned – and met them man for man; indeed it was less than that, for they outnumbered us. But we held out until there came a trumpet call – from inside the camp.

Kurt, with two others, all good fighters with field-craft skills, had disappeared early on, and then moved invisibly right around the camp, sneaking in behind the defenders, who thought they had put us all to flight, and they now held the flag. It was, as so often in the history war. '*Those who run away – can turn – and so they do win the day.*

There was no doubt we had won, but the individual battles went on, nobody wanting to stop if there was a chance of beating his opponent. *Rottenführer* Hugo was giving me a hard time. Erich came and watched, but he had the good manners not to interfere until I got the upper-hand. Then, taking my time, and using my favourite headlock and strangle – I finally forced Hugo to submit.

That afternoon two Air-rifles, targets, and a good supply of pellets were delivered with the day's rations. We soon had a makeshift range ready for use, with a sandy bank behind the targets. Gerhard – acting as Range Officer – was most safety conscious, laying a rope on the ground, and making it very clear that nobody would go beyond it except on his order.

"You will shoot in pairs. Five shots each. Then go together to collect your targets and bring them back for scoring. The next pair will go, at the same time, to set up their targets – and nobody else will move. Is that understood? I did ask **'Is that understood?**"

"Jawhol! Herr Oberscharführer!" came the loud reply.

The standard of shooting was generally good. Franz and two *Jungen* scoring 'possibles'. Then it was our turn. The rifle was new to me, having a safety device, a very powerful spring, and an unusually hard trigger pull. After firing our five rounds, Erich and I were ordered forward, together with Heinrich and Fritz, to collect and replace targets.

Whilst our scores were being recorded, they lay down to shoot. Fritz fired and Heini's target fell over. There were howls of derision. Heini mumbled something, dug the butt of his rifle into the ground and used it to lever himself up onto his knees. The idiot must have had his finger on the trigger – because the rifle fired. There was a moment of horrified silence. Then a yell from Otto, who stepped forward and punched Heini full in the face – knocking him to the ground.

"Stillgestanden!" Roared Gerhard, bending down to take possession of Heini's rifle ... which was the one I had just used. *"Kameradschaftführer* Hils. Escort this – this creature – I cannot call him a *Hitler Junge* – and set him on to peeling potatoes for the evening meal. I will deal with him myself later."

Otto had been very lucky. Heini's pellet – having travelled barely two yards – had put a fair dent in the thin metal of his belt buckle. Had it gone a couple of inches in any other direction we would now be rushing him to hospital. Gerhard loaded the rifle, and banged the butt on the ground; next he tested the trigger pull several times, and he got others to do the same. We all agreed that the rifle could not have fired itself.

Then – as though nothing had happened – the shooting continued until everyone had had his turn. Afterwards Gerhard gathered us around him.

"This incident has brought great shame on all of us – on *Schar Eine*, and on *Gefolgschaft Sieben*. Therefore, we in Schar One, will deal with it. Indeed it must be a matter of honour that nobody outside Schar One shall ever know what happened here today. Otto did what a man might do – and we will say nothing more about that. And remember this – nobody is to speak to Heinrich, unless to give him an order.

After the shooting finished there was general agreement that Heinrich had indeed brought great shame on our *Schar*, and because of that Gerhard was encouraged to punish him very severely. Whilst we enjoyed the evening meal, Heinrich – now sporting a definite 'blue-eye', as the German's term it – had to stand beside the flagstaff, rigidly at 'Attention' but with head bowed, for a full hour. Immediately afterwards, to complete his disgrace, our *Oberscharführer* publicly deprived him of his *Halstuch*, for the remainder of the camp – at least. (Two whole days were to pass before I fully understood just how much the loss of that black Honour Scarf must have meant to a 'Super-nazi' like Heinrich – who's father was an important leader in the *S.S.*)

The lads had been looking forward to another gentle day amongst the vines, but after the Flag-lowering ceremony, Gerhard gave us some advice.

"Before 'Lights Out' tonight, make sure your boots and stocking are *In tiptop ordnung*, ready for a long march. Also have your water-bottle filled, your breadbag ready packed with mess-tin, swim gear, notebook and camera." Despite saying this, he firmly refused to answer any questions. "I should not have given you even this warning – but – and only because I am such a kind and considerate leader ...." The remainder of his sentence was lost in some very undisciplined catcalls – which he'd been fully expecting.

Franz and I turned in well before the last trumpet – both being pretty well exhausted after a long and tiring day – knowing we had early *Feldküche Dienst* in the morning.

* * *

It seemed no time at all before Willi Schmidt was shaking me awake. I cursed him and buried my head in the blanket. Next came a roar from Franz ... and I joined him in throwing fat Willi bodily out of the tent – because that idiot had awakened us a full ninety minutes too early. Only seconds later he was back, and begging – from a safe distance – that we should both get up at once. Gerhard had sent him from Sentry Duty, to call us, because an early breakfast – for the whole camp – must be ready in little over three quarters of an hour.

Well before the normal Reveille time, we fell in for the Flag-raising Ceremony, after which Gerhard addressed us.

"Heinrich – being in disgrace, and without his *Halstuch* – cannot be allowed accompany us. He must remain in camp, peeling potatoes for our supper tonight. The rest of us – having made our preparations – will now march the few kilometres to Main Camp, for a 'Special Day' ... and whatever that may mean, you will find out soon enough *Meine Jungs*. But I do demand of each one of you, that we do really well at whatever lies ahead, for all eyes will be on us. Woe betide any *Junge* who lets us down – even a quarter as badly as Heinrich did yesterday!"

The march took us through a long wide valley, where boys of the *Flieger H.J.* were flying in gliders from a hillside above us. Gangs of lads, six or eight to a side, would run forward stretching heavy elastic ropes, that catapulted the machines into the air. Those gliders were very primitive, being nothing more than a simple wing and tail unit, joined together by a flat wooden skeleton – inside which sat the pilot, completely exposed to the elements. Most of the pilots managed a short flight and then turned back towards the launching site.

But one possibly over-ambitious youth – probably attempting to gain extra height – soared steeply up, and then hung almost motionless. This 'pilot' next achieved a series of erratic descending swoops, in our general direction. Our *Oberscharführer* – seeing the possible danger – shouted ***'About Turn! Double March!*** We did as ordered, whilst other bystanders scattered panic-stricken in all directions. Meanwhile the glider skimmed over the roadside fences – and landed heavily, demolishing several drying racks piled high with hay – before coming to rest in the middle of the farmer's pond. We gave the Pilot a tremendous cheer, though his fellow *Flieger Jungen*, and doubtless his Leaders and Instructors, would have been very much less enthusiastic about this remarkable performance. Nevertheless we could not stay to see how they recovered the glider from its watery resting place. Instead, we marched steadily on, though I at least had no idea where we were going – nor what we'd be doing for the rest of the day.

11. The Special Day.

At Main Camp, *Gefolgschaftführer* Horst, together with his superior, the *Lagerführer,* came and inspected us closely. Only then were we allowed to join the rest of *No 7 Gefolgschaft* on the parade ground. Eventually, after much shouting and reorganising, the band struck up and we set off behind *No 5 Gefolgschaft* who were our great rivals. After five or so kilometres we came to a river, and the steamer that would take us upstream. Loudspeakers on board gave details of the scenery, which was magnificent. On either bank were steep woods, or cliffs, often topped by fantastic castles, some ruined, others still inhabited, but all built long ago by Teutonic Knights or Robber Barons. Cameras and notebooks now came into their own, because the H.J. encouraged the keeping of camp dairies, and some of the photo albums I had seen were works of art – every snap being captioned in white crayon, with often humorous sketches added, to fill in the story.

Rounding a bend in the river we sighted the newly completed *Zweiturmdamm,* named for the tall fairy-tale castles on either side of the gorge, built by feuding Princelings some four hundred years earlier. Our ferry entered the open lock gates, and in a few minutes – passing from one lock to another – it had been lifted more than 40 metres so it could enter the lake formed by the dam. There it would take the younger *Deutsches Jungvolk* boys on an extended cruise. But two hundred of us older lads were disembarked, for inland water training with the *Marine Hitler Jugend.*

In their white sailor suits and round hats, with long blue ribbons dangling down their backs, the older boys of the *Marine H.J.* looked just like the *Kriegsmarine* – and some of them certainly thought themselves every bit as experienced, and even more important. With an excessive amount of shouting they detailed us into groups for canoeing, rowing or sailing. A number of big white rowing boats lay at the jetty, where our crew of ten was greeted by a lordly *Marine Kafu*. He ordered us to see that our boots were clean before stepping aboard his *Kutter*. Next he sarcastically suggested.

"If any of you should feel inclined to be sick – do please do it over the gunwale!"

We settled ourselves, five to a side, two to a thwart, with a heavy oar each – and that was the first time many of those lads had ever touched an oar. The two *Marine Jungen* with us pushed our boat away from the jetty, and then did clever things with their long boat hooks, whilst the *Kafu* – who stood at the stern – started yelling one instruction after another. He was using quite incomprehensible nautical terms, as if deliberately trying to make us *Algemeine H.J.* appear stupid. The result was utter chaos. Erich and I pulled together, and well enough, even though others got their oars entangled with ours. No wonder the *Kafu* complained that our boat looked like a demented spider. But, after a while, we all managed to get the hang of it – and even to keep the stroke – except for Willi, who often couldn't stay in step on dry land. Heading up the lake, our two *Kutters* overtook a huge Red Indian style canoe, which was making erratic progress as a dozen *Gefolg* 5 lads paddled frantically in an attempt to stay ahead of us. When our cutter was past the headland, and thus out of sight of his superiors, the *Marine Kafu* became much more reasonable, the more so when he realised we were really trying. Within half an hour things were going quite well, and he said as much, whilst ordering us to take even longer strokes – leaning right back each time as we heaved on the long oars. Things were not going so well in the other cutter manned by *No 7s*, and so we soon left them behind. Eventually we beached the boat on a small island, for bathing. Our young *Kapitän* warning that the water was very deep, and colder than we might expect. Because of this he kept the boat manned, with both his Life-savers at the ready.

When we started back, the *Kafu* took Gerhard's oar, telling him to steer. Then the second *No 7* cutter came out from a bay and they were obviously trying to catch us. Tired although most of us were, everyone pulled harder when Gerhard urged us on, and I heard him telling the *Kafu* he felt like a Viking Chief, standing there at the tiller. Then a shout from our Lookout warned that the big canoe was ahead, and on a course to cut right across our bows. The *Kafu* glanced quickly over his shoulder, and then told Gerhard.

"The Rule of the Sea says – that you have the Right of Way. So – you must hold your course and speed." That was said with authority, and Gerhard did as ordered – looking straight ahead – as though the 5's and their strange craft did not exist; but of course they wanted us to be the ones to give way. It was a near thing, for at the speed we were going, that canoe could have been cut in half. However, at the very last moment, their *M.H.J. Kapitän* got scared, or sensible – and tried to turn away – or to stop ... perhaps both at the same time ... because paddles were going in all directions. Two real landlubbers jumped to their feet in panic, upsetting the balance of the canoe, which began to rock so wildly that the pair of them went overboard. It was a great moment for *Gefolgschaft 7*, and Mops swore gleefully that the 5's would never be allowed to forget it, nor that their two sodden *Jungen* suffered the ultimate indignity of being dragged – on the end of a boat-hook – into *No 7's* second cutter.

Back on shore we were hurried to the smoke-belching *Gulaschkanone* – as the Army Cooks called their horse-drawn Field Kitchen. They grumbled that we were late, saying the stew was burnt – and it was all our own fault. But I for one, was so hungry I'd never have noticed if it had been. The Steamer was not due for some time and the *Stammfürer* decided we must give the local people a show, by marching round – and round – and round the little village. The inhabitants must have been thankful that the *M.H.J.* had only one trumpet, and that all our band instruments had been left aboard the Steamer. The return voyage was mostly spent singing the half-shouted boastful songs beloved by the H.J. Leadership. But three younger lads, who had fine voices, did give us an occasional quieter and much more pleasant alternative.

When all units were ashore and formed up for the march back to Main Camp, the *Lagerführer* shouted for *'Oberscharführer Götz!'* Gerhard promptly sprinted forward, received some instructions, and then ran back, head held high, and looking very pleased with himself. Shouting his orders loud and clear, he marched us, at a brisk double, to the back of the column – which moved off the moment we were in position. With perhaps some three kilometres to go – and without any word being said – Gerhard broke away from the main body, leading us up a side road, in what I took to be the direction of our own little camp. As soon as the others were out of earshot Gerhard halted us.

"*Kameraden!* That we do not have to march to the Main Camp to be dismissed, is ordered by the *Lagerführer* himself. This is given as a special privilege, because we have all done well today. And because he is satisfied that I have you all – and our exceptional little camp – well under control." He paused to let that sink in, then, "I too say 'Well Done – *und Vielen Danke!*"

During long marches Gerhard was in the habit of following behind the *Schar,* and calling a single boy back to join him. This always aroused speculation. Would the chosen one be getting advice, words of praise, or a private warning about his past or future conduct? More often it was just a chat, because a Leader was expected to know his boys as individuals, and even to visit their families occasionally. This time he called me back, asking had I enjoyed the day?

"Yes Gerhard, very much. And I'd have liked the chance to go up in one of those gliders too."

"So, you want to fly – *und* me also. *Und* I will soon... You keep a secret John? For months I want join *Flieger H.J.* And at long last they say *'Ja'.* First day next month I become *Flieger.* It is good yes?" This came as a shock to me, and it would be a much greater shock to the rest of the *Schar.*

"Very good Gerhard ... for you ... but who ... will take ... ove' ... ?" I stopped, lamely, for it was not for me to ask such a question.

"You keep another secret Johann – you promise?" I nodded. "Is bad news for *Schar Eine,* I think. *Kameradschaftführer* Hils, he becomes *Scharführer.*" I just did not know what to say. I knew this was a secret that must be kept, because such news would certainly ruin the remainder of *Sommerlager* for my friends. (I suddenly realised that I didn't know Hils' Christian name, or even a nickname. It was some indication of his unpopularity that he was always referred to as *'Kameradschaftführer Hils'* without even abbreviating the rank to the more familiar *'Kafu'.*) Although I didn't say as much, I was glad Gerhard had had to wait. He was keen, and hard, and a real disciplinarian when it mattered, but nobody could say he was a 'Super Nazi' – and after I'd learned not to tread on his toes – he'd become a real friend to me.

After the evening meal on that my last night, we all fell in before the flagstaff for the ceremony of lowering the Hitler Youth's own swastika'd flag. When the last trumpet note had died away, Gerhard called Kurt and myself to stand beside him, in front of the assembled *Schar.*

"Kameraden. Der Engländer will be leaving us tomorrow," he announced, "and I – We – will be sorry to lose him. John has marched like a *Junge.* He shoots like a *Junge* ... and he fights like a *Junge!* That being so, Erich's friend is well worthy to wear the honoured *Schwarz Halstuch* of the *Hitler Jugend.* Indeed he should become a member of the *Hitler Jugend* – then he would really be one of us!"

I felt enormously proud when Kurt placed the black neckerchief under my shirt collar, holding it there until Gerhard had slid the brown leather

Knotte up to my throat, to keep it in position. My brief but sincere reply was warmly applauded, by *Jungen* and Leaders alike – even though I had said nothing about joining the H.J. myself. (Although I had enjoyed their activities and greatly appreciated the easy friendship shown me by the *Jugend,* I had – even then – a deep loyalty to my own King and Country, which would prevent me from ever sharing their unquestioning devotion to Adolf Hitler.)

As twilight turned to dusk on that beautiful evening, we gathered around the big fire. Gerhard ordered a pale youth to open the evening's entertainment. Reluctantly he stood and tunelessly sang a short item from the official song book. It was all about blood and sacrifice – an unpromising beginning to our concert. Next, following what I quickly learned was a *Schar Eine* tradition, the singer piled more wood on the fire, and then slipped off his shirt to show he had made his contribution. In turn others stood and recited, sang songs, or told long unfunny jokes. But, as time went by, things became much less formal, and towards the end of the evening many of the songs were distinctly ribald. After my turn, the lads gave me more applause than the song deserved, and my log sent a great cloud of sparks dancing up into the starlit sky. Then, with duty done, I was able to relax beside my friends – shirtless in the warm glow of the fire – but very conscious that the dark token of their friendship still hung around my neck. Erich then rose and told a number of jokes that he most certainly would not have dared to tell at home – and because of this they were very well received by the boys.

A buzz of anticipation greeted the arrival of a couple of youngsters who set up two tent poles, between which they stretched a thin cord at about chest height. Rudi beat a quick roll on his drum, and there was a cheer as a figure came into the firelight. Even behind an enormous burnt-cork moustache, and a towelling 'turban', I could instantly recognise Mops. He bowed deeply. "Introducing – My World Famous Flea Circus, featuring the intrepid Adam, who, together with his partner, the beautiful and utterly fearless Eva, will perform – upon the High Wire – acts of unparalleled skill and daring."

With a flourish, Mops took a small tin out from his pocket. Next, two torch beams focussed on one end of the cord, and there he placed the two non-existent performers. Guiding them with his finger, he made them *'Parade-Marsche'* – *Goose-stepping* – along the wire.

"Legs Out!" He boomed. *"Eins - Zwei,* One - Two!" Like perfectly rehearsed spotlights, the two torches followed their progress to the other end of the cord. When the clapping had died down, Mops told us that Adam would now walk backwards, with Eva standing on his shoulders – and only she would be carrying a balancing pole. Twice they had to pause, waiting until the wire stopped swinging, and once – so we were told – they almost fell.

Next came the most dangerous part of the performance, never before seen in public, during which we were urged to keep completely silent – lest the concentration of the Artistes be broken. Adam and Eva were to cross the wire, leap-frogging over one another as they went. Rudi gave a slow roll on his drum, and then they set off – at a fine old rate – each leap being described by Mop's finger. But – at the halfway point he gave a great cry of dismay – for Eva had fallen!

Immediately one of the torch-holders swore he'd seen her land on Theo's head. Mops promptly began a none too gentle search through the fat boy's hair. Theodore was unpopular, and up to then he hadn't even offered to perform, so there was general approval when Mops asked for help. Gunter eagerly grabbed Theo's ear, jerking it to and fro, saying he was 'trying to get some light inside.' And Franz searched underneath his shirt. So, between the three of them, he had a pretty rough time of it. Only when Heinz shouted that they ought to see whether Eva was inside Theo's shorts, did Mops push the others away. Very solemnly he tried to comfort Adam, before retuning him to the tin.

Mops was visibly sobbing as he walked away into the darkness. But his return, without the fancy dress, was greeted with thunderous applause and much laughter; then – having added his log to the glowing fire – he came and sat down beside me.

Some twenty minutes later, while Theo was floundering inharmoniously through a rather silly *Rubezahl*, he was suddenly interrupted.

"Eva Gefunden Ist!" Shouted Mops excitedly. *"Meine geliebte Eva zürueck-gecommon ist!"* Then, when all eyes were upon us, he carefully lifted up my black *Halstuch* – and picked Eva from my chest. Poor Theo didn't know whether to shut up, to sing on, or to sit down. And nobody was the least bit bothered what he did. Because Mops was busy talking to Eva, and I was assuring anyone who would listen, that she was quite unhurt, and the whole *Schar* were loudly congratulating us of her safe return.

When every one had done his party-piece, Gerhard rose and thanked us. "To-night," he continued, "has really been John's night. So, instead of closing with a German song, I am asking John to lead us all through the *Engländer's* ceremony of Friendship and Farewell." I felt sure this was intended as a real compliment – but it caused me extreme embarrassment – because I had absolutely no idea what he was talking about. Eventually I gathered he had once seen a film in which the party ended with 'Auld Lang Syne'. It was pointless my trying to explain its Scottish origin, and much too late to teach the words, so I gave a solo rendition – whilst trying to guide some forty utterly bewildered *Jungen* through the motions – which must have convinced many of them that most *Engländers* really are quite mad.

The following morning Gerhard brought Erich and several others to see me off at the village station. Kurt put my luggage on a seat, and then I looked down from the carriage doorway whilst we said our farewells. Very slowly the train began to move and I shook hands with Erich again. He stood to Attention with the others, and raised his hand – as if to give the Party Salute – but he changed his mind and waved to me instead. When I could no longer see them, I lifted my suitcase to put it up on the rack. Underneath, where Kurt must have hidden it, lay a small paper package. Inside I found a red be-swastika'd Hitler Youth Armband, and a pair of red edged shoulder straps, numbered 324, for the *H.J. Bann* at Fürth; they even had the correct grey metal buttons, numbered 7, for our *Gefolgschaft*. I could see no reason why anyone would have taken either to camp as spares, and that meant they must surely have been taken from somebody's uniform ... and for that reason I valued the gift all the more.

Hours later, when my train was speeding through France, I opened my suitcase in search of a book. There lay the treasured black scarf. '*What,*' I wondered, '*What will Gesfu Horst say when he learns that this, and the other insignia, have all been presented to me?*' Regardless of that, I knew I'd be wearing the scarf again next year, when Erich planned to take me on a walking tour through the Black Forest, or perhaps up into the Harz Mountains.

Back at school I had a number of clashes with our Geography Master, who admitted he had never been in Germany. This fact was seized on by my classmates, and thereafter they too often quoted me – during his classes – as the expert on all matters German. In response he usually came up with some crack about 'Our Young Fascist', and I didn't like that at all.

It must have been on one of those occasions I first realised that deep down inside, and remembering my own recent experiences, I felt ashamed that I – like the rest of the world in the late 1930's – although knowing, and disapproving strongly, of the evils that were commonplace in the *Third Reich*, was prepared to do precisely nothing about them.

Little did I know then, how much that situation was about to change.

Hand-launching *Grunau G 9 glider*

12. Will We Be Enemies?

All our planning had been in vain, because war clouds were gathering over Europe that summer of 1939. Instead of holidaying together, Erich and I were forced to spend our time preparing for hostilities – on opposing sides. Erich and his family had returned to Germany, but we exchanged letters quite often. He wrote of his service in the *R.A.D.* ' I almost sleep with my German spade, its my constant companion; if I'm neither drilling with it, nor digging, then I' ll be polishing the *verdammt* thing ready for the next parade. Most of our time is spent in forestry or drainage work; shirtless, burnt brown as an Arab; but I'm stronger than ever – and fighting fit too.'

I had already told Erich about my job in an Insurance Company's office. Although it was deadly dull, most people said I was lucky to have a job with a future, but he was much more interested to learn that I too was in uniform – once a week at least – with the Territorial Army. Amongst my friends, it was the fashionable thing to do at that time. Most of us went in a bunch to volunteer, and that threw the clerks into confusion; which probably accounts for the Army always believing I was exactly two years older than my actual age. (Several months passed before I myself realised this – and by then the many advantages were far too apparent for there being any question of my 'noticing' the mistake, and getting it corrected. In particular, I had been accepted for Officer Training, whilst my contemporaries were all told to apply again in six or twelve months time.) We 'Terriers' were issued with the uniform of 1918, and had they let us spend as much time on the Rifle Range as we did in cleaning our boots and brass buttons, we'd all have become crack shots. But polish and drill always came first, with realistic battle-training a very poor second.

Erich's next letter was something of a surprise. 'I'll be going into the Navy in October.' He wrote. 'I had to go to Keil, to take a big exam, and thankfully I passed for officer training, at the *Kriegsmarine Akademie* at Mürwick – that's Flensburg to you. But at least it means I'll not find myself shooting at you John. Although everyone here says England will never come into a war.' On reading that I had to ask myself '*Why the Kriegsmarine? He never expressed any great interest in the sea, nor any thought of transferring to the Marine H.J. Maybe our afternoon together as crew of their Kutter had put him off.*

Anyway, just three days after that letter arrived, I had been mobilised, and was permanently in uniform – carrying my gas mask and tin hat wherever I went – which just showed how wrong 'everyone' can be. That meant I no longer spent seemingly endless days calculating other people's premiums, and I was too young to be unduly worried about my own personal War Risk loading. From then on there was of course no more news from my good friend ... whom I must now think of as my enemy.

Our Officer Training Centre was based on Greaton Hall, a run-down stately home in Shropshire. The Commanding Officer had the basic concept that '*An Officer should know something about everything*', though there was rarely enough time allowed for us to learn anything very thoroughly. Even so, time was found to teach us how to salute with a sword. This was considered essential, because – as we were constantly reminded – each one of us was being trained to become an 'Officer and a Gentleman.'

Amongst my class of Cadets, questions were often asked as to how 'Cecil' – as we had come to know him – could have been passed by any Selection Board. He was vain, and worse still – stupid. He quickly rubbed most of us up the wrong way, by repeatedly asserting that he was bound to be commissioned, and would go straight into a Guards regiment. (Eventually the explanation leaked out. He was the nephew of a highly placed V.I.P – who shall remain nameless.) 'Cecil' was short-sighted, but refused to wear spectacles, believing they would affect his chances of promotion. And how right he was about that!

Halfway through our Course, Cecil was leading my Section in an attempt to ambush others from the same Platoon. He gave his orders in exemplary fashion. '*Intention ... Method ... Right Flanking ...* ' and all that stuff. After a swift move on hands and knees, he had us in position, and eagerly awaiting his next order, which was, '*Enemy troops advancing, on road to your front. Load five rounds blank ammunition. Sights at 200 yards. Five rounds Rapid ... FIRE!*'

The Troop of Boy Scouts were more than a little surprised by all the noise, and two of the youngest were quite badly frightened. Their

Scoutmaster – who wore the 'Pip, Squeak and Wilfred' ribbons of the last war – was at first very indignant, and then quietly amused. But that was as nothing to the withering blast that came at us all from the Commanding Officer later in the day. But even he was silenced by our Barrack Room Lawyer, who had ambitions to become a Barrister.

"Permission to speak Sir?" He asked respectfully. "Is it approved practice, to question an order to open fire, when given by a superior rank, on the field of battle, and in the face of the enemy? Would that not be construed as Mutiny, and carry the death penalty, if the offender be found guilty, by Court Martial, Sir?"

Two days later Routine Orders recorded 'Cecil' as 'R.T.U.' (That's to say Returned To his original Unit.) Though neither explanation nor reason was stated.

* * *

My eye had fallen on the End of Course group photograph that hung, half- hidden on the side of the chimney breast. It's hard to known why it stays there, for I doubt if I've seen three of those young men in the last ten years. Five at least were killed in action ... and old age must have taken others by now ... My war wasn't so enjoyable that I wanted to attend Annual Re-unions, and I've lost touch ...

I sensed my Grandson was growing impatient, though even at fifteen, he has the understanding – and what I value even more, the good manners – not to break in on my private moments.

* * *

I found that our instructors varied enormously, from elderly languid officers whom nothing would hurry, to solid dependable Regular N.C.O.s. And there were the 'Specialists' too – many of them having been designated as such, just to fill an unpopular, or vacant post. However, some attempt had been made to find square pegs for square holes. Most notable amongst these was the newly appointed 2" Mortar Instructor. He was a Head-in the-clouds young Lance-corporal – with an Honours Degree in Chemistry. (He would actually have been more useful, and – as we were soon to learn – probably much safer, had he been given work in a munitions factory, instead of being sent into the Army.)

When it came to our turn, he spent two hours giving us excessively detailed facts and figures about propellant charges, fuses, and the assorted types and use, of the small bomb those mortars fired. Having over-run in the Lecture Hut, the Lance-corporal decided there was no longer enough time to march us all the way to the Range for the live-firing demonstration. Instead, he used his own initiative, and set up the mortar in front of the Hall – with a long uninterrupted view out over peaceful parkland. Having told us he'd first fire a Parachute Flare, he proceeded to load with High Explosive ... to our suppressed delight. Then – believing himself to be a Good Instructor – he paid more attention to our numerous questions than to his aim. The bomb soared upwards, almost vertically. It was then caught by the wind – for which he had made no allowance – and it appeared to be coming back to its point of origin.

We began to scatter *Sauve qui peut,* but our instructor, in his blissful ignorance, was quite magnificent.

"Not to panic, please Gentlemen – its quite obviously a dud – no danger unless it actually hits you on the hea ...." I was already down behind a low stone balustrade when his words were cut short by a dull roar – a tinkling of window glass – and a cascade of dirty water that drenched him from head to toe.

That demonstration was generally considered to be good entertainment, some even said it was the High Spot of the whole Course. It had its positive side too, because the large ornamental fountain pool was still well stocked with big fat carp. Such fish, when freshly killed, and cooked by a Soho Restaurateur-cum-Infantry Officer – even one who has only a coke stove, mess tin, freshly stolen herbs, and a pack of illicitly traded cook-house butter – can taste quite delicious, especially after months of monotonous Army fare. As I ate that fish my thoughts went back to Mops, who would certainly have appreciated the skill with which it had been prepared. *'He'll still be wearing the uniform I knew so well, but when the time comes for his call-up, will the Germans let his talents go to waste, as the Army had done with our 'Fellow Cadet'.* (It was of course considered to be the height of bad form to speak of one's 'Mates'.) *'And what of the older lads I shared that Sommerlager with? Many would now be wearing very different uniforms. What if I were to meet them on the battlefield? How would they be thinking of me now? And ought I still to think of them as Kameraden?'*

On completion of that hurried, and often hilarious training in Shropshire I was due to be commissioned as a Temporary Second Lieutenant. ('Temporary', because when the war ended, so would my commission.) On the evening before the Passing Out Parade, we sat on our beds, pressing and polishing every bit of our uniform or weapon that could be pressed or polished, and I found myself wondering what Erich was doing then.

Even in wartime, a Passing Out Parade had to be a big affair, and our's was no exception. We spent almost an hour Marching, Counter-marching, Wheeling, and even Inclining, each done 'By the Right', 'By the Left' and 'By the Centre'. As we neared the finale, disaster was narrowly avoided. We were about to pass the Inspecting General, for the last time. He was up on the dais, on our right, but the Officer Cadet, i/c Parade, gave a very clear 'Eyes Left!' Nevertheless – with commendable disobedience to orders – most of us did manage to correct that for him.

Having wangled transport for the evening, a group of us celebrated – well, though not too wisely – over dinner at the Mytton and Mermaid Hotel at Atcham. This being highly recommended by one of our number, whose parents had stayed there during his school days.

After the normal confusions in the Orderly Room, I found myself commissioned into the Moundshire Regiment, and joined their 5th Battalion shortly before they were sent to join the British Expeditionary Force in France. We took over positions on the Belgian border – only a kilometre from where the Maginot Line ended. This time was rightly described as the 'Phoney War'. We spent our time waiting, watching and wondering. As the winter hardened a major problem was keeping the men occupied, and their quarters – in dilapidated farm buildings – even tolerably warm. Indeed I was fortunate to be sent home on a full week's Leave, followed by a seven day Course of training in 'Aircraft Recognition and The Use of Infantry Weapons in an Anti-aircraft Role'. I quickly realised that by far the best chance of success with a Bren Gun was to fire on an enemy aircraft as it flew straight at one – but this was the very moment when common sense said 'Take Cover', because most German planes had two or more forward-firing belt-fed guns, opposed to the fire power of the lone gunner with his single barrel, and a thirty round magazine. However, when I returned, I did at least have something new to offer in the way of training, and we rigged up dummy aircraft as targets. These swooped down from the tallest tree in the district – much to the delight of the local children, both boys and girls.

13. Kriegsmarine.

'Meine Herren Offizieranwärter! This is *Kriegsmarine,* Let me tell those of you who are fresh from *Arbeitsdienst,* that your days of standing about leaning on your shovels are past. And if you have any hopes of becoming an officer, and taking command of one of *Der Führer's* warships, you will have to work hard, and when I say 'Jump!' You will all jump, and jump very high too. Is that understood?'

'Jawohl, Herr Obermaat.' Replied Erich, in unison, with his fellow Officer Candidates.

'Is that understood?'

'Jawohl – Herr Obermaat!'

'I cannot hear you!'

'JAWOHL – HERR OBERMAAT!'

'That is better. If you give your orders like a girl, the helmsman will not hear you, and he will do nothing, and your ship will go straight on to the rocks!'

Such was Erich Falkenberg's welcome on the First of October 1939, when he reported for Officer Training. Having travelled by train to Stralsund, he, and the rest of his Intake or *Crew,* are taken by bus across the newly constructed causeway to the Baltic Island of Rügen. And thence to barracks on the smaller island of Dänholm.

For their first few days, the newcomers are constantly kept on the run, often doing seemingly needless tasks, hounded by Petty Officers who were intent on weeding out those who could not meet the physical demands that would be made on them during the coming weeks of Initial Training. A number of these are promptly sent home. The next 14 days see a further culling, until only those likely to make good officers remain.

Their activities include gymnastics, boxing, fencing, soccer, and of course classroom instruction in all fields of on-board duties and activities.

Dressed in naval field grey uniforms, similar to those of the Army, they found that their rigorous basic land training was much the same. And here Erich finds his experiences in the Hitler Youth to be helpful. Rain, and even snow, are not allowed to interfere with their training. This, coupled with intensive work in the classroom, is intended to eliminate all but the fittest – mentally as well as physically.

Initial Training, at Rügen, ends on November 30th. Those who have survived entrain at Stralsund at 0300 hrs. Engineering and Administrative candidates going direct to the *Kriegsmarine Akademie* at Mürwick. Most others, including Falkenberg, leave the train to join the pre-World War One Battleship *Schleswig-Holstein*, at Keil; where a smaller number go to her sister-ship *Schlesien*.

Arriving as dusk falls, they board a barge which takes them to their ships. There they find very little personal space. Their first problem being to remember how to navigate the numerous passageways and ladders, then learning to sling and sleep in a hammock. Next morning those hammocks have to be tidily stowed in the approved style. Afterwards each Candidate is shown to his Action Station. Some are envious of Falkenberg, who is positioned half way up the foremast, at the optical range-finder. From there he will see everything that is happening, when many others are stationed below decks to handle ammunition. However – whilst they will be protected inside – the range-finder was on an open platform exposed to both winter weather and enemy fire.

Training continues. Everything has to be cleaned, polished, oiled or saluted, as appropriate. But at the weekend a picket boat lands them at the Hansa Pier, for a run ashore into the town. The training is always hard, sometimes working in the blacked-out ship, dashing in response to 'Action Stations!' or 'Close watertight Doors!'; fighting imaginary fires, and always the routine daily chores of cleaning ship, collecting food from the galley and washing up afterwards. Then they are introduced to the *Kriegsmarine* rowing *Kutter* – shades of *Sommerlager* for Erich – and this provides a good close view of the other ships in harbour, in addition to both warming exercise and competition to enliven their day.

Schleswig-Holstein goes on War Patrol in the Baltic, stopping ships which might be carrying contraband. There Erich spends a very cold four hours on the Quarter Deck, on Lifebuoy Duty. Nobody fell overboard, but – when most of the Candidates are having their meal – he is ordered to throw the

Lifebuoy overboard. The ship is stopped, so the *Kutters* can be launched, and sent – in rough seas – to recover it. By mid-December the weather has turned very cold. *Schleswig-Holstein* leaves the safe and blackout-free Baltic, returning to war conditions in Keil, where some Christmas Leave is granted to the older married men. But the younger ones are only allowed three days without any training. Absence from their families at Christmas is made all the worse by bad failures in the Mail Service.

In the New Year, *Schleswig-Holstein* moves slowly through the Keil Canal, acting as ice-breaker for following U-boats and other small vessels; passing through locks and below the high level bridges, including the famous one at Rendsberg, where the railway line spirals upwards, and then down again, after passing over the canal. No gunnery training was possible because – by long tradition – it was forbidden to rotate, or even elevate the guns whilst on passage through the canal, but everybody on board is looking forward to the Live Firing that is promised, though only if their training goes well enough.

Prior to leaving the canal, when *Schleswig-Holstein* is being manoeuvred into the last lock at Brunsbüttel, one of the tow ropes is caught – and rapidly wound in – by her own propeller. Five hours later she has been docked, though still blocking the canal. So cold is it inside the trapped U-boats that their crews are hurriedly brought on board *Schleswig-Holstein* to sleep in hammocks. Eventually a diver freed the rope from around the screw, but the *Kadetts* were not allowed to watch this; a hurried lecture on 'Communications' being set up to keep them all more usefully occupied.

That night there is an Air Raid Warning, and eager probing searchlights sweep to and fro across the sky. Erich – feeling very vulnerable – has to remain at his exposed action station, even though there is no possibility that either the 280 mm [11inch] guns, or their range-finder, would be of any use against aircraft. No bombs were dropped.

Back at Keil, Falkenberg's training continues despite very cold weather and snow. Then *Schleswig-Holstein* is ordered to escort smaller vessels through the Little Belt, between the Danish mainland and the Island of Fyn. In a blinding snowstorm – whilst trying to avoid minefields – the vessel goes onto a sand bank. Drinking and washing water is pumped overboard to lighten ship, but it still needed full power and six tugs to get her off. As a result she suffered a crack in her side, and had to be Dry-docked. This enabled the Candidates to see how large the crack was, and some feel it comforting that even with this much damage, she still stayed afloat. During her time in the dock, all washing facilities and the 'Heads' are closed, so everybody has to walk a long distance to reach these essentials on shore, but no extra time is allowed for this. It is also necessary to take a tram into the town, and the last one back at night usually has many sailors hanging on the outside.

By February the repair has been completed, but whilst the ship is being un-docked, the engines fail, and she is again damaged. The Candidates are now moved into the accommodation ship *Monte Olivia*, which is also very cold. Despite deep snow, training continues on land, but one 'War Game' exercise ends up in a big snowball fight, with even the Petty Officers joining in. By early March *Schleswig-Holstein* has completed sea trials. Only then, after Torpedo firing in Eckeförde Bay, do they at last experience Live Firing by Main Armament. Erich being surprised by the blast and how much the mast moves each time the 11 inch guns are fired below him.

Schleswig-Holstein is suddenly recalled to take part in the invasion of Norway and Denmark. After working hard taking on the extra stores that are needed, many of the Candidates are put ashore, but Erich remains on board, expecting to see some real action. However, the ship goes aground again. (There must surely have been at least one 'Jonah' amongst her complement.) The *Kutters* then have the dangerous task of taking out the ship's heavy anchors; the weight of cable increasing significantly for every metre they pull away from the ship. Even with her own winches, and the aid of tugs, *Schleswig-Holstein* is not able to take Erich Falkenberg to war.

March 20th being Adolf Hitler's birthday, a big parade is held at which all the Candidates are promoted to *Fähnrich Zur See*. (Midshipman.) Although in their smart new 'officer' uniform, with dirks at their side, they are firmly reminded that this did not make them 'Officers', but only qualified them to become such – after possible sea time, and further intensive training at the *Kriegsmarine Akademie* at Mürwick.

14. Le Quescourt.

In May 1940, the Germans started their invasion of the low countries and we Moundshires received immediate orders to cross the frontier in support of the Belgian Army. But after only three frantic and confused days of fighting in Flanders, my Battalion was heading back towards the French border again. Suffering persistent attacks by large numbers of enemy dive-bombers, we lost vehicles, officers and men – including my Batman. As a result – dead men's shoes – I had been appointed Acting-Lieutenant. However I did have the satisfaction of watching one of my 'pupils' bring down a *Stuka* Dive-bomber that came too low after dropping its bombs close to a group of refugees on their horse drawn carts. The Colonel put Roberts name forward for a 'Mention', but unfortunately the man didn't live long enough to learn that it had been confirmed.

Orders arrived that the Army was to establish a 'Stop-line'. We Moundshires, as infantry, had been allocated a sector around the little French frontier town of Le Quescourt, where – so it was said – there should be some concrete pillboxes on which we could base our defences. I was sent back alone on my motorcycle, and without a map, to reconnoitre and make preparations for the Battalion, which would follow on several hours later. Both Belgian and French Frontier Customs Posts were already deserted, and about a kilometre beyond them I found the first pillbox. It was strongly built and well positioned to cover the road, but its steel door was securely locked. Before I could set off to examine the others, I was surrounded by a group of agitated Frenchmen. One pushed forward and drew himself up.

"Je suis Soldat Francais. Vétéran de la guerre de quatorze-dix-huit, with a *leetle* English." He went on to tell me that some three months previously a young couple had moved into an isolated cottage, hidden amongst trees, very close to the frontier. Most unusually they had made no attempt to

make friends, or even to contact their nearest neighbours. Those few who had managed to speak to them were very suspicious – some being convinced that she at least, was most certainly German. They all insisted that I must go – *allez immédiatement!* – to investigate.

As I set off, a distinctly scruffy British Sergeant came in view, riding fast, and on a civilian bicycle too. I held up my hand and he screeched to a stop.

"Sergeant. I don't know – or care – where you are going. I need you, and your weapon now. So leave your cycle with these good folk and come with me." He dismounted somewhat sheepishly, leaving me wondering whether he was perhaps just on the run, or possibly in the act of deserting. The fact that he had a German Luger pistol holster on his webbing belt did not greatly add to my confidence.

The couple at the cottage – both of whom were noticeably blond – were far from pleased to see us. They made a great point of not understanding any of my questions in English, nor when repeated in French, even though my pronunciation had improved considerably in the past two months. However, when I 'accidentally' slipped in a German phrase, I spotted a momentary jerk of recognition, then they were both back to *'Je n'y comprends rien!'* Clearly I had to try another tack.

"Come on Sergeant, they're right enough. We're wasting our time here!" And with that we left, but as I passed the window I looked in, and it was obvious the pair of them were arguing fiercely about something. "Well Sergeant?" I asked, at the garden gate.

"Dodgy, Sir. Very dodgy. There's something about her accent, reminds me of a neighbour back home, came from somewhere near Dusseldorf, married a Tommy in the Occupation Force, spoke good enough English, but she never lost that something – even her kids had it – same as that woman in there has."

"Right. Follow me!" This time I did not knock, but just burst in. Speaking louder and more authoritatively than before, I repeated my questions, demanding to know. "Who are you? Why are you here? Where have you come from?" Suddenly they could both understand my French.

"Claudette Delage and my husband Pierre. We are from Amiens." She said, and then the man continued.

"Her drunken father, he hates me. After her aged *Grandmere* died, Claudette inherited this cottage." Then the wife spoke – as in a well rehearsed double act.

"We plan – *Sale Bosche* permitting – to run a smallholding *Monsieur.* And to live a happy life here with our many children *si Dieu le veut.*" It all came out far too pat, like a carefully prepared story.

I changed abruptly into the German I had been rehearsing in my mind.

"*Wer?*" I almost shouted. "Who sent you here? And what are your orders?" There was no doubt they both understood that.

"*Scheisen!*" She whispered. "Hans – they know!" With that she made a grab for the large kitchen knife on the table in front of her, and he spun round stretching out a hand for something on the shelf behind him. I reached for my revolver, but before I could even draw it, four shots rang out. When I turned to look, the Sergeant's holster was still closed, though smoke now curled up from a small Walther automatic in his hand. He must have kept it concealed – held ready in his pocket. Quite deliberately, he now leaned forward, knocking the oil lamp from the table, so that the ornamental glass reservoir shattered on the stone flags.

"Oh Dear! My mother always did say I was a clumsy kid." As he spoke he produced a box of matches, and indicated the door. "Would you like to lead the way – Sir?" I was only too happy to leave that cottage, and I was thankful he was such a good shot – even with a totally unauthorised enemy weapon.

Moments later he caught up with me as I walked away. "Pity a good-looker like that had to get in the way of a bullet!"

"I take it you're referring to the woman, Sergeant?"

"Of course, Sir. But if you like 'em like that – he was quite handsome too!"

"Yes. I suppose Herr Himmler would have considered them to be an ideal Aryan breeding couple. Did you know Sergeant, that its the duty of a married German woman to have a child every year – for her *Führer?*"

"Oh yes Sir, and she'd get a medal if she produced four, another after six, and a third after eight – the poor cow!" I recalled Erich telling me about the 'Mother's Cross', and knew he was right ... *but why would a man like him know that?*

The Sergeant kept looking back over his shoulder. Smoke, then flames rose from the cottage. I did not feel inclined to comment directly on those facts.

"After what happened back there, Sergeant, it would be best if I forget I ever met you. When we get back to your bike, you can leave me to explain the smoke, and I suggest you should ride off immediately, without answering any questions."

"If I may say so, Sir. Very wise decisions. We in the S.I.B. are more used to asking questions than to answering them." After that we strode on in silence.

He obeyed my instructions, and I never saw him again. Whether that man really was a Sergeant, and in the Special Investigation Branch, I still can't be sure. It was only after he'd gone that I began to assess him, and his appearance. The obviously new, but almost unnaturally dirtied battle-dress carried neither Regimental nor Divisional insignia, which would also serve to mask his Military Police identity. He was certainly brighter, or better educated, than the average soldier – but that could have emboldened him enough to assume the identity of those who might have been pursuing him. To this day, that man remains in my memory – as a complete and utter enigma.

Frustrated after reaching the fifth pillbox, and finding that all the steel doors were equally firmly locked. I knocked – louder and louder – at the nearest cottage. The door was cautiously opened by a frightened incoherent old woman, who seemed to believe I was German. Realising I was going to get no sense there, I turned to the cowering 10 year-old beside her. But he appeared unable to understand me either. I grabbed his arm and dragged him – protesting loudly – to the nearest pillbox.

"Ou est la clef? Ou – est – la – clef?" I repeated it endlessly, pointing to the locked door – but he only understood when shown my own keys.

"Monsieur le Maire." He mumbled through his tears, pointing in the general direction of Le Quescourt..

Throughout the drab dirty streets I saw signs of rapid departure; furniture and household goods littered the pavements, probably discarded as too bulky to go on what little transport was available. A sad unshaven Policeman – who was obviously burying valuables in his garden – gave me an odd look when I asked for directions to the *Mairie*. He said it was on the far side of the town, but he made no offer to escort me there.

The Mayor, small and shifty-eyed, wore the symbol of his office – a frayed and grubby tricolour sash. At first he denied all knowledge of any *fortifications* – saying such matters were for the Military. Only when told that I had visited five pillboxes, barely two kilometres from where we stood, did he change his tune.

"Oh – THOSE *reduits!"* He simpered, *"Monsieur L'officier* should be more clear." He was adamant that he had no keys ... "A boy has said so? What could a peasant boy know of such important matters? If keys there are, they will be, *bien sûr*, in the hands of *Les Militaires*, at Arridot – a mere ten kilometres away."

However after following his directions exactly, I met up with some Belgian troops who showed me, on their map, that Arridot was at least twenty kilometres from Le Quescourt – in a quite different direction.

Les Militaires, when I did finally locate them, were most emphatic that local Mayors always held one set of keys for unmanned defences – and the others were kept locked in the safe of the Area Commandant. But where, *à ce moment,* he or the key to that safe might be – nobody could even guess. *"C'est la Guerre, Mon Vieux!"* When I asked for petrol they said they had none. Again it was *"C'est la Guerre!"* which excuse – so it seemed – relieved them of any, and indeed, all responsibility. I got the impression that most of them had already given up the struggle. One very junior officer did suggest I should try the *Station Service* at the back of the building.

There a notice told me 'No Petrol'. But when I pressed my need, they claimed that what little stocks remained in their tanks were reserved for *Les Militaires.* When I politely suggested that I was *Militaire,* the response was a very insolent and emphatic. *'Militaire Francais!'* I just kept my temper, though putting on a big show of fury.

"Je Suis Militaire!" I thundered, moving my hand to my pistol holster. *"Militaire Anglais, votre allié. Cinq litres d'essence - Vitement!"* I looked down, whilst opening the holster flap, then up at the attendant. *"C'est la Guerre, Mon Vieux!"* I just could not resist the temptation – and that was enough to get my tank filled – however grudgingly. Remembering the *Entente Cordiale,* I asked how much I owed? He stated an astronomical number of Francs. Luckily the normal price was still partly visible beneath the figure now marked on the pump, and – despite his loud protestations – I licked my finger, rubbed the chalk away, worked out what was due, and paid him ... to the nearest *sou.*

Now in a really foul temper, I rode off back to Le Quescourt, where I saw British uniforms around one of my pillboxes. The door had been blown open by men of the 3rd North Ridings, who were settling in there, and – so far as I could gather from the Corporal – into all my other positions too.

"The battalion is way below half strength." He told me. "Two Companies were detached – but God only knows where they are now, Sir. We had heavy losses, men and vehicles – especially the Officers and Senior N.C.O.s ... all those left are now at H.Q."

He pointed to a big house with a distinctive turret, just visible amongst the trees a few hundred metres away. As I re-mounted my motorcycle, three *Stuka* dive-bombers came in sight. One after another, with sirens screaming, they hurtled down on the house and each dropped a single large bomb, before turning back towards their own lines. A moment later the building disappeared in a cloud of dust and smoke.

Junkers 87 'Stuka' Dive Bomber

15. With the 3rd North Ridings.

I roared up the drive to find two 15 hundredweight trucks burning and the house half-demolished. An elderly officer was being brought out, supported by two privates. Blood streamed down his face, and one trouser leg was ripped open to the thigh. He spotted me, and ordered – in a weak but authoritative voice.

"Organise a rescue party ... for the officers – all my officers – in – in ... back there."

I found N.C.O.s and men were already swarming over the wreckage. One bomb had landed just beside the house, stripping away much of the outer wall. The room inside was a shambles, most of the visible bodies being officers or senior N.C.Os. Stretcher bearers were checking to see whether there were any survivors, and I helped them with one Captain – but he died as we moved him.

When I reported back to the Colonel, he was sitting against a tree, with one arm in a sling and his head heavily bandaged. He was already in command of himself and the situation – but only then did he realise that I was a stranger. He was surprised to learn that my unit had also been ordered to man the positions he had just occupied. Then a young Second Lieutenant and a Sergeant approached. The Subaltern came to the salute, but just stood there, swaying, open mouthed, ashen faced – with his fingers twitching nervously. A moment later the Sergeant cut in.

"Casualty Report – Sir!" He spoke with the unruffled dignity I had come to expect from N.C.O.s who had seen service in the 1914-18 war. The Colonel was visibly shaken when he heard all his officers were dead, with the exception of the shell-shocked Subaltern, and a Major who was unlikely to live – even if an ambulance could be found to take him to a field hospital. The Sergeant believed himself to be the senior surviving N.C.O. who was fit for duty. Fortunately casualties amongst the men were small, for most of them had been busy digging in, well clear of the house.

There was a pause, then the Colonel swallowed hard, and nodded at the Sergeant, who gently led the lad away. It was only too clear that he would be of no use for many hours or even days. After another pause the older man began talking to me – in a quiet but fatherly way.

"It would appear, Hardwicke, there has most probably been a change of orders, and your Moundshires have been sent off elsewhere." I nodded, because they were already long overdue. "On the other hand," he continued, "it must be patently obvious, to anyone, that I would have more work for you – in the next few hours – than your own C.O. might give you in a couple of months." He was right enough about that. Furthermore, I had no means of communication – and in the prevailing chaos it would be very difficult for me to locate the Moundshires. Then, before I could say as much, his tone suddenly changed; he had come to a decision.

"Hardwicke. This is an Order! You will stay with us, as Second in Command." He hesitated, thinking deeply. "Nobody listens to Lieutenants – especially when things are going wrong – so – you'd better assume the rank of ... Major ... at least until further notice."

Late that evening I put up my crowns, but took no comfort that they were taken from a dead man's shoulders; I could only hope he would forgive me for that last indignity. In fact I slipped off his rank slides, and found three stars on the shoulder strap underneath – which left me wondering if I was the third Major the unit had had in far too short a time. Luckily I also had the foresight to get the Colonel to confirm both his orders in writing. The rest of the night was peaceful, except for one small air raid, and most of the men got some badly needed sleep – but I was far too busy gathering up the reins of my new command. At 0400 hours orders arrived for yet another withdrawal, and by dawn we were on the move – without having fired a single shot. I chose to travel alone, and on my motor bike, because I still had unfinished business in the town.

The door of the *Mairie* was locked, but whilst a Bren-gun carrier clattered noisily past, I put my shoulder to it – and then I was in. The thinly carpeted stairs creaked under my heavy boots. As I reached the landing my attention was caught by a dimly lit square in the ceiling, where a ladder led through an open trap door. It was then that I heard it – and knew I was right to come. Cautiously I drew my Webley, cocked it – and crept silently up the ladder. *Monsieur le Maire* was seated, hunched over a table, with his back to me. Only when I stepped onto the bare boards of the attic floor did he become aware of my presence – and the tapping stopped as his fingers froze on the morse key. Very slowly he turned – to find my revolver barely a yard from his head. The look of dismay on his colourless face told me everything, but – if proof was needed – the eagle and swastika on the maps, and the codebook too, confirmed that I had caught a Fifth Columnist at his treachery. Remembering the unerring way the three *Stukas* had picked out our Headquarters – and the carnage that resulted – I had absolutely no doubt what had to be done.

My first bullet ended the careers of *M. le Maire*, and the next two destroyed his transmitter. Stuffing maps and the book into my pocket, I left, but – try as I will – nothing can blot out the terrified half-comprehending face of the sleepy-eyed child I brushed past, as I leapt from the ladder before pounding on down the main stairs. Shells were already falling on Le Quescourt, and I rode off hoping – indeed almost praying – that one would score a direct hit on the *Mairie*. That way at least, the child would never be taunted with her Father's treachery.

Every road was choked with refugees so we made slow progress. Our Second Lieutenant had appeared to be recovering, until *Me. 109's* shot up our column. Everybody jumped from the vehicles, seeking safety in the ditches, but he just froze, standing in the middle of the road – staring up at the first *Messerschmit* – and before anyone realised his danger it had opened fire. Parallel spurts of dust and sparks stitched along the *pavé* – passing by on either hand – leaving him quite unharmed. As if interested in the plane, he turned to watch it go – and was almost cut in half by fire from the next in line. We had been a legitimate target, but later there were repeated attacks on groups of civilians, many of them being women and children. No man who had passed an Air-crew eye-test could possibly have thought they were anything but refugees.

In spite of his other worries, the Colonel could not forget what we had seen.

"What sort of a man would behave like that?" He asked me again, and again. I reckoned I knew, but didn't tell him about sharing sentry duty with one. Axel had made it very clear to me that he, and his brothers, would have absolutely no hesitation in doing anything – no matter what – which they knew, or believed to be 'The will of *Der Führer*'.

*   *   *

For the first time my Grandson interrupted me. "Gramps. Was the war really as awful as you say? And did you really shoot the Mayor – just like that? I thought the French were on our side."

"Bill. The man who wrote '*War is Hell*' had it just about right. Most of war is just plain boring, and the remainder is pretty beastly. And just because a man is labelled as your 'Ally' or 'Enemy' – it isn't necessarily the truth, and certainly not the whole of the truth. Remember there were Germans who were my good friends, but that French Mayor was as much my enemy as if he'd been wearing a German uniform and shooting at me ... and have they never told you at school, about the only Master who didn't come back from the war? No? Well, you should ask about it. I forget the full detail now Bill, but it is certain – that when he died – there was Frenchman's bullet in his back!" The boy just nodded, and I continued with my tale.

* * *

That evening a Humber Staff Car drew up in front of our lead vehicle. An Officer, bristling with red tabs, got out and shouted for our Commanding Officer. Moments after they had met, I was called to join them.

"What the hell are you lot doing here? That's what I want to know." So barked the Brasshat, as I got near enough to hear him. Our C.O. still had his head bandaged, and I believe it was giving him considerable pain.

"If somebody in the higher echelons does know what the hell's going on – and they could be bothered to tell the p.b.i. – then I'd be able to answer your question, Sir! Our last order was to pull back – until further orders – and that's what we have been doing. Though I expect we'll soon stop doing that unless we can find some fuel for our vehicles! Can you perhaps manage to help us in that respect Sir?" I stood silent, in expectation of some vicious blast from the red-tab. But he ignored what the Colonel had just said, and replied more quietly, as if he did not want the men to hear what he was telling us.

"All I know is that the situation is pretty grim, and there's a damn great hole in the line behind you Colonel. Goodness knows who ought to be there, but your men will have to go back and plug that gap, to hold the line until others come. Here, look at my map. See this long straight road? That's the line I want you to hold. I'm told there are good ditches on either side, so you'll not need to dig in. You'll be our front line – everything beyond that road will be enemy. Just hold it until relieved. There should be units on your flanks – from where the road bends in each case."

"Do you realise, we only have small arms, nothing bigger than Brens?" I could see the Colonel was horrified by the new orders.

"What about mortars?"

"One three inch, but no ammunition, Sir." I reported to Red Tabs. "And two two inch, but most of their bombs are smoke or parachute flares. Any chance of getting some H.E. – for either – or both, Sir?"

"I very much doubt it, Major, but I will try to get something sent up to you."

The Colonel interrupted him. "Yes. But how do you expect us to stop tanks? We did have one Boys A.T. Rifle – for what little good that was – but it was lost when we were bombed at Le Quescourt." There was an awkward silence until Red Tabs continued.

"There is talk of some French being on your right flank, but I wouldn't put much reliance on them. And I know there's a unit of some sort being cobbled together to move up on your left. And beyond that, all I can ask you to do is to remember you are Yorkshire Men. And I know you'll do your best to at least delay Jerry's advance. They've already reached the sea at Abbville, so we're cut off from the rest of France. There are plans to get as many of our troops as possible to Dunkirk, and thence back across the Channel. So, any time you can win is going to be very valuable. I suggest you leave the vehicles here, and get moving quickly whilst there's still light enough to see where you are going. Good Luck North Ridings!" And with that, the Staff Officer saluted us, and was driven away.

The Colonel shrugged his shoulders. "You heard what the man said, John. Get the men organised and moving to the Front – if there is such a thing. I'll have to stay here on the road – with our wounded – just in case an ambulance passes by, or any more ridiculous orders do catch up with us, and I have to drag you back again."

The first of the ditches we'd been promised was in fact dry and deep enough for our needs, though it reminded me uncomfortably of tales I'd been told about life in the trenches during the last war. Beyond the roadway I found a wide water-filled ditch that just about qualified as a waterway, and it would certainly stop tanks. The only bridge I could see, in the failing light, was intended for farm traffic, and might very well collapse under the weight of any armoured vehicle. In fact our position was not nearly as bad as I'd feared. Having spread the men out – all too thinly – along our stretch of the road, I sent scouts out 400 yards beyond the bends on either flank, but they found no neighbouring troops. I had manned the Front we were given, and could do nothing more. Having sent a runner back to the Colonel with a situation report, I posted sentries, and told the rest of the men to get what sleep they could.

As they say in the best books 'Came the dawn', and I ordered 'Stand To'. Then word was passed that I was needed, urgently, on the left. There

I was told, and could see, the vague outline of something visible through a straggly hedgerow some 150 yards to our front. As the light improved the shape hardened, until there could be no possible doubt, it was a tank ... and the Staff Wallah had been most emphatic that everything beyond our road would be enemy. And he expected us to do our best!

"Sergeant. I want you and three volunteers, with at least three grenades apiece – and the same for me. Quickly and very quietly now." It was just possible – with a large amount of luck – that we could surprise them, even though there was only tall grass for cover on the flat hayfield between us and that hedge. I'd been told the nearest 2 inch mortar had only six bombs, four of them being smoke. My orders were simple

"Tell them to stand by to fire smoke to give us cover if we have to get back fast, and save the single H.E. until there's a decent target. And the four of you who are coming with me ... No rifles. We go, silently, over the bridge and crawl to that hedgerow – two either side of me. Then watch me, and do exactly what I do with my grenades. And there will be a 'Mention' for anybody who drops his second one inside that bloody tank. Its the only way we can hope to cripple it. But I want a spread of first throws, to get the crew, before they can start firing at us. Remember – dead silence all the way!"

That crawl seemed endless, but we reached the hedge together, and undetected, though I could hear snoring close by. I laid two of my grenades ready to hand; then held up the third so it could be seen. The men either side of me did the same. I raised my other hand and drew out the safety pin. There was a loud Clang, followed by a soft but most un-german expletive.

"Hold Your Fire!" I yelled. "British Troops are behind you tank men! Everybody! **Hold Your Fire!** I had no great faith that I'd be believed, because many Germans spoke better English than the average soldier, and it was not unknown for them to take advantage of that fact. However, all went well, and no harm had been done. The very surprised Tank Commander showed me the line drawn on his map. This proved he'd been ordered to man a Front at 30 degrees to ours. The end of that pencil line came just short of the halfway point of our road, so the two fronts overlapped considerably. Thank goodness we'd not had a decent anti-tank gun, such as the one brought up by the much better equipped, and relatively fresh Scots, who arrived to relieve us some twenty minutes later.

We made our way back to the vehicles, where the Colonel was amused by my account.

"If that foolhardy attack had succeeded in taking out an enemy tank, I'd have put you in for a 'gong' for sure. But there's no honourable recognition for the 'own goal' you were lucky enough to avoid." During that day there were a few shells overhead, but – for once – they were going in the right direction, fired by our own artillery.

At dawn we were ordered back again. Around mid-morning we arrived only minutes after a refugee column had been straffed. Amongst the wrecks was a petrol tanker, both the driver and his French army escort were dead in their seats, though I could see only a couple of dents where bullets had ricochetted off the tank itself. We drove off the excited French and Belgians, before filling our own vehicles and any spare cans we had with us. The natives were definitely getting restless, and I saw two of our men had fixed their bayonets, but I did not rebuke them for that. As each of our trucks was filled, it was sent on ahead to get some cover where the road wound its way through a wood. At the next stop the sergeant came to me.

"When the last truck was filled I ordered the guards to get on board and we left those jabbering Frenchies to help themselves. But we was barely four hundred yards away from there when I heard a bang, and saw a bloody great sheet of flame, as the whole ruddy lot went up. I've no idea what those idiots done, an' I wasn't going back to find out!'

We were now well off for petrol, but I had no idea where or when we'd get our next supply. Nearby I spotted a motorcycle-combination, abandoned, but apparently undamaged, with its side-car piled with domestic items.

"See if you can get that going Sergeant, and if so dump all that junk. I've got a use for that machine." All it needed was petrol, and it started second kick. I picked a Lance Corporal I knew to be a motorcycle enthusiast, and another sound man.

"You two are now Petrol Scavengers. Find a crowbar, spanners, a funnel, rubber hose, and some empty cans. Each time you see a damaged vehicle, get underneath if you can, and break the petrol pipe, or rip it out of the tank, and catch what you can in the funnel. Don't waste time on undamaged vehicles, because they've probably got dry tanks.'" It was a risky job I'd given them, because some of the engines and exhausts were still hot. But those two did good work, and helped to keep us moving. Next evening, the Colonel asked me, very seriously, if I thought he should put their names forward for a 'Mention'.

"You could do so, Sir. Though it might cause problems with the Citation, and with those higher up too." At that point I put on my very best 'Brigade of Guards' voice.

"I really don't think that's on Old Man – decorate a man for stealing from our Allies? Not quite the thing, What?'" His only response was a wry smile and an understanding gentle nod. The matter was not mentioned again.

Next morning, shortly after setting off in the lead vehicle, I was flagged down by an Officer and a Lance-corporal.

"I've just lost 'Annie', my beloved Austin Utility. Direct hit from a 150 millimetre shell." The Lieutenant told me. "I'm an Observation Officer, with the guns. See that smoking church over there? We were up in that tower – only place in this flat country where I could get high enough to see beyond the Hun infantry, to where their tanks are massing. But its the old old story. As soon as I start correcting the fall of our shells, Jerry knows someone can see them. And they can almost certainly see where I am, and the Hun's not stupid. Their gunners are good – a damn sight too good. Their first single ranging shot usually falls behind my Observation post – be it church or windmill. This time right on poor Annie. That's when the Corporal and I come down those rickety old ladders, faster than you'd believe possible, and we've left a wireless and several telephones behind in our hurry. But at least this time I'd got our lot right on target before we had to scuttle out. The second Hun shot normally falls short, and – just as we're getting clear – their third one brings the building down. I only wish our gun-layers were as good." He looked back at the shattered tower. "I do feel a bit bad about those fine old churches being ruined in that way. But if we don't use them, so getting them destroyed by Jerry; then – as Jerry moves forward – he'll put his own observers up there, and we'd have to destroy them ourselves. So – however ancient, and beautiful – most of them are doomed anyway ... *Je suis desolé, Mon Vieux – mais c'est la Guerre!*" He shrugged his shoulders in truly gallic fashion, then paused for a moment as though reflecting on the matter. "But, to look on the bright side, this bloody war is giving me a chance to use some of what little French they managed to force down my throat at school."

For four more days we were forced back South-westwards. Towards the sea. Often driven back by tanks, but sometimes falling back without even seeing the enemy – when others had been overwhelmed, so leaving us out-flanked. Dive-bombers harassed us much of the time; our casualties were heavy, and sleep a luxury we rarely enjoyed. Chaos and confusion were our constant companions on the road. The Colonel's condition deteriorated, and I had to assume a greater share of responsibility. We had 'run off the map' and no replacements could be provided, but I was fortunate enough to find an old *Guide Michelin* in an abandoned car, so we had a map of sorts again. One night, as we made our way towards Dunkirk – driving at a snail's pace, with only a minimum of lights – word was brought to me that there was a feint red light, something like three-quarters of a mile ahead. It was definitely moving, at about our speed, and could perhaps be a vehicle rear lamp.

The whole situation was so fluid that it was more than possible German armour had swung in ahead of our own troops. So I desperately needed to know whose rear lamp it was. I judged it would be too risky, and too noisy, to send one of our soft-skinned trucks forward to find out; but we did have a pedal cycle which was near enough silent. Lance-corporal Paddy Patterson was always on the lookout for a chance to get himself a medal. That made him my natural choice for Scout. I halted the column whilst he rode forward alone. He returned with good news; that light was in fact on a British Cook Wagon. By an amazing chance, we were following the other half of the North Riding Battalion. Welcome though they were, it was another bad blow for the Colonel, because they turned out to be a pitifully small remnant, under the command of a Second Lieutenant.

Refugees were everywhere, weary exhausted groups, of all ages and classes – walking pushing or riding anything with wheels – and always overburdened as they desperately tried to save their heirlooms and other essentials. Hampering our movements, these hapless fugitives were often more trouble than the enemy – and we got little enough help from our Allies too.

From the sand dunes I looked down on a long open beach that was repeatedly straffed by *Luftwaffe* planes. Thousands of khaki-clad soldiers – some up to their chests in the water – queued patiently for boats that would ferry them out to waiting ships, one of which was sunk as we watched. A great pall of black smoke hung over Dunkirk, where the outskirts had already become choked with abandoned vehicles of all sorts. As German bombers roared overhead, almost unchallenged, I wondered who was the idiot who had so prematurely ordered the destruction of the many heavy Ack-Ack guns we saw, now blindly pointing their fanned-out muzzles skywards.

A Military Policeman told us to save what weapons we could carry, but to destroy our vehicles and other equipment. As our trucks blazed up, fresh orders arrived, sending us North East, to join the perimeter defences – some five miles back – pretty much where we had just come from.

We set off on foot. In a field close to the road, I spotted a three ton lorry being emptied; its load of new boots being thrown onto a heap of burning uniforms. I tried to persuade the driver that it was his duty to transport us to the Front.

"Left to me, I'd take you and welcome, Sir. But you know how things are at any H.Q. The Major who sent me here threatened me with a Court Martial if I didn't come back, or if I sloped off to the beaches – as so many others have done. So I've got to go straight back and load more stores to be burned here."

"But why do they have to be brought here? Why on earth can't they be burnt where they are now?"

"Procedure, Sir! A load of bull if you ask me. But after the order authorising Destruction has been signed, it has to be counter-signed, stating that the listed stores were seen leaving for the Approved Destruction Site. And that – for some reason known only to the bloody Staff – is here, Sir"

I did debate whether to use the persuasive powers of my revolver, but the wretched man was only obeying orders, regardless of how stupid they were, and anyway I felt that such 'persuasion' was best reserved – as hitherto – for our French Allies.

16. Safe in Norfolk.

I awoke between clean white sheets in a Norfolk Hospital. My memories of those early days in the hospital are confused. I seemed to come and go, without rhyme or reason, so I hardly knew where I was – nor was I at all certain who I was ... but it slowly became clearer. Several bomb or shell fragments had been removed from my back. All my kit was lost, and my papers were missing, so were the two middle fingers off my right hand – and at least three days from my life in France. Just how I came back to England nobody could tell me. Somehow those Yorkshiremen must have got me onto one of the last ships to leave the port of Dunkirk, but most of those who'd helped me would almost certainly have to spend the coming months, and probably years, whiling away their time in some wretched Prisoner of War camp.

For the first fortnight or so, the Staff gave me the privileges due to my rank as 'Major' – which they knew from my uniform, and casualty label. Then pointed questions began to be asked about my age, the more so when somebody found only two stars under the slide with the Major's crown. Unknown to me, enquiries were being made outside the hospital. The North Riding's Regimental Depot had never heard of me; and my own Moundshires – being one of the first units to be pulled out of France – had recorded Acting Lieutenant Hardwicke as 'Missing – Possibly A.W.O.L.' Accordingly I was moved into the Junior Officer's Ward – in disgrace – because nobody would believe my story. And even when my wallet did come to light, somewhere in the hospital, the Colonel's orders pencilled on the back of a now filthy Signal form, were viewed with great distrust, and I knew no confirmation would be forthcoming from him.

Amongst my nurses there was one Dutch woman. Maria van Dieman was as firm as she was efficient, but happily she did sometimes let her young sister come into the ward as a visitor, and later as a volunteer helper. The sister was a shy beautiful girl, with an almost permanent air of sadness. At first I tried to cheer her up, but every time I made her laugh, Anna seemed on the very brink of tears. When I was well enough, she took me for walks in the grounds, and later we went further, out into the countryside – where she found my shoulder was a comforting one to cry on. And for a girl not quite 18 years old, she certainly had enough to weep about. I fell in love with Anna then ... and its been that way ever since.

*   *   *

Young Bill glanced up at this; he nodded in approval and let me continue. The boy had been close to his Grandmother, and her sudden death had been a bad blow to him, and rather worse than to those of us who were older, and had more understanding of sickness. I had always felt it best that Eric should tell his children about their own family history – though he had never done so in my presence. But I knew it couldn't hurt the lad to hear it again, and this time perhaps he'll learn something new – from me.

*   *   *

The van Diemans were a successful and close-knit family, who all lived near each other in the old part of Rotterdam; most living in flats over their shops or business premises. When the Dutch Army was mobilised to meet the threat of German invasion, Maria's father, brother and two cousins were all called to the colours. Three days later the entire family had gathered in *St Laurens Grote Kerk* to mourn the deaths of two of their menfolk, and to pray for the other two – unreliably reported as 'Missing – possibly killed.' Only Maria was absent – having placed the needs of the living before those of the dead – by remaining where she was much needed, on duty at the City Hospital.

Whilst the family prayed, Dutch and German officers were meeting nearby, to negotiate a surrender, but – in spite of this – the *Luftwaffe* launched an unprecedentedly ferocious air attack on the almost defenceless city. Some of the first bombs demolished the *Kerk*, others started fires which burned for many days, destroying a great part of the ancient city. Maria returned from the Hospital, to learn all her family had perished, together with hundreds of other civilians. But – several hours later – Anna was discovered, almost unhurt, having been miraculously blown into a corner, where a massive oak table had given her protection from tons of rubble which fell from the roof. Maria had already been invited to escort a party of Jewish refugee children to England. Now that her home, and everything she treasured, had been totally destroyed, she decided to go – bringing Anna with her.

* * *

Many of the less seriously wounded officers were sent home to recuperate, and there was talk of Medical Discharge for me. But I pointed out I was able to walk, salute, and – being left-handed – I could still write, load and even fire a revolver. They decided nothing more could be expected from a Junior Officer, and so I was kept on as 'Lieutenant', in Norfolk, on what were officially designated as 'Light Duties'. This involved walking for miles – assisting contractors who were rushing up coastal defences nearby. As a first protection against the threatened invasion, strange forms of floating barriers had been hurriedly installed off the beaches – only to be thrown ashore by the first real storms. Land mines had been sown haphazard; quite often these had to be located and then lifted, before our vehicles could reach the beaches. The builders obeyed rough-drawn plans, with the result that a few concrete pillboxes were constructed facing the wrong way, or down in hollows where the occupants could see nothing to fire at.

Then hundreds of miles of steel pipes were clamped together – as in scaffolding around a building – this being erected between High and Low water marks, to form continuous defences against German landing craft. One day I came upon a young Royal Engineers Lieutenant who appeared to be attempting to demolish one of these structures with his bare hands.

"Look how it moves, how the whole thing wobbles – these are bloody useless!" There could be no doubt how strongly he felt about the matter. "They do say Jerry will use rubber boats for the first wave, and maybe that bit of barbed-wire might puncture them – but anything heavier would go through this lot like a hot knife through butter!" He was definitely pleased to hear that I'd been saying much the same thing, and then he eyed me up and down. "You don't look much like a Regular. How would you like to have some fun? That's if you're not afraid to stick your neck out with the Brasshats?" I listened, with growing admiration, as he went on to tell me he'd been so worried about these doubtful defences that he'd risked making his view widely known – and far up the Chain-of-Command. So far in fact, that the Higher-Ups had most reluctantly allowed him to organise a test – though with dire warnings of what could happen to his already slender promotion chances if he should fail to prove his point. *And now,* I thought, *he's so very generously inviting me to share the same fate. But – with my own military career at such a low ebb – I don't suppose that I've got a lot to lose.* And that is how we came to join forces.

Four days later I was on board a Dumb Barge, a 'Thames Lighter', usually towed about the Pool of London; but now fitted with a powerful engine, so turning it into a makeshift prototype Landing Craft. (Even when most of us were fearing an invasion by the Germans, there were those who had faith that we could survive, and they were already looking ahead to our own invasion of German-occupied France.)

The previous evening my Sapper friend had selected what he believed to be a particularly weak point in the barrier, and had marked it with a big flag. Around that spot were now gathered a large crowd of high ranking officers, together with their Staffs, and the Contractors who had rushed up the scaffolding. There was also an Army Kine Unit on hand, to record our predicted failure on film.

The barge headed out to sea, then turned on course for the flag, our bows lifting as we sped shorewards – with the controls set at 'Full Ahead'. The Sapper ordered the men to take cover below deck, and to brace themselves against the coming impact, whilst he and I lay on deck, to get the best view. By now the 'Brass' had moved down onto the shingle, directly behind the barrier, smug in the certainty that we would fail to get ashore – and thus they would be amply justified in the creation of such an apparently flimsy defence. And I am sure some of them had already prepared their speeches, or written their reports to that effect.

"Here we go Hardwicke! Hold on tight!" Pipes flew in all directions when we crashed into the scaffolding. A hideous clatter followed as our unprotected propeller hit the steelwork – but we swept on like a tank through standing corn. By now the spectators were scattering in panic. The last pipe disappeared beneath our bows and the barge carried on up the beach – with a portly Staff Officer running ahead of us. The stupid fool couldn't even make up his mind whether to escape to the right or the left. In the end he tripped and fell, but fortunately our craft stopped too – though only a matter of inches from him.

"Follow me Hardwicke!" So saying, the Sapper leapt down onto the shingle, where I joined him. He then strode over to the scarlet-faced General, and saluted diffidently. "Reporting ashore, as ordered, Sir!" We had not, of course, expected many thanks for our demonstration, but I was more than a little taken aback by the torrent of lurid language with which the General told us to get our unspeakable selves, and our unprintably disgusting boat of his blood-stained beach. The Sapper turned slowly, and then called up to the grinning crew of the barge. "Cox'n, the General requests that we ..." Poker faced, and in a clear parade-ground voice, he repeated, verbatim, every single coarse or obscene phrase the General had just addressed to us. It was beautifully done – and it completed the discomfiture of the Brasshats. Within minutes, all the spectators, together with their film unit, had slunk away.

A big squad of Canadians arrived the next morning, and began to fasten land mines onto the barrier – in a belated attempt to make it more effective. Naturally enough, nobody would admit that this was in any way connected with our little demonstration. But, even now – more than 50 years later – I have yet to find a single person who ever saw 'The Invasion of Norfolk' as recorded on Army Kine Unit film.

Although officers with battle experience were in short supply, I was still considered to be something of an embarrassment – the more so after our Invasion fiasco – and was conveniently 'got rid of' ... as an Instructor with the Local Defence Volunteers. My first days reminded me of my activities with the *Hitler Jugend*. Only now I had to deal with a mixture of youths, and much older men. Most of them had been issued with Denim uniforms; which were much beloved by the seventeen year old youngsters – who had to be reminded these were to be worn for 'Fighting and NOT for Flirting.' On the other hand, men up to sixty five despised them as being 'mere boiler suits' and nothing like the smart brass buttoned uniforms many of them had worn 'in the last show'. Again I had to differentiate between lads who knew nothing, but thought they knew everything – and their seniors, many of whom probably knew more, and certainly had as much, or often more, battle experience than myself.

Our local L.D.V. Commander, who had 'fought' most of his last war behind a desk at the War Office, was determined to show what a wise warrior he was. The nearest Common was being converted into an airfield, and he judged this would be an ideal landing site for large forces of Germans, arriving by air. This despite the fact that every night construction machinery was deliberately left scattered over the whole area, to frustrate any gliders or aircraft that might attempt a landing. On his orders, single sentries – each armed with a Ross rifle, long bayonet, and five rounds of ammunition, were posted at diagonally opposite corners of the Common.

These two sentries were to be relieved at 2 am, when the weapons would be handed over. One night, a teenager, a recent arrival in the district, had the first watch. When his relief did not report for duty, the Sergeant of the Watch decided it was pointless to take the long walk to the far side of the field, just to tell the lad this unhappy fact, and that he would not be relieved. Nevertheless the youngster did hear footsteps at the expected time.

"Is that you Sarge?" He asked in a friendly way, quite forgetting he was meant to challenge anyone who approached – especially if from outside the perimeter, as did these footsteps. No reply came. Again he called out. Still no reply, but the footsteps were getting closer. Suddenly he remembered the correct procedure, and gathered what little courage he had. "Halt! Who goes there?" He challenged loudly. "Advance one and be recognised!" He was really quite pleased with that, though not by the lack of any response. There was silence save for advancing footsteps in the grass. He was debating whether he'd be justified in 'putting one up the spout', when 'Mooo! Mooo!' and then further 'Mooing,' from several different directions. Clearly he was surrounded by bulls. And – being a city boy – that scared him far more than a whole glider-load of heavily armed Germans would have done.

As dawn broke, the Sergeant found him, trembling, in the centre of an inquisitive herd of gentle Jersey cows, which had found a way out of their own field half a mile away.

Having uniforms, and many being armed with rifles – though in a variety of calibres – the Local Defence Volunteers were not quite so much a figure of fun as they had been in the early days, when most had only an armband and a pitch fork, or perhaps an ancient shotgun. Some Brass Hat decided that there should be a big parade of the L.D.V. Presumably this to reassure the local population that they were now safe in the event of enemy paratroopers dropping from the skies – even if dressed as nuns. I was called upon to help organise the parade; and every big parade does need a band. Wraxton, the nearest Public School had their Junior Training Corps [formerly Officers Training Corps.] with its own band. The Headmaster was willing, and so it was agreed that their band should lead the procession past the Town Hall steps, where the much decorated local hero – a superannuated Cavalry Officer – had promised to take the salute. I decided that my wounds, and my status as an Officer in the Army, precluded my marching in any Volunteer column. So, having got the various detachments into something like the planned Order of March, with the smartly turned out band at their head, I took a short cut to the Saluting Base. There I joined the General and various Civic Dignitaries, amongst whom I recognised the Headmaster.

There had been no opportunity for rehearsal. But I had been told that the Wraxton band had a good reputation, and could be relied upon. I was left in no doubt about this when they struck up – in the distance – with a fine loud military tune. Unfortunately nobody had told me that Wraxton J.T.C. was affiliated to a Light Infantry Regiment. Whilst never marching at full Light Infantry rate, the Corps had taken on a little of their ethos; and the boys – being young and fit – did like to march at a brisk pace. By the time the parade reached the saluting base at the top of the long hill, many of the older Volunteers were in obvious distress as they tried to keep up with band. I saw two drop out immediately after passing us – their pride had kept them going until they had received the great man's salute. Beside me the Headmaster was fuming. "I'll have words with that big-drummer. He's the one who sets the pace. What does he think these old men are – machines?" I could sympathise with the Head's anger, and yet the lad himself – sweating under his leopard-skin apron, and the load of his enormous drum – was only doing his best; twirling his drum sticks magnificently, demonstrating the 'bags of swank' that anyone in his position is expected to show. Marching beside him, his younger brother struggled with large and brightly polished cymbals, that produced a most unusual note. Talking to the pair of them after the parade, I learned that these ancient instruments – reputedly captured from the Turkish Army in 1917 – had both turned inside out, as they usually did if played with any degree enthusiasm.

[Note. It was not until August 23rd 1940 that Winston Churchill renamed the L.D.V as 'Home Guard'.]

17. 'Sealion' & Special Duties.

The *Kriegsmarine Akademie* at Mürwick is a huge and imposing red brick building, standing high above Flensburg Fiord. Erich Falkenberg had been there about four months when he was told his name was on the notice board.

<u>*Unternehmen Seelöwe.*</u>

The following Fähnrich z. See will report immediately to Kriegsmarine H.Q in Boulogne, for temporary duty.

Dress: Field Grey Uniform.

BAUER. H. HAHN. W. LENK. G. SCHOTT. K.

F.z.S. FALKENBERG. E. in charge.

Having reported for duty at Boulogne, the group from Mürwick were addressed by a *Korvettenkapitän*. 'Gentlemen, you have been sent here to assist in preparations for *Unternehmen Seelöwe*. Some of you may already know that *Der Führer* has approved plans for the invasion of England; what the English will come to know as 'Operation Sealion', when the time does come. However, you will find that you – as *Kriegsmarine* – are not very welcome here! The whole matter of transporting troops from here has been placed in the hands of the Army. And, in their unfathomable wisdom, they have given the task of providing sea transport to a battalion of Engineers – from Bavaria! Where, as you will be well aware, they have rather more experience of mountains and edelweiss, than with the tides and waves of what the English so proudly proclaim is 'Their Channel'. So far we have seen big rafts, made from wooden wine barrels, others made from old aeroplane floats, and some from river-bridging pontoons. What's more – would you believe – there is even talk of powering some of these monstrosities with obsolete water-cooled aeroplane engines and their four bladed propellers!'

Falkenberg was directed to a fleet of Tugs and Landing Craft. He was at first intrigued, then horrified, to learn that each river tug was to haul two inland waterway barges, which had been crudely adapted into makeshift landing craft. Most were huge, known as *Kähne* and used on the big rivers. *Präme* were about half that size and used on canals. Some of both types did have their own engines, though the majority could only be towed. Falkenberg finally reached a group of even smaller *Challand* barges, as used on the older narrow French canals. There he reported to the *Leutenant* in charge of Barges number 16 and 17.

"I understand you are here as an 'Observer'," was the curt greeting he received, "and observe is all you need to do. Everyone here knows exactly what has to be done. Everything has been most carefully planned. Provided Göring's *Luftwaffe* and your *Kriegsmarine* manage to keep us free from attack on the great day, all will go well. Tomorrow, I will be on barge 16, which has an engine. You can go on 17, which does not have one – but you will be under My orders."

Falkenberg knew he was outranked and could only 'observe', though with little faith in the outcome of the exercise. During an earlier briefing it had been explained that these smaller craft – being more manoeuvrable, and drawing less water – would be used for the first landings, and each would mount a heavy machine gun at the bow. A tug would tow two of these *Challand* – making up a *Schleppzug* – and when it was almost aground the tug would cast the barges free. They, having tied up alongside each other, would continue to the shore under the power of the engined one. The tug would remain offshore, waiting for them to refloat. Then, the re-united *Shleppzug* would return across the Channel, for more troops or supplies.

Falkenberg watched whilst a hundred soldiers embarked on each barge, encumbered with their life-jackets and full equipment, including a wheeled 37mm *PaK* anti-tank gun and cases of ammunition. He 'observed' how this load set the barge low in the water, and also that no form of seating had been provided. *They're going to get very tired standing up all the way across to England.* He told himself.

A *Feldweble* was in charge of number 17, with a corporal at the helm. Falkenberg stationed himself beside them. Even before they cleared the harbour the helmsmen were having difficulty keeping the two barges apart. Out at sea there was little more than a gentle swell, but this was enough to have several men puking. Falkenberg too leaned over the side (though not for the same reason) and he was alarmed to see how little free-board they had. He then suggested the men should all sit down. The Sergeant objected to this, because the concrete flooring was wet.

"Better a wet arse than a swim in full equipment!." Falkenberg told him. "The men will all sit! That is an order Sergeant, but you of course may stand if you wish." He did just out-rank the Sergeant, though he was much younger. Reluctantly the *Feldweble* ordered the men to sit.

When the tug turned through 90 degrees to approach the shore, 17 was caught by a swell and spun around further – as though about to ram 16. Falkenberg leapt across and seized the helm, and a collision was averted by barely a metre. Nevertheless, most of the men standing in 16 had seen what was happening. They panicked and rushed away to the far side. That sudden movement of at least ten tonnes caused the barge to heel over. The next wave increased this, so that water began to pour in. Less than two minutes later the barge had sunk. A quick-thinking crewman on the tug grabbed a fire axe and cut 16's tow rope. Following vessels stopped to pick up many of those in the water, but the Belgian skipper of the tug continued on his way with 17. He was blindly obeying the order that he was '... to treat this exercise as the real thing.' The tug grounded with 17 still in tow. The barge was cast off, and having no engine, it was carried ashore, beam on, by the waves. There was then difficulty in lowering the ramp before the troops could wade ashore – leaving the PaK behind them.

Despite this, and many other problems, the whole exercise was declared 'a success.' At the subsequent enquiry, the *Leutnant* insisted that his barge 16, had been rammed by 17 – under the command of Falkenberg. Fortunately for Erich, a higher ranking *Kapitän-leutnant* had been 'observing' from the following tug, with a clear view of what happened to both barges.

"In fact," he declared, "it was only due to the swift and decisive action of *Fähnrich* Falkenberg, that such a collision was actually avoided. Furthermore, had the men in 16 been ordered to sit – like those in 17 – their vessel would not have capsized ... and nine good men would still be alive today."

As a result of this incident, most of the small *Challand* barges were declared to be un-seaworthy and they were returned to their French canals. Nevertheless, invasion exercises continued at Boulogne, but the *Schleppzug* was reorganised so that two barges were towed in tandem, with the powered one furthest from the tug. When the time came, a motorboat would appear, from somewhere, and secure alongside the other, so that the two barges could hit the beach together.

Erich and the other *Fähnreich z See* were involved in more action before they returned to Mürwick. On several dark September and October nights, MTBs or larger ships of the Royal Navy entered or bombarded channel ports like Calais, Boulogne, and Cherbourg, sinking ships and barges as well as damaging shore installations. *F z S* Lenk died from wounds thus received, on 11th September. No British ships were sunk during these raids.

* * *

Shortly after his return to the *Akademie*, Falkenberg was surprised when the loudspeaker boomed out. *'Fähnrich Falkenberg to the Commandant's Office – im laufschritt!'* Not knowing what to expect, he dashes to the Headquarters area.

"Come in Falkenberg. This officer wishes to ask you some questions." The Commandant nods towards an elderly officer in *Luftwaffe* uniform. Erich noted that he wore the Knight's Cross at his throat, with a Pilot's wings and silver wound badge on his chest.

"Falkenberg. You have seen *'Fiende Hörte'* posters – warning you to be careful what you say because the enemy may be listening?" That was asked kindly enough.

"Yes, *Herr Hauptmann.*"

"Do you think, in the last few days, you might have said anything, in public, that you should not have done?" That was asked rather more sharply.

"No, *Herr Hauptmann*. I never discuss my training outside the *Akademie*."

"But I am told you had a good deal to say about the *Luftwaffe* in the Golden Eagle, two nights ago."

"With respect, Sir. Some of your airmen are very boastful, and I, I just told the truth." Only then did the Commandant intervene.

"Falkenberg! A word of advice. When you are in a hole – do not dig yourself deeper into it. Leave that to the Army, most of them spend their lives digging holes."

The *Hauptmann* ignored this. "Falkenberg, I am given to understand that you, with your knowledge of the English coast, could well conduct the coming invasion of England single-handed!"

"Herr Hauptmann. As I recall it, I said that while the *Luftwaffe* may drop a few men from the sky, the *Kriegsmarine* will have to deliver the rest, together with their vehicles, horses, guns, and ammunition, not to mention

Panzers. I did not say – what I know to be only too true – that the *Heer*, being landsmen, have only the strangest ideas, of how that is to be done. It is true that I did say I know parts of the English coast better than that of my own Country. My homes in Augsburg, and then Fürth, are far from our own shores, which I never saw until I joined the *Kriegsmarine*. And, as some of us now know, the invasion of England will be launched from ports in the occupied countries, not from the Fatherland. However, I was careful not to mention that I had been involved with Operation Sealion, nor – as a result of that – that I have more knowledge of *Der Führer's* plans for invading England than do most people. Furthermore I did not repeat what was being murmured, amongst senior *Kriegsmarine* officers, that *Feldmarschall von Rundsteadt*, who is in overall command – remains in his Paris Headquarters – and has not yet been seen at any amphibious training exercise."

"Just as well too, Falkenberg." The *Fregattenkapitän* now rose. "I will leave you alone with the *Hauptmann*, who has some very specific questions to ask you. Now Falkenberg, so far as the *Kriegsmarine* is concerned, you are free to answer all his questions. But I do ask you to remember that the *Luftwaffe* is a large and proud service, and you – are a very junior officer – even though you are in the *Kriegsmarine*."

* * *

Some five days later the *Akademie* loudspeaker oscillates, then clears. *'Fähnrich Falkenberg! Fähnrich Falkenberg! Report to the Commandant's Office – im laufschritt – Im Laufschritt!'* Following this unusually urgent summons, Falkenberg arrives breathless at the Commandant's Door. He knocks.

"*Einkommen* ... Ah Falkenberg. Sorry about this." Said the Commandant. "Bad news I think. You are to report, immediately, to the *Kriegsmarine Medical Centre* at Wilhelmshaven. There is concern about something in your medical history. It sounds as though your future may be in doubt. Take all your kit with you. As soon as you are ready to leave, report to this office for your travel documents. Now hurry!"

Twenty minutes later Falkenberg returned to collect those documents, and – to his considerable surprise – the *Fregatten-kapitän* escorted him out of, and away from, the main building. There he handed over a large blue envelope.

"Sealed orders, Falkenberg. Not to be opened until you are on the train. Speak to nobody as you leave the Academy. Good Luck, Falkenberg!"

As soon as his train leaves the station Erich opens the stiff envelope. The orders, written on red paper, come straight to the point. 'Ignore all mention of a Medical Condition. Do not proceed to Wilhelmshaven. Instead report, soonest, to U-boat Headquarters at Kiel Wick, for orders. Travel documents are enclosed herewith. On your return to the Academy, you will be silent about your activities during the next few days. But, as your cover story, you will grumble – loudly and often – about the half-blind Medico who kept you hanging about for days, making you swallow quantities of clay-like muck. And only then realised he had you confused with an Erwin Falkenburg – who is suspected of having stomach ulcers.' Erich is much relieved by the first instruction, but has his own suspicions about the purpose of the remainder.

At Keil there is confusion as to why he is there, because he is forbidden to show his immediately recognisable sealed orders. Phone calls are made, then an *Oberleutnant* appears and hurriedly takes charge.

"Report aboard U 114. Familiarise yourself with that boat – she's a type II – lying alongside the Turpitz Pier. You will return to this office 0900 tomorrow, for briefing – and do not be late." Erich has a long walk along the pier, passing a number of larger submarines before he can find U-114. On board he is greeted by an older *Fähnrich* who proudly shows him around.

"There's not much room – especially for you – you being on board as an *Extra*. U 114 was intended to be a huge *Untersee-kreuzer*, and would have taken ages to build, but they shrank her down in size so we could get into the war before it finishes."

Next morning Falkenberg is shown into the office of the Commanding Officer of U-boats. There he is introduced to *Oberleutnant zur See* Graffunder, *Kapitän* of U-114, and he is also surprised to see the friendly *Luftwaffe Hauptmann*.

"So we meet again young man. Our technicians have prepared the device I told you about. Two men have been detailed to go with you to install it."

The Commanding Officer of U-boats then nodded at Graffunder. "Your duty is to get the three men and the device ashore, and not to leave until it is fully established and tested. That done, unless U-boat Command send other orders, you will return here. And you, Falkenberg, after landing will go straight back to the Academy. *Oberleutnant* Graffunder knows he must be guided by you. But do not forget, he is in command. His orders are not to attack anything on the away out – unless a major warship crosses your path. But on the way back you may hope for some excitement. Any Questions? No? Then, Good Luck, Falkenberg. You will sail within the hour. Dismissed."

Erich salutes, and leaves, hurrying back to the pier and his new boat.

18. Special & Secret Duties.

After little more than a month with the L.D.V., I was recalled, because somebody had decided I was expendable – and therefore ideally suited to lead an 'Auxiliary Unit'. Few if any survivors were expected from these small 'stay-behind parties'. Our job was to disappear as soon as the invaders arrived, and to come out of hiding later, to launch attacks on their rear, and Lines-of-Communication troops. To go 'Scallywagging', as Colonel Gubbins, our organising officer, so tactfully worded it.

I found a derelict house on the edge of Kelling Heath, and began to convert it into a secret 'Operating Base'. One dark night we staged an Air Raid. Three explosive charges laid in the front and back gardens produced satisfactory 'craters' – as from a stick of bombs straddling the house; and several smaller charges collapsed much of the building itself, though leaving a high lookout position. The three cellars – from which we had already dug a well hidden emergency exit – remained intact.

Under a veil of secrecy I was ordered to Coleshill House, in Wiltshire, where I was the only Army trainee amongst a bunch of civilian 'Auxiliers'. On return to Norfolk I put my new training to use, and had my six men out and about most nights. We practised silent approaches to bridges or locations which I thought the enemy might use for his fuel or ammunition dumps. Our first real raid was on Weybourne, where we left a dummy bomb on the Army's normally defective Bren Gun Carrier. This was done almost as a challenge to a local farmer who told me of the old saying *'He who would all England win, must at Weybourne, Norfolk begin!'* After that we ventured further inland, 'attacking' other 'well-guarded' military sites, even leaving 'bombs' on three aircraft at the nearest R.A.F. Station. Unfortunately I was never able to be a 'Fly-on-the-wall' when any of our embarrassing packages were discovered. Early on, having achieved a small degree of competence ourselves, we spent our weekends training civilian Auxiliers – and they, being keen to learn, soon became capable of making themselves a thorn in the flesh of any invaders who might occupy their locality.

* * *

Late one evening a Despatch Rider arrived, asking for Lieutenant Hardwicke and insisting on speaking to me personally. He handed over a mysterious and quite unexpectedly heavy canvas Royal Mail sack, and then rode off, without asking for a signature – which was most unusual. Inside the bag I found a Thompson Sub-machine gun, and a generous supply of ·45 ammunition. Attached was a hand written label inscribed *'Ask No Questions!'* I searched amongst the wrappings and eventually found paperwork which suggested the gun should never have reached my local H.Q. I could only surmise that they – knowing we were short of weapons, like everybody else – had decided not to look a gift horse in the mouth. And they passed it on to me; thereby conveniently 'losing' what they would doubtless profess – 'We know nothing of it. We neither requested, nor expected to receive, any such an item.' I took that Tommy Gun for my own personal weapon. It was finely engineered, though heavy. But once I'd come to terms with its powerful urge to swing the muzzle to the right, and upwards, when firing automatic, I found it satisfactory. And so very different to the 'rogue' Sten Gun I encountered later on. (This one always fired a short burst when set for 'Single Rounds'; and only a single round when I needed full 'Automatic'.) But with the Thompson, I now had a really effective reply if we were ever discovered in the open, having failed to achieve our objective by stealth.

Our more specialised weapons and supplies arrived in dribs and drabs. These included reels of fine Trip-wire, and Pull-switches, used to set off explosive booby-trap charges. Less technical, and more silent in use, were rubber truncheons, and even 'Garrottes' – consisting of two crude wooden grips, joined by a loop of thin wire – to go around the neck of an unsuspecting sentry. Over-enthusiastic practice with these produced cuts that could not have been caused by shaving, and so had to be discontinued.

* * *

The weeks of the Battle of Britain passed, but still the Germans did not come. Slowly the Army gathered itself together, and – even more slowly – equipment began to arrive; so making good some of the enormous quantities of weapons and transport left behind in France. Hitler had already lost his best chance of launching a successful invasion, but reports kept reaching us of preparations being made across the North Sea. The R.A.F. daily bombed large concentrations of barges, and we regularly received warnings that an attack must be expected when the tides next became suitable. Our O.B. was about half-completed, but already well stocked with food, arms, ammunition and explosives, when – on September 7th – we received the one word signal that everyone was expecting.

The codeword 'CROMWELL' meant that invasion was 'Considered Imminent'; and that all troops were to go at once to their battle-stations. I ordered my men down into the cellars, and early next morning our sentry reported – from the look-out post in the ruin above us – that church bells were ringing in the distance, and he could hear heavy guns firing as well. For two days we lay low, according to our instructions. Only then did a Despatch Rider come to tell us that 'CROMWELL' had been cancelled at 1600 hours the day before. Due to a widespread misunderstanding of the real meaning of 'CROMWELL' – church bells had been rung, to call out the Home Guard, and the 'gunfire' had been demolition charges set off under several bridges, by over-zealous Royal Engineers. Worse still, an officer and his driver had been killed nearby, when their motor-cycle combination ran over a hastily placed and super-sensitive anti-tank mine. Despite all this, some 'knowledgeable' historians still maintain that the 'CROMWELL' signal was never sent, (Only years later did I learn that in the chaos of 'Cromwell', over seventy lives had been unnecessarily lost.) And all of this without one single German even having attempted to land – by air or water. Nor did they ever come.

Living full time in the cellars soon became unbearable. So – entirely without reference to any of my superiors – I commandeered an empty holiday chalet in the woods close to our base. In order to justify my action – using means best left unrecorded – I acquired a District Headquarters letterhead. My cook-cum-batman, a trainee Solicitor's Clerk, quickly converted this into an official looking requisition document, 'signed', or so it appeared, by a Lieutenant-General. This we displayed inside the front window, and it was never questioned. As ever, a high enough rank went unchallenged.

It would appear that amongst 'Auxiliary Units', my O.B. was almost unique in being manned entirely by military personnel. And being located barely two miles from a probable invasion beach, we would certainly have been overrun on the first day – had the Germans been at all successful. Most other Auxiliary Units were based further inland, being discreetly recruited from older men, or those in reserved occupations, who had an intimate knowledge of their own immediate district – local poachers being much in favour. Some were forced to resign from the Home Guard, others saw their H.G. records being torn up in front of them; and, having been sworn to secrecy on appointment to an Auxiliary Unit – they were quite unable to explain their perceived 'desertion'.

Because of this, they were held in contempt for many years afterwards. A harsh judgement on men whose expectation of life, when activated, had – unbeknown to us at the time – been officially assessed at a mere 14 or 15 days. And, as a further injustice, many of those who served in what ultimately became 'The British Resistance Organisation', did not even receive the Defence Medal which was granted to all with three years service in the Home Guard.

By mid October it became clear to me that Hitler had already missed his best opportunity for a successful invasion. Long periods of boredom led to ingenious designs of personal weaponry. One Private made what he proudly described as 'a readily-concealed, ivory-hilted, folding thrust-weapon'. This was a short length of polished pig's leg bone in which he had mounted a viciously sharpened six inch nail that swung out at a right angle. The weapon was much admired, and he found time to make one for each of us. I have mine to this day.

* * *

"I beg to report for duty, Herr Commandant." Erich Falkenberg had returned to the Academy at Mürwick.

"Welcome back, Falkenberg. But ... but ... can you please explain that new ribbon of *E.K.II* in your button-hole?"

"This Iron Cross was awarded to me, and also to the *Luftwaffe Electiker* and the *Bergsteiger*, by *Vize-admiral* Doenitz, who happened to be at Kiel Wick when we returned, Sir."

"Congratulations Falkenberg. But ... as you are very well aware, your Special Duty was Top Secret – and it must remain so. I have made it known here that you had to go for a medical examination, and might not be returning. Nobody earns an Iron Cross – even Second Class – by standing around waiting for a Medical Board. I greatly regret that I must order you to remove that ribbon, and to do it before you leave this office. And thereafter you are to stick to the 'Medical' cover story, as in your written orders. However ... I do promise you, that on the day you and your *Crew* pass out, I will explain to them, why it is that you have not been wearing the ribbon, and although – for reasons of security –no details can be given, the award was very well merited. For the rest of that day, you are to wear the *Eisernes Kreuz* itself – regardless of tradition to the contrary. But until that day, your Cross is to remain a secret between the two of us. And both your Cross and its ribbon will have to stay here, in this office."

"Understood, Herr Commandant. May I please trouble you for a knife or scissors? This ribbon is well sewn in."

"Falkenberg! You really are a most inconvenient young man!"

* * *

Although the civilian population of London endured Air Raids every night for two and a half months, I spent a peaceful winter – seemingly forgotten by Higher Authority – in command of my own 'Private Army'; doing little more than joining the men in cutting up fallen trees for our fires – because I dared not draw attention to the whereabouts of our unauthorised living quarters by indenting for regular coal or coke deliveries. Even though it was a boring and un-heroic way of soldiering, it did give me opportunities to see enough of Anna for her to accept my proposal of marriage.

Although I had virtually disappeared for several months, Higher Authority were firmly reminded of my existence when amazing news arrived. *'H.M. King George has been graciously pleased to approve the award of the Military Cross – to Acting-Major John Hardwicke, Moundshire Regiment .'*

And that, to some extent at least, did lift the cloud that had hung over me for so long, but it did little to solve the mystery of those missing days. The citation gave no more than a suggestion that I had done something rather better than the right thing – whilst leading a counter attack, somewhere near Dunkirk – three days before he evacuation came to an end ... though I very much doubt whether I would have stuck my neck out so far had we known that Hitler – in his role as 'Military Genius' – had actually been holding back the advance of his *Panzers*, which could so easily have kept on, pushing us right into the sea.

There was no explanation of how, or from whom, the recommendation was received. Be that as it may, I had one more good reason to be grateful to the friendly Colonel, and his gallant little band of Yorkshiremen.

Anna was delighted by the award, perhaps the more so because I received the Cross just in time to wear it at our wedding, in the tiny village church close to my Grandparents home in Warwickshire. Because Anna had no relations except Maria, we had decided to keep it a small affair. Even so, my relatives rallied round, and put on a surprisingly good Wedding Breakfast

– though the small almost fruitless Fruit Cake appeared hidden under an imposing 'iced' cardboard cover.

* * *

Not until early summer did the Powers-that-be decide that I should return to my own unit, then patiently guarding the South coast of Devon. Or, perhaps it was the fact that I now had a 'gong' which persuaded the Battalion to accept me back where I properly belonged. Regardless of which, this new posting was not as good as it might appear, because Granny had died, and her cottage – like most of Noss Mayo – was now full of people from Plymouth whose homes had been destroyed, or who were seeking safety from the heavy and persistent German air raids.

On arrival I reported to the Adjutant, a beery-faced regular who believed that officers – such as myself – who were serving 'for the Period of Hostilities Only', were merely 'amateurs'. And he held the oft expressed opinion that 'Without a Sandhurst Training, one cannot be a real Officer, nor – except in very rare cases – a Gentleman either.' He began by asking probing questions about my last days in France, making it very clear that in his view I had deserted the unit – if indeed I had not been a deserter in the full sense of the word. Knowing as I did, that the 5th Battalion Moundshires had been one of the very first units to be withdrawn from France; I stood it for just so long before quietly reminding him – perhaps somewhat unfairly – that whilst he had been knocking it back in some cosy English pub, I was still on very Active Service in France. And there – in my amateur way – I'd been losing bits of myself ... and picking up other things too. Reluctantly, his eyes followed mine down to the little white and purple ribbon on my chest.

He said nothing more, but sat fidgeting with my papers. I waited impatiently, then – without any hint of a salute – I turned on my heel and stalked out of his office ... leaving the door wide open behind me. Never again did Captain Ward mention France to me. Neither – being sworn to secrecy – could I tell him, nor any of my fellow officers, anything about my nefarious 'underground' activities in Norfolk.

More importantly, it was quite impossible for me to ask them to answer the one question that had been nagging me for months – especially since my return from France.

19. Devon Again.

Very shortly after my arrival in Devon, my own Captaincy was gazetted, to the fury of the Adjutant – for yet another 'amateur' had caught him up in rank. On that same day an unusually elderly Second Lieutenant joined us. At once I spotted the bronze oak-leaf cluster he wore with his World War One trio, and knew he'd be an interesting character. Hanson appeared to be a somewhat reserved but self-confidant gentleman. Slowly his past became known to us, though – as is so often the case – leaks from the Orderly Room ensured that the men knew more, and sooner, than their officers.

As a very young Lieutenant-Colonel, Henry Hanson had gone up into the front line trenches intending to end the war with his men. At around 1030 hours on the 11th of November 1918, when most activity had died down in their sector, a stray shell exploded overhead. Nobody was sure whether it came from the Germans or was a premature burst from nearby French artillery. Hanson had taken a large splinter in his shoulder, and was stretchered from the trench, protesting that he must stay until eleven o'clock, to be able to congratulate and thank his men, at the moment the Armistice came into force. But that was not to be, and after a long period of treatment, he left hospital as a civilian.

At the outbreak of war in 1939, Hanson volunteered for service, and was repeatedly turned down on medical grounds, but that did not prevent him from later raising and leading the Local Defence Volunteers, and subsequently – ranked as Captain – he commanded a Home Guard Company. But all the time he was badgering authority to let him get back into 'The Army Proper.' The story goes that they finally relented, but only after he insisted on being re-commissioned as a Subaltern – on the grounds that ' ... things have moved on a long way since my last war, and I've got a lot of catching up to do.' Because of that, and his natural gentlemanly manner, he was quickly accepted – and respected – by all ranks; becoming known, affectionately, as 'Uncle Harry'.

Since I was to some degree a 'newcomer', it was easy for me to strike up a friendship with him, and that was in no way affected by the fact that – though with much less Service – I now visibly outranked him. Not surprisingly the Adjutant made the most of his own 'superior' status, even objecting to the slender Malacca swagger cane that 'Uncle' habitually carried. It is my belief that Ward's primary gripe was that it's silver thimble bore the badge of Uncle's last Regiment. The 'Shiny Silvers' had a much longer and considerably more distinguished history than us Moundshires, and they enjoyed an unquestionably higher social standing too. Despite the Adj's repeated hints, Uncle continued to carry that cane, and it was noticeable he had developed a possibly sub-conscious habit of indicating approval, or displeasure, by the way he handled his cane. For the latter, holding its mid point in his left hand, he would variously tap, or even pound the silver thimble into the open palm of his right hand. A gesture I quickly recognized, and one which – whilst he held his former rank – must have brought fear and trembling to any young Subaltern who was falling down on the job.

At first I was too busy learning about the defence plans in my own sector to worry about the situation further West. However, at a conference I met a Lieutenant of Marines, and he turned out to be responsible for my old stamping ground – along the Nine Mile Drive. It had often crossed my mind that Erich might have informed his superiors about Porthyn Pryva, but I had never actually got around to doing anything about it myself. The Lieutenant's answers, to my tactful questioning, made it clear that our own forces knew nothing of the little beach, so they had taken no precautions there. And that left me with some difficulties. The Adjutant was still gunning for me, and my 'invasion' of Norfolk had not yet been forgotten in certain quarters. So it did seem unwise to raise a possible false alarm, especially about a situation that really ought to have been reported many months earlier.

Though little was said initially, I soon sensed that Uncle shared my low opinion of the Adj: and as we grew closer, we did on several occasions conspire to cause him some small embarrassments. It was naughty of course, but it did help to relieve the boredom of our days. Uncle was the only fellow-officer with whom I ever felt I could discuss my days in Germany, and my friendship with Erich and his *H.J. Kameraden*. Uncle was very understanding, having himself spent a happy year at Heidelberg University, and he knew that two of his closest friends there had been killed in1917.

Fortunately my problem with Porthyn Pryva was partially solved when I bumped into an old Schoolmate, who was then serving with the Navy, in Plymouth. Over a drink he readily agreed it would be useful for me to get an 'attacker's eye view' of the shore we were meant to be defending. In spite of that, it did cost me a lot more in drinks before he could be persuaded – on a strictly unofficial basis – to provide a boat which would pick me up at Fort Bovisand. This vast brick fortification, was built in mid-victorian days, to house twenty four huge muzzle-loaders. Now, with just three 12 pounder guns – installed as long ago as 1898 – and 6 modern searchlights, it still guarded the approaches to Plymouth Sound.

Feeling more than a little self-conscious, I stood, in warm sunshine, waiting beside the Fort's tiny harbour, with a rolled up towel under my arm, and a G.S spade in my hand. I clearly overheard – but chose to ignore – the comments of a couple of West Country gunners who were working nearby.

"Just like a muckin' orfficer. 'E's forgot 'is bloody bucket. Shil I get 'un one?"

"Naa – let'n bide. 'E's got 'is liddle shovel so 'e can still make 'is sandy-castles without 'un."

The battered grey painted cutter came gently alongside the quay. A youthful Midshipman clambered up the vertical iron ladder and saluted me.

"Good Morning, Sir. I'm Jeffcott. Am I to have the pleasure of your company for this morning's Jolly?" I gave him my luggage and, in spite of the handicap, the fair-haired youngster went down the ladder like a monkey. I followed, very much more cautiously, because my hand was still weak; my missing fingers hidden by the leather gloves I habitually wore – despite the warm weather. And maybe that explained the disdainful glances of the two ratings when I finally boarded the rocking boat. At the tiller stood a bearded Leading Seaman who, to judge by the three Good Conduct badges, was probably a recalled pensioner. With practised ease, he reversed out of the harbour and – seemingly without changing gear – he headed us South, towards the open sea. As the Mewstone came abreast, the Midshipman produced a chart.

"Just what part of the coast is it that you want to see, Sir?" He asked politely, and I put my finger on the spot, to avoid confusions over map references and chart co-ordinates.

"Just there, Mid. ... and when we get there, I'm going ashore for a few minutes." He looked closely at the chart.

"Not with those rocks Sir, I can't "

"No!" I interrupted him. "You certainly cannot take the boat in – that's why I brought these." I indicated my swimming gear. "You go as close as you think is safe, then I swim ashore, and you stand off in deeper water until I've done."

"Nobody gave any orders about you going ashore, Sir."

"Nobody told you Jeffcott. But as I understand it – nobody tells Midshipmen anything – they're expected to find out for themselves – to use their own initiative. Correct?" His only reply was a rather sickly grin. And at least I'd prevented him from asking questions that could not be answered, because the trip ashore would be made entirely on my own initiative.

"You'll find there's near enough slack water, for about an hour," I told him,"just before Low Water at Plymouth." The poor lad could hardly accept such information coming from a mere 'Pongo' (as the Navy refer to us soldiers.) Neither could he risk challenging the word of a much superior officer. I watched him searching the chart, seeking in vain for confirmation of my statement. "But," I added – just to show the Army could have an understanding of such matters, "The tide will still be running when we get there, so you'll have to anchor, or else keep motoring. Whilst I'm ashore."

"We'll be there in about 45 minutes, Sir." He observed, without any sign of enthusiasm. Leaving the Mewstones astern we headed Eastwards, across Wembury Bay, and it was there I realised we were not flying any sort of a flag.

"The Coast Defences should know we're coming Mid. But I'd be a lot happier if we could let them know we're on their side." (In actual fact, I thought it most unlikely that my friend would have alerted anybody. Knowing that he ought not to have let me have the boat, he'd not have wished to draw attention to the fact.) One of the ratings produced a grubby White Ensign, and mounted it at the stern. With only a gentle following wind – that exactly matched our low speed – the ensign just hung limp against its staff.

"Can't you find a bit of string to hold it out?" I asked the rating. "So the Coastguards, or even the Home Guard can recognise it?" The Middy was scandalised by my suggestion.

"Couldn't do that Sir – the White Ensign must be worn properly at all times. I'd be on the mat within an hour of landing – if I were to allow that, Sir!"

"Use your initiative Mid." I urged. "Don't hazard your ship. In the Army its only the Guards who'd rather be dead than 'improperly dressed'. And remember, its the Marines who own this bit of coast – not your lot." The rating was grudgingly ordered to do as I had suggested.

"Ay Aye, Sir." He replied, poker faced. "Not to worry Sir ... Worse things do 'appen at sea!"

I debated whether to take the spade ashore with me – and decided against it. In all probability I was on a wild-goose chase, and the Middy was correct in describing our trip as a 'Jolly'. It didn't take me long to swim to the rocks. Porthyn Pryva was just as Erich and I had left it, though perhaps a little smaller than I remembered; and at first I felt nobody could have been there since. Nevertheless I began to search closely, seeking for any sign to the contrary. And then I saw it ... a thin wire stretched up the rocky face of the alcove! Almost twenty feet up it divided, to form a huge 'Y'. Whoever put it there must be a very experienced climber. The lower end of the wire disappeared into the sand, at the foot of the cliff – barely a yard from where I estimated the cave entrance to be.

Erich! I thought. *It must be that Erich is involved in this – surely no other German could know of this beach – let alone the cave. But ... Erich was no climber, and he'd not have learned that in his Naval training ... But – does it have to be German wire?* (In those days many of our own people were doing the strangest things – and telling almost nobody about them. So it was more than possible – even if improbable – that I had stumbled upon one of our own Top Secret installations, whilst making my own totally unauthorised landing.)

Feet scrunched in the sand behind me. I spun around, feeling trapped, and very conscious that I was totally unarmed. There stood a naked youth, with wet hair darkly plastered across his face, his tanned skin glistening in the sunlight.

"ERICH!" I exclaimed. *"Warum ist du heier?"* Even as I spoke came the realisation that he was not Erich – who had been so much in my thoughts – but the young Midshipman.

"Sorry I made you jump Sir. But I – I – er – you left your spade behind. I thought you might need it, Sir, so I brought it ashore for you." Jeffcott had absolutely no business to be there, and I was annoyed by his intrusion; because there'd soon be plenty of trouble from my own superiors – without having the Navy putting their oar in was well.

"Do the officers in charge of His Majesty's ships normally abandon them?" I demanded angrily, but even then I knew the question was quite unjustified. "As you were, Jeffcott! At sea you are in charge. But ashore you are my subordinate – and seeing you are so concerned about spades, you can come over here, and bloody well use that one!" I showed him where to start digging – over the mouth of the cave.

The Midshipman set to work and immediately spotted the wire, pointing to it. Before he could ask any unanswerable questions I warned him not to damage it. Within moments his spade was beginning to work in under the cliff.

"I say Sir, it looks as if there's a sort of an opening here."

"I don't need you to tell me that Mid." I snapped back. "Don't talk – Just Dig!" I needed time to think – remembering the night Erich and I had spent in that cave. *Can it be someone is in there now – waiting – and armed?* Unfortunately it was – without any doubt – my place to find out. Pushing the Middy aside, and taking the spade from him, I opened up the entrance. Nothing happened, and all I could hear was the sound of the sea beyond the rock wall. When the hole was big enough I wriggled through into the cave. It was unoccupied, and I could see no trace of footprints in the sand, though a tide or two would have taken care of that. But there was still the so well remembered smell, of stale damp seaweed in the first stages of decay. My eyes were just beginning to get used to the gloom – but suddenly the light was cut off.

"Dammit Jeffcott!" I shouted. "Get away from that blasted hole – and let the daylight in!" The lad was too keen by half ... *and why the hell does he behave so much like Erich – as well as look like him too?*

The wire inside led upwards, as I had expected, to the rock shelf – and then to a large metal box. Alongside that, joined by thicker wires, were several smaller boxes – which I took to be batteries. *Ought I to cut the wire, or to disconnect the batteries?* For a while I could only ponder, knowing full well that this installation – if it was an enemy one – would most probably be booby-trapped, because that was a German speciality. My final decision was to leave everything untouched, and to report immediately to my superiors; hoping they might be disposed to agree with me, that in such a situation, No Action, was in fact the correct course of Action. I left the cave and ordered the Midshipman to fill in the hole and to bury the spade there too.

Whilst he was doing that, he reminded me the tide would soon be running and we should be getting back to the cutter. I had a final look around, then followed him out through the rocks, pausing to collect the life jacket he had used to float the spade ashore. By the time I was in the water he was half way back to the boat, and, as they hauled me on board, he gave the order for our return to the Fort.

My clothes were at the bows, under the canvas spray-dodger. I felt certain my towel had been left spread over them – but now it was underneath.

Whilst retrieving it, I noticed that my webbing belt with its holster and ammunition pouch was missing.

"Who the devil has moved my revolver?" I demanded.

"I have!" Came a voice from behind me. "Put your hands on your head – and turn around, very slowly ... Sir." I did as the voice commanded. That blasted Middy was holding my revolver in his right hand, pointing it straight at my head, whilst he inexpertly drew back the hammer with his left. Seen as close as that one was, the muzzle of a Webley ·455 looks bigger than a twelve bore ... and I don't think I've ever felt nearer to death than at that moment; for it is doubtful if that kid had even had hold of such a weapon before. Each time I tried to speak, he told me to keep quiet, and it was quite obvious he was getting more and more jumpy by the minute. In the end I did just as he said, because I'd a better chance of staying alive that way. He made me move to one side of the boat, to get dressed. Perkins, the Leading Seaman, searched my garments before throwing them to me, one at a time. It was ludicrous – being held like that, by a boy in his birthday suit, who was nervously gripping a gun that was far too big for him to handle – but I was not laughing then.

"And now, Sir, I'll have to trouble you for the loan of your towel." He murmured apologetically. (Not for nothing does the Navy call them 'Young Gentlemen'). He handed the weapon to Perkins, and to my intense relief the grizzled seaman aimed it to one side of me whilst he carefully lowered the hammer. In that state it was no less lethal, but now there would have to be a much more determined squeeze on the trigger before it could kill me.

As we were entering Bovisand Harbour, the Leading Seaman shouted for the Guard to be turned out, and this time he brought the cutter in alongside the steps. I found the stones were slippery, and when I stumbled Jeffcott jabbed the revolver into my kidneys – proving he'd a lot to learn about escort duties, but he lacked nothing in keenness. A sentry, with rifle and bayonet, was waiting for me on the quay, and others were running towards us. Without my battledress blouse – and so bereft of visible rank – I was marched off to the Fort, taken down into an underground ammunition magazine, and left there in the care of two armed sentries. Shortly afterwards, Jeffcott arrived, still clutching my revolver, and accompanied by a very unhappy looking Artillery Second Lieutenant.

"What the hell's going on here?" I stormed. "Has this boy gone out of his mind?" The Subaltern was courteous, though trying hard to appear firm.

"I regret that my Battery Commander is absent, but you will have to be detained here, until he returns – at some unspecified hour this evening."

"Seeing that you are so very clearly unused to accepting any responsibility, this would probably be your best course of action ... unless you'd care to examine the identity card in my wallet, which the Navy – as represented by this boy here – has refused to return to me." I continued making myself thoroughly objectionable until the Subaltern unwillingly agreed to have me taken, under armed escort, to Army Headquarters, where my identity could be firmly established. I insisted that 'Young Horatio' should accompany me – to explain his insulting behaviour to a Senior Officer. Up to then nobody had offered any form of explanation for my arrest, nor yet the slightest suggestion of an apology.

My Brigadier received us in his office, where the Lieutenant seemed to be unsure, or at least unable to explain why we were there. Irritation showing, the Brig: turned to the overawed Midshipman.

"Well, can You perhaps give me a coherent explanation?" The lad told of his doubts when I had unexpectedly insisted on going ashore alone, and of his suspicion when I addressed him in what he believed to be German, and at my refusal to allow him into the cave to see what lay at the end of the wire. Knowing the signs, I thought the near-apoplectic Brigadier was about to bawl the lad out, but I jumped in before he could start.

"In retrospect, Sir – after listening to all that – I now believe this young man acted with initiative – and in the best traditions of his Service." That silenced the Brig: temporarily at least, but I knew somebody would feel his wrath before the day was out – and that person would almost certainly be me.

When my captors had been told to wait outside, I was ordered to give my side of the story. The Brigadier amazed me by listening, almost without interruption, right to the end. Then, having let me sweat for a little while, he had the other two shown in again.

"What did you tell your boat's crew was your reason for arresting this officer?" He barked at the Midshipman.

"I said I thought he was a spy, Sir."

"Did you mention the beach, or the cave to them Jeffcott?"

"No Sir, only that I thought he was a spy – there wasn't time to say anything more."

"Good!. Now Lieutenant, get the two of you back to the fort, just as fast as you can, and see that this whole matter is hushed up, and treated as Top Secret. Do you understand me when I say Top Secret? You can say the man who was arrested is being detained by the Army – because we'll need Captain Hardwicke until the end of the war, or even longer. Midshipman, you must make absolutely sure your crew don't talk. Tell them that they sailed along the coast, and back again – and they never stopped. Never Stopped ... Understand? Now, on your way gentlemen – and hurry. I shall be in touch with your Superiors, and in your case at least Mr Jeffcott – it will be a favourable report." They saluted and turned to go. But the Brigadier called the Midshipman back.

"Mr Jeffcott," He boomed, not unkindly, "if you don't return this officer's revolver, he will have to face a Court Martial for losing his weapon." Sheepishly the lad handed it back to me, saluted yet again – and bolted from the room. That left me alone with the Brigadier, and I braced myself for the expected blast.

"Now, Captain Hardwicke. I want the whole story again. Write it as a report – at once – but leaving nothing out. I'm not sure if you have disobeyed orders, or just exceeded them. Not that it matters at the moment, not until we know whether you have breached our own security or – as seems much more likely – you've made a most important discovery of enemy activities."

Some three hours later I was recalled to meet a mixed group of very senior officers. It was clear the Navy found it hard to believe that H.M.S. Hood could have been sunk, taking many of their friends with her. (But at least this grim news would be the main topic of conversation amongst the ratings, so – with any luck – their trip in the cutter, and my arrest, might perhaps be pushed into the background.) In a very sombre atmosphere I had to tell my story again, in the greatest detail.

Then I faced a barrage of questions, about Porthyn Pryva and the equipment I had found there, and particularly about Erich. They wanted to know if he was 'Officer Material', and was I sure about him joining the German Navy? I had to say 'Yes' on both counts. Next the Brigadier attached me to his Headquarters until the matter was sorted out, and he ordered me to guide a small group of specialists to Porthyn Pryva in the morning. Since it appeared I was in some degree of favour, I took full advantage of that, turning to the Commander R.N.

"May I suggest, Sir, that we have the same boat again, on the grounds that it will help security if we use men who are already involved – in preference to newcomers?" This was readily agreed, and then I ventured a more personal note. "I do hope that 'Young Nelson' will be in charge of the boat, Sir. That young man's got guts. Remember he could have met with a nasty accident when ashore – had I really been a spy. As it is, I'll be happy to sail under his command again ... always provided ... I am allowed ... to keep hold of my own revolver." And at that the meeting broke up in some much needed laughter.

I completed my report, with no feeling of guilt over divulging the secret of my idyllic little beach, because the age-old peace and tranquillity of Porthyn Pryva had already been brutally violated – but by whom? Much later that night I turned in, with my mind still in turmoil. And when sleep did eventually come, for the first time in many months, Erich joined me in my dreams. He was his pre-war cheery self, and we made repeated visits to Porthyn Pryva. Of course we always went into the cave – and each time we found ourselves trapped in there – by the same terrifying but unrecognisable danger. Then my friend would silently disappear, leaving me in the darkness, to face its stealthy approach alone – until I suddenly awoke, trembling and bathed in sweat, with the smell of seaweed still strong in my nostrils.

20. A Trap Is Set.

I was almost late in arriving at Devonport the next morning, and the dockside shed was already crowded. Whilst my identity was being checked, I quietly asked the Sub-Lieutenant whether everyone there was hoping to go on my boat trip. He nodded grimly, ticked off my name on his list, but said nothing. They really were an extraordinary lot – Officers, N.C.O.s and Other Ranks, from all three Services ... many holding exalted rank, and being dressed in uniforms that were quite unsuitable for small boats. There was even a Lieutenant-Colonel resplendent in breeches and highly polished riding boots, with a hunting crop under his arm. His cap badge explained everything, for it was widely known that the 'Gorgeous Gallopers' had never become reconciled to exchanging their horses for tanks. And, even in wartime, they had clung fiercely to their reputation as 'The best tailored Regiment in the British Army.'

A small door at the far end of the shed opened, and Midshipman Jeffcott peered in. He looked around, spotted me, and beckoned – with one finger.

"Sorry about that, Sir." He apologised, as I joined him outside. "But I didn't want to get in amongst all that 'Brass'. Meet our man from Naval Intelligence." The elderly R.N.V.R. Lieutenant-Commander looked distinctly worried.

"Why are all these senior Army Officers here?" He demanded abruptly. "And why the devil have you brought them with you?"

"Nothing to do with me." I assured him. "They look like a bunch of dug-out Staff Wallahs – who think they'd like a day out, and a trip in Mr Jeffcott's *Skylark*. Be glad enough the see the back of 'em myself." He seemed relieved at this, and asked me to wait in the shed with the others.

I introduced myself to a middle-aged Captain who wore a 'Bomb Disposal' flash on his sleeve. He came straight to the point.

"Now then Hardwicke, they tell me you suspect, or expect, a booby trap? My Corporal will have to come ashore with you. Afraid I'll have to stay in the boat – otherwise I might get rusty." He struck his leg with his swagger stick – producing a hollow clang. "Tin leg you see. If it filled with water I'd probably sink like a stone. But my Corporal will be right enough, water polo international before the war." Whilst he was speaking I recognised the tiny silver George Cross in the centre of the dark blue ribbon he wore before his W.W.I. trio. And then I knew we had at least one good man to help us.

A bespectacled Pilot Officer explained that the R.A.F. were also interested, in case I might have found some sort of radio beacon, and his two men were radio specialists – as were as were the two Naval ratings standing nearby. Almost everyone else seemed to have difficulty in explaining his purpose for being there, and several were distinctly indignant that a mere infantry Captain should even enquire.

Jeffcott entered, followed by a couple of ratings carrying a large wicker hamper. Next, the Intelligence Officer climbed onto a packing case and very respectfully asked for silence.

"Gentlemen, I hardly need to remind you that this Operation is Top Secret, and therefore calls for the strictest security at all times. I feel sure everybody here will appreciate the unhealthy attention that must be aroused, if a party of high ranking officers, from all three Services, were to be seen leaving the dockyard – in a small open boat. Therefore the Port Admiral has ordered that everyone – except junior Naval personnel – must go in disguise." He nodded to a smirking matelot, who opened up the hamper, and held aloft a paint-smeared boiler-suit, and a rating's round cap. Before anyone could object, the Lieutenant-Commander continued. "I must apologise for the fact that these boiler-suits are all equally dirty, in fact they were on their way to the cleaners – and no others are available. There is a war on ..." he explained very solemnly, "as you Gentlemen will be well aware."

At this point the Rear-Admiral suddenly announced that he was only there to see us on our way. Immediately other senior officers appeared to loose interest, or else they adopted his attitude.

"Well, I shall need a boiler-suit. A decent fit if possible!" All eyes turned to the 'Galloper', amazed that he would deign to wear such a garment – even if brand new. "Well Dammit!" He barked, defensively. "Someone's got to see this show through – What?" Jeffcott glanced up at the Intelligence Officer, and slowly drew a finger across his own upper lip. But the Commander pretended not to have seen him.

"Of course you would be most welcome to join us, Sir – but I'm afraid you'll have to shave off that moustache – or else grow a beard in the next fifteen minutes ... there are spies around ... and even an alert Girl Guide would spot that you couldn't be a seaman – not looking as you do at the moment, Sir."

'Tin-legs' and I were struggling into the filthy garments when the I.O. came and joined us.

"I'm terribly sorry about this Gentlemen. But you two do pose something of an extra problem. You see we don't get many ratings with a limp or leather gloves. However, we'll have to overcome that, because Jeffcott will definitely need you both." He gave me a broad wink, before taking a bandage from the nearest First Aid box; and in a couple of minutes my gloved hand was hidden inside the boilersuit, supported by a sling. "Now if you'll both amble along behind, whilst I march the rest of our motley crew. Then, with a bit of luck, the Dockyard Mateys will think you two tried to take on the Marines – and came off second best!"

In bright sunshine the cutter made its way down the placid waters of The Sound. No wonder so many others had wanted to come for the trip – for a 'Jolly' as Jeffcott would have put it. But that young man was taking it all very seriously and, to judge by the lanyard about his neck – and the large automatic pistol at his hip – he was taking no chances either. This time we were paddled ashore ashore to Porthyn Pyryva on a Carley float, getting almost as wet as if we had swum. Inside the cave, working by torchlight, the Corporal searched for booby traps, then the Naval and Air Force technicians examined the transmitter, but none of them could find anything more sinister than the crumbling remains of a tin of Corned Beef. Of course, that could readily have been explained, had I chosen; but there was no explaining my certainty that we still faced a very real danger, and that one – or even all of us – could well be dead within minutes.

The row of cased batteries stood ranged along the rock shelf, each joined to its neighbour by a thick lead, and finally two more very heavy wires connected them to the transmitter. The batteries were ordinary enough, and similar to British issue. They were all alike but – holding the torch close – I checked each one in turn. Something made me check them all again – but more carefully – and only then did I spot the difference. Six of those cases bore an identical group of numbers and letters – stencilled in white. But the one closest to the transmitter had a partially erased, though totally different coding – in red. I reasoned that those markings could well be Stores Reference Numbers. *But Why?* I asked myself. *Why would the methodical Bosche use different numbers – for identical items of equipment? And what – if any – could be the significance of red?* After a brief discussion about my discovery, the Corporal went back to the boat to consult with 'Tin-legs'.

"You were quite right, Sir," reported the Corporal on his return. "We went through the manual, and it confirms your suspicion. The Seventh case is half battery and half bomb, and it should detonate as soon as the circuit is broken. But not to worry, I can easily set it to 'Safe', by giving a quarter of a turn to the screw head that's concealed beneath one of the filler caps. Though the Captain insists you must all leave the cave until I've dealt with that switch."

Several minutes passed before he came out, with a worried frown.

"It is already set at 'Safe', Sir! At least I'm almost sure it is – but I wouldn't put it past Jerry to alter the settings if he thinks we've got to know how it works. I'll have to go and have another word with the Captain." There was nothing else the rest of us could do whilst he was enjoying his swim, so we lay dozing in the warm sun – as Erich and I had so often done in happier times. I was beginning to wonder what had become of the Corporal when we heard him calling for assistance. We hurried to the water's edge and found 'Tin-legs' struggling ashore from the float, and finding it hard going amongst the rocks.

"Nasty one this Hardwicke. I want to take a look myself. You'd better come in too – and the blue-jobs had best go back to the boat, for the time being." With or without his George Cross, that man could have been invalided out, with honour, but he still behaved like a fully fit man half his age.

The Corporal and I waited whilst he dragged himself painfully through the small opening. Together they checked the screw slot. It was lined up along the length of the case, and 'Tin-legs' confirmed that according to the manual – that was SAFE. Then he began to explain the problem to me, but it was clear he was actually talking it out with himself.

"Jerry can be clever – diabolically clever at times – but if we believe he's cleverer than he really is, we could end up losing the whole ruddy lot. So ... we assume it is set at SAFE ... but we'll couple up our own leads, just to be extra safe – and only when that's been done, do we break the circuit – whilst we're outside – with our heads well down." Two pairs of hands were needed to change the leads, so it fell to me to hold the lamps. And, although it was always cool inside the cave, I was wet with sweat by the time we returned to the sunshine.

There – moving as far away as possible – we took cover behind a large rock.

"You found it Hardwicke – so you can have the pleasure of blowing it up if Jerry has managed to out-smart us." 'Tin-legs' handed me the end of a cord that led from the cave mouth. I pulled it tight, hesitated, then gave it a hard jerk. A Herring Gull screamed angrily, as if objecting – but there was no explosion. I continued pulling on the cord and dragged out a jumble of wires and crocodile clips. The booby trap had indeed been left at SAFE. And – deep down inside – I wasn't greatly surprised by that.

An hour later we were heading back to Plymouth, with the transmitter, now wrapped in two layers of rubber sheeting, to be extra safe from salt water ... and from prying eyes too. Then, for more than 24 hours, I was left to my own devices; the matter having passed into the hands of those with much greater rank. During this time news came that the loss of Hood had been avenged by the sinking of *Bismarck*. I learned this with very mixed feelings. Erich had by then served long enough to have been on board her, but there were plenty of other ships, or shore stations where he would have been safe. There was no way of knowing, so I put the matter out of my mind.

Very late that evening I was called to another high-powered Joint-Services conference, and it was quite evident some of those in darker blue had been celebrating the sinking of *Bismarck*. A Vice-admiral rose and called us to order.

"Gentlemen. You have been summoned here, at this inconvenient hour, to begin coordinating plans for the forthcoming Operation – which has been approved ... at the very highest level." He paused, before continuing more slowly, speaking – in a Churchillian manner – gesturing with an imaginary cigar as he did so. "Topmost Priority – For Action This Day!" He let that sink in. "Now, let us hope, for all our sakes, that Captain Hardwicke knew what he was doing when he started all this nonsense. The Operation will be known as ... " He paused, giving me a long hard look, " ... will be known as ... Operation Judas!"

'Judas'! It came as a knife in my guts. Instantly I was filled with hate for the sadistic swine who had chosen that name. Whatever the outcome might be, I would – I knew – have to live with that word to the end of my days. I had put my Country first, and this was my reward – from some anonymous desk-bound pen-pusher, with a perverted sense of humour. Slowly my rage subsided and I became aware of the Admiral, who was still droning on.

"The equipment brought back from the cave is definitely a beacon – set to transmit for limited periods only – to guide *Luftwaffe* bombers so they can continue knocking hell out of my home City of Plymouth, and the Naval Dockyard at Devonport." He paused, leaving me wondering whether he had lost relatives or friends in earlier raids. "Now, when its mechanism has been re-set – to transmit at times that will be virtually useless to the enemy – the beacon will be installed again, as soon as possible, back in the cave. This action – so some optimist believes – will induce the Germans to make a second landing, to correct the 'faulty' timing device. If that does happen, and I do emphasise the 'if', we will be waiting – and the trap will be sprung. Then the returning U-boat – if such it was – should be either captured or destroyed."

The Army still insisted on being represented when the beacon was replaced, so once again I boarded young Jeffcott's ferryboat. But this time nobody even suggested we should be wearing fancy dress. When I pressed the Midshipman about this, he hesitated, and only replied after asking if I would keep a secret.

"You see, Sir, the Intelligence Officer did ask for help in getting rid of all those Brass Hats, but he was just told to use his own imagination, and that's exactly what he did do!" Ashore at Porthyn Pryva, our Naval signallers had no difficulty in replacing the transmitter just as we had found it. After everyone else had left the cave I spent some time there, and smoothed out the trampled sand. When my toe stubbed against something solid, I dug down cautiously with my fingers – and uncovered the hilt of an *H.J. Fahrtenmesser.* Its chrome still shone brightly, but the scabbard was turning red with rust; and the broken leather suspension strap made it clear how it came to be left behind. A coating of grease had protected most of the blade *'Blut und Ehre!'* read the familiar motto, but I already knew what the other side would show ... Erich, so proudly – or would it be, defiantly – staring me in the face ... *'A boy as hard as Krupp steel.' Yes!* I thought, *He's that, right enough – to come ashore, right on the very doorstep of the Royal Navy.* Now I had proof positive, of what I'd always believed, from the moment I first saw that wire stretched up the cliff face.

It was indeed Erich who'd led our enemy to Porthyn Pryva, and so, in part, he was responsible for the devastating bombing of the city and dockyard. I now had to face the fact that – in serving his own country's interest – Erich had betrayed both our friendship, and the secret that I'd so willingly shared with him.

Calling from outside, Jeffcott broke in on my reverie.

"Time to be going, Sir. The weather's worsening, and the sea's coming up." I concealed the knife, intending to keep it secret, as my own personal souvenir.

On the way back we encountered a series of nasty squalls, and the movement of the cutter became distinctly uncomfortable. Before long both the W/T ratings were hanging over the gunwale, in all too obvious distress. The Leading Seaman did his best to excuse this.

"They're just H.O's, Sir. From a stone frigate ashore – not real Matelots – not what you'd call regulars."

"I'm Hostilities Only, myself!" I retorted firmly. "But I'm feeling fine!" To be quite honest, that was a long way from the truth, but I just had to get my own back for the time the Navy had held me prisoner at the point of my own revolver. And I did just manage not to disgrace myself before we landed.

My next task, as ordered by the Brigadier, was to set up an Observation and Listening Post overlooking the sea at Porthyn Pryva. Under the pretext of Security, I got his approval for the Pioneer Corps to bring in men from a distance, to do the initial work. He also agreed that I should be allowed to choose a small squad of Moundshires who would man it when completed. This was accepted without comment by our Colonel, but naturally enough it was resented by the Adjutant. I quickly realised this unusual state of affairs carried a definite bonus, in that whenever I disliked an order as posted by Ward, I could, and did – unhesitatingly – declare my subservience to the Brigadier. And so I came to command my second Private Army.

Building that O.L.P. was a tricky business, which could not be done in darkness, though it had to be completed before enemy reconnaissance aircraft could spot it. With this in mind Fighter aircraft patrolled overhead from dawn, whilst the Pioneers lifted the turf before using pneumatic drills to dig down into the rock, creating a large slit-trench close to the edge of the cliff. This was roofed over with timbers, which were covered with soil, on which the grass was carefully replaced. However there was no easy way to remove the ruts made by their heavy vehicles, all of which led directly to our new position – a certain give-away in any aerial photographs that might be taken later. My over-hasty solution was to persuade the farmer to dump several loads of dung close to our dug-out. And then to spread some more over the top end of the field.. (The cause of those wheel marks was now patently obvious to the enemy – and persistently apparent to any one who did duty in the O.L.P.)

Next we installed a generator and a permanent telephone link in a derelict barn about half a mile inland. After dusk each evening, a field telephone and a small searchlight were moved forward to the O.L.P. Then we watched, and listened, and waited – until dawn when the cables were wound in and the equipment hidden in the barn again.

Twice, when there was no moon, a single plane flew past us several times, unchallenged by the nearest Ack Ack Battery. It came lower and lower, over both land and sea – as if searching for the beacon. After that we could at least assume that Jerry was aware of the failure of his gadget. That posed an unanswerable question. Could we be sure – inter-service rivalries being what they were – that the *Luftwaffe* would be able to persuade the *Kriegsmarine* to risk losing one of their U-boats whilst a landing be made to correct a faulty *Luftwaffe* device?

The Royal Marines were responsible for the defence of that sector of coastline. And their men on the spot viewed our activities with bewildered hostility. (It had been decided, for Reasons of Security, that apart from their most senior officers, they were to be kept 'in the dark' – until the very last minute – and not surprisingly we were considered to be unwelcome trespassers on their patch.) On the other hand, the Royal Navy were fully involved. Their anti-submarine forces had been instructed that any U-boat entering the area was to be shadowed, but only attacked if a major warship was at risk, or unless the intruder attempted to enter The Sound proper, when it would betray its presence by passing over the Asdic Loop. (This six mile long sea bed detector cable stretched from Pier Cellars, right across the mouth of the estuary, to the eastern side of the Yealm.) Each night a small force of M.T.Bs and M.G.Bs were to be held at short notice for action at Porthyn Pryva. Should they fail to deal with the U-boat there, it was hoped other vessels would ensure its destruction when it made for the open sea.

Perhaps it was inevitable, during those long unrewarding watches, that my thoughts should turn to Erich. *There can be very little doubt he came ashore from a U-boat, but does that mean he was serving full time in their Submarine Service? Not necessarily so; he could have been put on board only because of his unique knowledge of Porthyn Pryva and its cave.* I rather hoped that was the case, because our Navy was getting steadily better at sinking U-boats.

21. Action.

The former French Naval College at Brest is a huge building, and Erich Falkenberg has had some difficulty in locating the Commanding Officer of the First U-boat Flotilla.

'*Leutnant zur See* Falkenberg begs to report for duty, Sir.'

'You are a whole day late Falkenberg!'

'My trains were delayed, or re-routed several times, Sir. I understand the British Airmen and French Resistance are to blame.'

'Yes. They often are. Now you have five minutes to gather a small bag of essentials, then report to the Motor Pool for transport. You can read these orders whilst being driven to the docks. I will advise *Kapitänleutnant* Ziggendorfer that you are now on your way to U-330. Hurry now. And Good Luck, Falkenberg.'

As soon as Erich is on board, the U-boat sails, watched by senior officers and waving nurses from a nearby military hospital. It is very soon made clear to Erich that neither he, nor the *Luftwaffe Techniker*, are welcome on board.

"Why do you have to do the *Luftwaffe's* work for them?" Demanded Ziggendorfer irritably. "And why drag us into it? Anyway, after you've had our necks into a noose, and completed your heroics ashore, don't expect to touch dry land for at least another six weeks. During that time we'll have the pleasure of showing the pair of you how we earn our living. And right now I've got to find duties for you and your *Luftfunker*. We do not carry any passengers on my boat!'

This came as an unwelcome surprise to Erich, who'd believed he was being sent on an out-and-back trip like his last one. Having no warning, he had made no provision for a prolonged voyage, and had only a part change of clothing with him. Although without any formal U-boat training, he now realises he will have to do duty as a junior officer of the U-boat, not to act solely as Leader of the landing party. And with a Commander like Ziggendorfer, who wears the Knight's Cross, those strange new duties will have to be learned very quickly.

'Last time they sent you in one of the Type II boats. Why the hell can't they do the same now?' The Commander broke in on Erich's thoughts. 'The Type II is smaller, and much better suited to this class of work than our Type VII. We'll have to make the most of a Spring Tide to get us close in. Luckily for us – if there is any moon – its a new one. You'll go ashore at 0100 hours, and with any luck Tommy will be tucked up in his bed by then. Even so, you two will have to get the job done as quickly as possible. Otherwise we could end up bending our keel on a rocky coast like that.'

'*Herr Kapitän!* Whoever told you we could work at high water – let alone at Springs? We cannot possibly dig away the sand that blocks the way into the cave entrance when it is a full metre underwater. We will have to be getting ashore three hours before, or two hours after, high water.'

'*Leutnant!* Who the hell do you think you are – to be giving me orders as to what to do with my boat?'

'With respect Sir. I am the only person on board who has been ashore there. I am the only one who knows where the cave is, and how to get into it. My orders are to get the *Luft-techniker* in there. And – as I understand it – your orders are to get the two of us ashore so that we can carry out our task, and then to get us back on board again. After that we are both at your disposal, Sir.' Ziggendorfer glowered, but Falkenberg continues firmly. 'I do have to point out that when we are travelling in the *Slauchboot,* there will be a strong tide running. Depending on how far out the *U-boot* is when it is launched, we must be at least 150 metres up-tide of the landing point. And on our return, for the same reason, the *U-boot* must be the same distance down-tide. We will need at least three of us in the *Slauchboot.* Myself, the *Luftmann,* and one, or better two, of your men, ones who are used to paddling those damned blow-up boats. And one will need a ten metre rope so that he can come ashore to hold the boat against the rocks whilst we work inside the cave. We cannot possibly carry that boat ashore with us.'

'I will only risk one of my men. You two will have to do your own paddling. I repeat – in case you may have forgotten – we do not carry any passengers on my boat.'

* * *

Our nightly watch at Porthyn Pryva had continued, week after week – becoming easier as the days grew longer – and enlivened by only one false alarm. We were alerted because a U-boat had been detected, but then word came she was not heading in our direction. From time to time we were able to stand the men down, but only when the sea was so rough it was reckoned that any landing from a U-boat would be impossible. And it was during one of these intervals that 'Uncle' Hanson seemed unhappy over what he phrased as my 'inaction' in that respect. He then told me a story he'd learned when studying his former regiment's history.

"Way back in the early 1800s they were serving in India and had some connection with the locally raised Madras European Regiment, who were very proud of their part in the capture of a Dutch spice island. The Madras's were on board H.M.S. Caroline, and three other British warships, off Banda Neria. the Dutch were aware of this, but – on one particular night – they decided it would be safe to stand down their normal guard, because the weather was so foul that no attack would be possible. Captain Cole did not agree; he brought his ships in close enough for the Madras men to be rowed ashore. Once landed on the island, and unopposed, they moved swiftly. So swiftly that the first the Dutch Governor knew about it was when the Madras soldiers burst in upon him as he sat at his dinner table. And you should remember this John, that some at least of the German Navy, can be brave and daring, just as our own sailors were on that filthy night so long ago."

I did manage occasional daytime meetings with Anna, who had got herself a job in an Exeter hospital so as to be near me.

"What news of Maria?" I asked her.

"She's in London." Anna's reply was unusually curt, and she offered no more information. Later, in spite of our joy at being together, it became clear to me Anna was under some sort of strain. Again I asked after Maria, and Anna gave me one of her looks. "I told you before – she is in London – don't ask me again. I will tell you when there is any news from her." That told me Maria was doing something more than just ordinary nursing and, so long as I knew nothing about it, there was no way I could give anything away. (Everywhere one went at that time there were posters warning *WALLS HAVE EARS!* or *CARELESS TALK COSTS LIVES!* – which all too often turned out to be tragically true.

Anna and I were about to part at the end of a later visit, during which she had been particularly subdued. She held me close and whispered,

"Maria is reported 'Missing'." I was about to ask her where, and how – but she held up a hand to silence me. She opened her handbag and passed me a pound note that was folded, in the way they did in Holland – to form a capital 'W' – as a token of continuing loyalty to Wilhelmina, Queen of the

Netherlands. That told me all that I needed to know then. Maria was back in Holland, and I asked no more questions. In fact Anna had been sworn to secrecy before they would tell her Maria had parachuted back into Holland, on a clandestine mission which appeared to have gone wrong. Anna would not break faith by telling me as much – yet she had to share her terrible secret with somebody, and had found her own way of doing it. No wonder she was worried, for if her sister was in the hands of the Germans she could expect imprisonment – if she was lucky – but her fate would probably be far worse.

* * *

The boy stirred himself slowly, then quietly interrupted me.

"But Gramps, wasn't it true what Granny told me – that *Tante Maria* was shot by the Germans, in the Hague?"

"Yes its all quite true Bill. The *Gestapo* took your Great Aunt to Schevening prison and tortured her for days, but – being the brave woman she was – she wouldn't name any of her contacts in Holland, and in spite of everything they did to her, she gave nothing else away. That refusal certainly cost Maria her life, though it must have saved many others working with the Dutch Resistance – and because of that, Queen Wilhelmina awarded her a posthumous medal. But of course we didn't know anything of this until almost the end of the war – a while after I'd married your Grandmother. That's how it is you have no living relations on her side of the family, and why she always found it difficult to understand how I can feel as I do about Erich Falkenberg, and so many of the German boys I met before the war." Bill seemed to be satisfied with this, and so I went on with my story.

* * *

There was another false alarm; someone couldn't tell the difference between E-boats and surfaced U-boats. However, the following night information came that a submerged U-boat had been detected off the Eddystone Light. No depth charges had been dropped, but after a short period of shadowing she was left alone, and reported to be 'proceeding slowly in a northerly direction.' Nothing more could be expected to happen for at least an hour, but I tested all our phone links and had the generator run up, to ensure it would start the moment we needed it. Soon afterwards we heard powerful engines below us – M.T.B's speeding eastwards, into Bigbury Bay. The Gunboats, I knew, should already be hiding inside the Breakwater at the entrance to Plymouth Sound. Although the Navy, now lurking on either side of me, had the trap fully set, they could do nothing until I passed the word that the U-boat had been sighted from my O.L.P.

A stiff breeze was blowing in from the sea, and I could pick out occasional white horses with my night glasses, but waves breaking against the rocks below us were visible to the naked eye, and this left me thinking that if the wind strengthened only a little, we'd probably spend the next night in our beds. The Sergeant and I took turn about, to watch, or listen through a headset, to sounds from microphones secreted on the cliff face below. Two hours passed, three hours, and I began to wonder if this was another false alarm. Yet again I scanned the heaving sea. *Even more white horses now ... Yes, tomorrow night we'll be comfortably tucked up in ... But – but – those, those waves – they're in a long straight line ...?* Hurriedly I focussed the binoculars – and there she lay – further out, and further along the coast than I'd expected – a submarine stopped on the surface. In that location, and with that silhouette, I knew she could not be British. *But how long has she been there? How much time have I already lost?*

I got busy on the telephone whilst my Sergeant kept up a running commentary.

"Some sort of a boat is coming ashore, Sir. Its coming straight for us. And the Sub is coming closer in too." Only then did I remember the effect the tide would be having on their movements. Above us a Corporal manned the un-lit searchlight, keeping it aimed in readiness at the U-boat. *The M.T.Bs and the M.G.Bs should be moving in by now.* My heart was racing – as I hoped they would be too. It was a long time since I'd been quite so close to the enemy and – for a change – the scales were heavily weighted in my favour.

The Sergeant nudged me, handing over the earphones. I took them clumsily in my right hand. *This time,* I thought, *it's they who are going to lose more than a few fingers ...* For a brief moment I savoured the idea of revenge, but I could not forget my friend Erich – who was the enemy of all those who were about to attack the vessel below me. *Perhaps he may not be on board her this trip.* The thought gave me little consolation, because – in my heart – I knew it was a false hope. I was there, and I felt certain Erich was there too. The secret we shared had surely brought us together again. Through the earphones I could just detect voices, although they were unintelligible above the background noise of wind and waves. *If only the Navy would arrive now – while Erich's ashore, and he'll be safe when the shooting starts.*

Again I phoned H.Q. urging immediate action. They replied that the order to attack had been given, and nothing they could do would hasten matters. Time passed so very slowly. The voices had ceased. Then we saw the boat being paddled away from the rocks. I ordered the generator started, relying on the wind to carry away its noise. Time was now running out fast, and with our small arms we could easily have sunk the rubber boat, but that would have alerted the U-boat, and we had no weapons that could prevent her leaving. The whole attack was in the hands of the Navy – and they were already late.

A green Very Light soared lazily into the sky. It was the signal we had been waiting for.

"Searchlight On!" I called. The well-aimed beam stabbed downwards, illuminating the whole foredeck of the Submarine, where a hatch stood open, and men were trying to pass a still partially inflated rubber dinghy below. Multi-coloured lines of tracer came winging in from the darkness – on the Bigbury side – cutting down the gunners standing ready at the U-boat's main armament before they could even aim at the attackers. A seaman on the conning tower pointed his machine gun up at us. "Take Cover!" I yelled. Moments later the searchlight above me was extinguished in a chaos of thudding bullets, hammered metal, and tinkling glass. "Both Mortars – FIRE!" I shouted. Two dull explosions beside me, and acrid smoke in the trench. "Re-load!" I ordered, as two parachute flares burst into brilliance high above the U-boat. Now I could see the whole length of the vessel – and in the distance the three low shapes that were hosing her with tracer bullets. But there was still no sign of the more heavily armed Motor Gunboats.

The U-boat was moving very slowly, swinging her bows away from the M.T.B.s *That will be to protect those working on her foredeck,'* or so I reasoned – until a single torpedo track became visible astern of her. I could only scream a warning into the telephone – but barely a minute later one of the M.T.B.s disintegrated, amidst a huge ball of flame. *What incredibly bad luck, to take a direct hit. But where the hell are those bloody Gunboats? They're needed more than ever now!* The sky above us seemed full of tracer as the machine-gunner sought to shoot out our parachute flares. He got one and when we sent up more, he turned the weapon on us, raking the position with three long bursts of well aimed fire. When it was safe to look out again I saw the foredeck hatch appeared to have jammed when only part closed ... men struggled frantically to shut it ... a body was dragged clear and pitched overboard. Our first flares had died and others were drifting over the land and so needed to be replaced. "Fire Both Mortars! Then keep your heads well down while you're re-loading!" Even as I shouted my orders, the

U-boat's deck was swept by cannon shells, which ripped into the open fore hatch and decimated the men who had been fighting to close it.

That fire came from the South – the Gunboats had arrived at last – though we didn't much welcome the gunner whose wild burst struck the cliff top, sending rock and metal ricocheting over our heads and thudding into the downland behind us. But by now the enemy vessel was moving faster, turning towards deep water – with clouds of spray all around her ... *They're venting her tanks – she's diving – but with that hatch still open?* A stream of men began to scramble out of the conning tower – abandoning ship – hurling themselves into the water to avoid bullets that still flew like hail.

A red Very light went up. All firing stopped and one M.T.B. began to close the submarine.

"Another flare Sergeant!" A figure on the conning tower grabbed the machine gun, but a well aimed shot cut him down as he swung it towards the approaching M.T.B. A final long burst of tracer arched erratically into the sky as his dying finger closed around the trigger. The M.T.B. came cautiously alongside, but she was too late to do anything but pick up survivors. When the U-boat sank – amidst a welter of bubbles – two men shot to the surface in a rush of escaping air, and joined the few others swimming there. The Navy turned on their own lights, but I sent up a succession of flares to help them in their work of mercy. For now the battle was over, there was no longer a foe to be fought, only fellow mariners to be saved, from their common enemy – the sea.

I heard a noise above me, and only then – to my shame – did I remember the Corporal who had been manning our searchlight. Luckily he too had seen what was coming and had got down in time – and he'd stayed well down from then on. A flying fragment had ripped the sleeve of his battledress, but he was unhurt. Half an hour later a white Very light went up, the signal for the boats to return to Plymouth. I reported the successful end of the action, and was congratulated, and told to stand my men down. They were triumphant, and outwardly so was I, knowing they could not begin to understand just how sick at heart I really felt.

On the other hand the local Marines were just furious. They had been ordered not to open fire unless specifically ordered to do so – and those orders never arrived – so all honours would be shared between the Army and the Navy. Then, insult to injury, in a heavy downpour of rain, they were sent to search the shoreline for survivors – and I felt sorry for any German they might catch – whilst in their ugly frame of mind.

The following morning I requested Leave for my men, and was dismayed to find they had all been Confined to Camp, on 'Security Grounds'. I went straight to the C.O. and was later able to promise them an extra long leave when they were out of 'Quarantine'. The Navy still seemed to think I was the custodian of the Beacon, so – in dense fog – I was taken to recover it. (Later on it was installed again, two miles along the coast, in the hope of routing Jerry's planes over a waiting Ack Ack battery. (Those guns did shoot down a *Dornier* – though whether the beacon had anything to do with it we shall never know.)

Off Porthyn Pryva, I could just make out a strange selection of ships, half-hidden by the swirling mist.

"Salvage vessels and Lifting Craft," said Jeffcott knowledgeably, "but of course you havn't seen any sign of them, Sir." I held an imaginary telescope up to my eye.

"I see no ships, Mr Jeffcott!" He gave me a pitying look – the sort of look the Senior Service reserve for mere Pongos. "I don't suppose they thought it was very funny when Admiral Nelson said it, but – as I remember Mid – it did go down in the history books."

"Do you want me to record it in the Logbook? Sir?" (With a cheek like that I should think he's either been cashiered, or came close to being made First Sea Lord.) On the way back to Plymouth we picked up the body of a German sailor. He was only a youngster, and he reminded me uncomfortably of Erich, and the lads I had known – and liked – in peacetime Germany. Inevitably that raised the question that had been dogging me since I first sighted that U-boat. Had Erich been on board her, and if so, what had become of him?

Back at camp, word was waiting that the Adjutant wished to see me, and I knew nothing good could come of that. He made no mention of my recent success, but imperiously ordered me to proceed, immediately, on seven days leave – an action that was calculated not to improve my standing with my own men, who'd had no leave, and no more than a handful of decent night's sleep in many weeks. When the men did finally get their leave, they'd be straight off home; but I had what could only be described as unfinished business – though I hardly knew what it was, nor where it was going to take me.

22. Dartmoor Hunt.

It was late in the afternoon before I was able to get away from the camp, having collected my leave pass and ration cards. By then I was absolutely certain – in my own mind at least – that Erich Falkenberg had been on that U-boat. And I felt that – being the Erich I knew – he would surely somehow have managed to survive, in spite of all our efforts to destroy him.

But where? I asked myself repeatedly, *where would he go as soon as he got himself ashore, and how could he hide if injured? Certainly he can't have forgotten the old church of The Poor Fisherman – unwelcoming though he'd think the shelter that offered.* But, after finding no trace of him amongst those bramble covered ruins, it crossed my mind he just might risk seeking another and possibly more hospitable sanctuary not far away.

Noss Mayo was it's usual peaceful self. Seemingly no explanation of the previous night's gunfire had yet reached the villagers, and certainly not the strangers from the city that I met there. Granny's cottage was crowded, and there was some delay before the new owner could be found. I identified myself, explaining my connection with the place, and asked if anyone had been enquiring for the Hardwickes recently.

"Only this very morning – early it was – he must have caught the first bus from Plymouth. A young man. Poor fellow, his ship had been torpedoed and his uniform was in a terrible state, still damp and salt-stained. He told me he was – Belgian would it be – and used to write to a pen-friend. 'At Noss Mayo, such a name I not forget', as he said. Somebody here told him this used to be Mrs Hardwicke's cottage, but when he learned she was gone, he wouldn't stay, not even for a cup of tea or coffee. They do drink coffee there don't they?" She was a garrulous soul and needed little prompting to make me quite certain it was Erich who had called at the cottage; but he had hurried away – even refusing her offer of breakfast – without mentioning either his name or his intentions.

I gulped down the tea she forced upon me, before setting off, to follow the route of our camping trip upon the Moor, in case he'd decided to hide up there for a day or two until things quietened down closer to the shore. It was the only plan I could think of, being fully intent on catching up with him if at all possible, and yet not knowing – if we should meet – whether I'd treat him as Friend or Foe. That would, to a large degree, depend upon Erich himself; because my sudden appearance would be proof – if any be needed – that I was the enemy primarily responsible for the loss of his ship, and so many of her crew. Be that as it may, I'd be dry, partly rested, well fed – and armed. With all those advantages I ought to have the upper hand this time, whereas in the past he'd too often been able to get the better of me.

Policemen stopped me twice, asking if I had seen any suspicious strangers. They told me of food having been stolen from a house, and a shop at Yealmpton being entered too, but the intruders were disturbed. Only a single man had been seen, though the whole crew of a shot down German Bomber were believed to be on the run somewhere in the district. That was distinctly bad news for me. With another hunt going on, my task would not be made any easier. Darkness was already falling, so I knew there was little enough chance the airmen would be captured before morning. After Bed and an early Breakfast in Ivybridge. I left my motor cycle there and set out on foot under threatening skies, prepared to spend the whole day on the Moor – should it be necessary. If I was right about Erich, he couldn't be too far ahead of me, because he would do best to travel in the half-light around dawn and dusk, especially out on the open moor, where a man can be seen from miles away – provided there's anybody else there to see him.

My problem was knowing where to search and where not to waste time – and that meant I had to think myself into Erich's mind. The night had been dark and stormy, so the only safe place for a forced march would be the tramway. By keeping the compacted ballast underfoot he'd know – however difficult the conditions might be – that he was still on the track. But somewhere he'd need to find shelter from view – and from the rain. I pounded on along the old track, knowing any attempt at concealment would slow me down too much. The rocks at Sharp Tor offer a hiding place, but no protection. And although I was tempted to ignore them, they gave me a good view of the Erme's valley and Piles Copse, where the old oaks were in full leaf. After hurrying back to the tramway, I pressed on northwards, keeping continuous watch on the surrounding hills for any hint of movement.

There was no sign of my quarry in the gaunt old buildings at Leftlake, nor under the nearby tramway bridge, and I remember thinking that for once Erich wouldn't be the least bit interested in taking a swim. I was virtually certain he had no map, and that meant he'd be tempted to follow our previous route. And that made for difficulties when I went hurrying down the slope towards Stoney Bottom and Erme Pound. One needs to watch every step on rough, tussocky, treacherous ground like that, but my eyes were always focussed on the distance, so perhaps I was lucky to fall only once – but nearly ricked my ankle in the process. The Blowing House was as deserted as the last time I'd seen it

But what of the Pound – any amount of concealment there? I searched our luncheon hut, finding a freshly emptied dark green tin marked 'Meat Loaf'. Although our own troops frequently exercised on the Moor, Erich could have had no opportunity to steal Army rations. And unless he had overcome his little weakness, no way would he have chosen to make an overnight stop there – *Zuviel Menschen!*

I already knew Erich had sought people since coming ashore. *What?* I wondered. *What was Erich after when he tried to find my Grandmother? Would it be he had hoped she would put him in touch with me? Or could it be he'd remembered my showing him Grandpa's Mauser Automatic pistol?* Unknown to my Grandmother, I had discovered this lethal World War One souvenir, on top of the wardrobe in our bedroom. It was kept 'hidden' here, complete with a fully loaded magazine, and its wooden holster, that could also be used as a butt. *Would Erich,* I kept asking myself, *have turned nasty if she refused to help him, or had tried to raise the alarm?* Erich had respected the old lady, and she had liked him too, admiring his good English, and his polite manners.

But, ever since her husband died, Granny always asked herself 'What would the Colonel have done?' and then she acted accordingly. (That was probably why she gave me so much freedom. My Grandfather had laid down a few strict rules for me – and they had to be kept. But I did overhear him telling her, 'Let John find out things for himself. The boy is not a fool – but he will be one if you keep him on too tight a leash, and if we take all his decisions for him.')

Again I found myself beset by doubt. *Am I on a wild-goose chase, or is he really up here on the Moor with me, and if so, where would he be heading – or hiding?* Faced with such problems, I reasoned that Erich could only know the one route, and as he was now most certainly a Real Man – wouldn't he find himself being drawn towards his 'Hard Country' up the Wollake

Valley? The nearer I got to the Tinner's Hut, the stronger grew my feeling that Erich was somewhere thereabouts, and not necessarily alone. With the German airmen in mind I drew my revolver, and began to search the area. Out of the corner of my eye I detected a dark movement further up the valley – well beyond the '*Trilithon*' – but a proper look revealed nothing more ominous than a group of cattle on the distant slope of Green Hill. The low walls of the hut could well have hidden a man, even a couple of men, and I didn't want to be ambushed by the *Luftwaffe*. My stealthy approach was wasted – nobody home. Although it did look as if some body, most probably that of a sheep, had flattened the grass whilst sheltering inside the hut. Then slowly onwards, up the little valley, heading towards the 'Warrior's Grave', but stopping every few yards to look and to listen. At each pause I felt a great impulse to call out to Erich, but what if some Home Guards were lurking near enough to hear me – might not one of them be sufficiently sophisticated to recognise '*Eerich!*' as a German name. And this time I'd not easily be able to talk my way out of a charge of 'Consorting with the Enemy.'

Moving cautiously, I worked my way forward until I stood level with the '*Trilithon*'. It was immediately obvious nobody was hiding in the cleft but, for the third or fourth time, my eye was caught by further movements of the cattle. Although not knowing much about such matters, I felt something must have made them uneasy. Possibly it could be flies, for they were annoying me; or could it perhaps just be me? There being no answer to that, I moved on down the slope, intending to cross over the swollen Wollake stream and then approach Phillpott's Cave from the blind side.

Trying to keep my feet dry I found a stepping-stone, and on that stone I got my answer. The top of a head – one that was most certainly not bovine – now appeared; the face and body being hidden by the rising ground in front of me. I froze, poised unsteadily on one leg. The top of that head kept appearing momentarily, as it moved to my left, taking a line that must eventually cross the Wollake – a hundred yards upstream. When it finally disappeared from sight, I leapt across to the far bank, knowing that by moving quickly but quietly, keeping low and using 'Dead Ground' down in the valley, I'd be able to surprise the new arrival then our paths finally intersected. Or perhaps – and even better – I'd come upon him from behind. In passing I managed a quick glimpse into the cave, but there was nothing, and nobody, to be seen there.

Minutes later, with pounding heart, I crawled forward, to peer cautiously over the grassy brow. No sign of anything human. I advanced, rising to my knees for a better view, and there I saw him – barely five yards away. At precisely the same moment he saw me. His hand flew to the F-S fighting knife on his belt – and I raised my Webley to cover him. It was indeed an anxious moment. If I'd not been lucky enough to catch that big Commando with his pants down – quite literally – I might have had to shoot him in self-defence. (In those days they were trained to strike first and ask questions afterwards – if it wasn't already too late!) But no man, however brave and well trained, is at his fighting best when surprised in that embarrassing situation.) As soon as I'd recognised him for what he was, I lowered my revolver.

"What are you doing?" I asked. "Are there any more like you doing it on the Moor today?" (Only later did it strike me that my choice of words could have been somewhat better.)

The Commando was alone, and engaged in an 'evasion' exercise – trekking from Dartmouth to a point on the north coast – where a mythical submarine was scheduled to pick him up in two days time. Equipped with only a map, a compass, and sealed emergency rations, he was expected to feed himself off the country – and not to get caught doing it. This was a policy which made for true self-sufficiency, but aroused fury in honest Householders, Poultry farmers and Gardeners in the area. Bearing in mind the nature of his test I ought to have marked his documents as having been 'arrested' – and then let him go on. But as it was, I desperately needed his goodwill – as well as his silence.

"I expect you'd welcome one of my sandwiches." I offered him one, taking the other myself, whilst giving advice on his best route. "Nobody need be told you encountered a friendly native up here in 'Occupied Territory'." He accepted my help willingly enough, though he must have wondered why on earth any officer should do such a thing.

Because I knew the area where I'd be walking, it had seemed unnecessary to lumber myself with either map-case or compass. Now, and equally foolishly, I had asked to use his map. And in doing so I drew attention to my own lack of one – which was unfortunate – as by then he'd been led to understand I was on the Moor to reconnoitre for a future exercise by my own troops. And what sort of an officer would set out to do that without bringing his own map? Naturally I dared not mention my search for one, or maybe even more Germans, lest the Commando feel duty bound to stay and help me round them up.

Grateful, though badly behind schedule, the Commando eventually moved on northwards, leaving me thoroughly rattled by the near fatal result of my actions, and also because I knew his suspicions must have been aroused by my strange un-officerly behaviour. In a belated attempt to make my story more credible, I now stood on a small rise – shading my eyes and peering in all directions, between making 'copious notes' in a pocket notebook – hopelessly over-acting-out my 'Recce'.

Once again I had put my neck in the noose by choosing to do my own thing. And all because of a firm but almost baseless belief – which could so easily be nothing more than just wishful thinking – that Erich had somehow made his way up onto the Moor. Surely the whole thing must be a Wild-goose chase, and certainly it was costing me time out of my leave – a whole day that could have been used for a duty visit to my parents; or, and even better, in joining Anna for her few off-duty hours at Exeter. Nevertheless I continued my search, moving on up the Wollake stream, getting steadily more weary and dispirited – and very conscious that I had another ten miles of hard walking to complete, before dropping down into Ivybridge to pick up my machine and my kit.

By now the valley had widened out, with open marsh below Duck Pool lying to the West of the stream, and – further away – on my side, the gentle boulder strewn grassy slope of Green Hill. Northwards and far ahead of me, as the Commando's map had shown, would be Two Bridges and Princetown with its grim prison. But closer to hand – between them and me – must lie the featureless expanse of Cater's Beam and beyond it, the treacherous Wastes and Mires around Fox Tor. That was country neither Erich nor I had ever seen. If he was ahead of me, there was no way of knowing which route he would take. But – without maps – each or either of us could easily get hopelessly lost, and with the sun now obscured by overcast, I'd have no way of checking my direction.

Again I cursed my folly in venturing so far from civilisation without proper equipment; the more so because it now looked as though darkness would fall early that night. There was only one sensible course of action to take. I must abandon my search, accept that I had indeed been on a Wild-goose chase – and turn back at once. It was either that, or run the risk of being benighted on the Moor, without so much as a groundsheet for cover.

* * *

I paused, deliberately, expecting that – despite the grim news of his Aunt Maria – Young Bill must surely have some comment to make, or question to ask about what he'd heard since. But he just sat there, staring into the fire. Eventually he turned to me.

"And ... ?" He asked, looking up with his cheeky grin, that so much reminded me of Erich, as I had first known him. "And what did you do Gramps?"

*   *   *

I realised there was no sensible alternative. Feeling tired and dejected, I had to admit defeat, bitterly disappointed by my failure to find any trace of Erich. But he had been bold enough to visit the cottage in Noss Mayo, so he'd surely have sufficient nerve to hitch a lift, or even take a bus. And so he could be miles away by now – using the same cover story though 'understanding' much less English, and probably speaking some German dialect, pretending it was the Flemish language.

Reluctantly I turned and began to retrace my steps. Having first checked that Phillpott's Cave really was empty, I was cautiously picking my way around it, when a *Heinkel 111* came out of the West, flying towards me fast and very low. It was followed, seconds later, by a lone Spitfire, which opened fire on it with all eight machine guns. I ducked for cover as spent cartridge cases fell around me. At the same moment something far heavier crashed down onto my back, hurling me to the ground, and – all these years after – I can still see the rock coming closer and closer as I fell towards it. ...

23. Decision On Dartmoor.

The next thing I can recall is a breathless urgent voice, coming from somewhere above me.

"Schnell - Schnell! On your feet!" *Hadn't I heard those words – those very same words – somewhere before ... long long ago ...?* With an effort I rolled over, and found myself looking up the barrel of my own revolver ... again. (It was getting to be a bad habit with me!) Above me stood Erich, bedraggled in a dark damp *Kriegsmarine* uniform – grim-faced – and stooping, as though for concealment.

"Raus!" He kicked at my boot. *"Schnell!* Into the cave – and out of sight. And do not try anything clever ... or we both be sorry!" I was in no position to argue. Inwardly cursing my own carelessness, I tried to see a way of getting the weapon back. But at that moment he was far too alert for any chance of success – and anyway my brain still felt more than a little wuzzy from the knock I'd taken. "Now MOVE!" He kicked me again – harder this time. *"Raus und MARCHE!"* I got to my knees, and crawled unsteadily over the rock, and into the cave.

Erich followed me in, and crouched down, so blocking the only way out whilst keeping as much distance between us as possible. He now held my Webley two-handed, and close against himself. He was still breathing deeply, but aiming unwaveringly at my guts. So far he hadn't missed a single move I'd made ... and, with the hammer back, and his forefinger tight on the trigger ... it was no time for heroics.

"The *Dummkopf Engländer* should have spent more time *mit der Hitlerjugend* – and he'd not have been caught so!" Whilst he was talking, Erich kept darting anxious glances outside, as if to make sure that I was alone, and that nobody else had seen us.

My old comrade hadn't shaved for days – I suppose it was easier not to in the confines of a U-boat. His *Kreigsmarine* uniform was muddy and badly creased, and I could see where he had torn the eagle from the breast of his tunic, but he himself was clean. Even in adversity, Erich's natural self-pride had kept him up to his old high standards. Now he stayed there, silently watching me, as though attempting to get control of himself, before he spoke again.

"This is not a good way for you – for us – to meet again *mein Freund.*" There was no denying that, so I nodded in agreement, but said nothing. One just does not excite or annoy a hunted man whose knuckles are white around the trigger. Slowly he began to relax. Moving my hand very slowly, I rubbed it over my hair where a lump was already coming up – but there was no sign of blood. "You should not have come, John – and you'd not have been hurt." That was the first time he'd used my name, and he was speaking more softly now, and in a somewhat more friendly tone. "If only we could throw away this *verdammt* great cannon of your's, and leave other fools to fight the war, whilst we enjoy ourselves as we did before they made me be your enemy."

"You and I can never be real enemies, Erich. But we do wear very different uniforms, and you know what that means!" Of course there was no need for me to spell it out. He'd know it was my duty to reverse our situations, even killing him in the process if needs be.

"I warn you John. Do not try anything – it would only be stupid. My little *Walther* – if I had it now – would kill you cleanly ... but this? This monster would blow your head right off, and most probably break my wrist too, and I wouldn't want that to happen."

"Nor me Erich! I certainly wouldn't want you to hurt yourself that way." If he could raise a joke at such a time, it was even more important for me to do the same, but it only led to an uncomfortable silence, until he spoke again, picking his words with great care.

"I have a problem – and so do you John. It is a matter of Honour – *Blut und Ehre* – you remember that?" He had spoken the words with a touch of pride, but then he dropped his voice, as though afraid someone might overhear us. "It would be dishonourable – quite impossible – for me to surrender to you whilst I hold your gun. And you are a brave man John ... if I went off, you would follow me – so sooner or later I'd have to shoot my friend. Maybe I ought to tie you up first ... though it would have to be done proper, or you might escape too quick ... but if you don't free yourself ... you might die before next person come here."

There was another long pause whilst he pondered. My head was still buzzing, so I just looked him full in the face, and waited to find out what he had in mind. Erich slowly squatted down on his heels, as though trying to look less dominating. The way things were, in that small cave, I could almost touch him, and now he'd be rather easier to tackle. But even if his first bullet missed me, it could still ricochet around inside that confined rock-walled space – like an infuriated wasp – until it lodged in a body ... and I knew it wouldn't be the least bit particular whose body. When he finally did speak, it was with a distinct air of hesitation – and uncertainty.

"We are both men of Honour ... but ... is it possible John ... for a little time at least ... we both forget ... the uniforms they make us wear?" (By now he was almost whispering, and perhaps that was the result of living where the walls really did have ears; because *Gestapo* agents were listening everywhere in the Germany of those days.) "I know, and you know John, because we prove it many times in our happy days before war, that you and I are very equally matched." He looked at me, hoping for confirmation, and I gave a little nod of agreement. "What John if – if you and I were to wrestle here? You remember our rules – in fair contest? I will give my word, as your friend, that IF you win, I will be your prisoner – and not try to escape ... and maybe you get another medal! But you must promise, as a British Officer, if you lose – to let me go – and never say you saw me, or anybody else up here today." By now he was speaking faster, and for the first time came a hint of his old grin, for he knew, just as well as I did, that such a proposal would horrify the Military Disciplinarians on both sides.

Once Erich was started on this theme, my thoughts were running almost ahead of his, and it seemed to me as if we had suddenly slipped back into our boyhood. And that whatever the outcome of this might be, it would get us both off the immediate hook pretty well. On a personal level I had no qualms ... but as one who 'holds the King's Commission' – even if only temporarily? Whatever would my superiors say about that – even if bearing in mind that I was already technically a Prisoner of War? They would doubtless worry about the amount of damage such a resourceful enemy officer might do before he was eventually captured ... which made it all the more important that he must not be allowed to win. After some considerable heart-searching I accepted his challenge. Then he lowered the revolver, pointing it at the ground whilst we agreed details of what I knew must be the hardest fight of my life.

The whole business was quite unreal, and I couldn't help thinking *C'est Magnifique – mais ce n'est pas la Guerre!* Although faced with a proven adversary, I'd not be able to use the lethal holds the Army had tried to teach me ... and yet ... with the stakes so high ... mightn't even Erich be tempted to foul? But first we had to find some place where the ground wasn't largely bare granite. With my weapon still in his hand, Erich followed me – but always keeping a full five yards between us. (I couldn't help thinking in that respect the *Kriegsmarine* or possibly the *H.J.* must have given him a better training than young Jeffcott got from our Navy.) We eventually found a large patch of short springy turf, and although it sloped down to a marsh, it was as good a mat as we'd be likely to find that day. Having moved apart, to opposite sides of the little arena, we took off our boots and stripped for the contest. When I was almost ready, Erich picked up my Webley and – for one long moment – held it aimed straight at my head. Then, and with a laugh, he turned it aside, flicked open the chamber, and emptied out the cartridges onto his open palm, before hurling them far out into the marsh.

"Now John Hardwicke! You and Me! Let your Motherland *und mein Vaterland*, and all *verdammt* Generals and Admirals take care of the war, until we have settled our affair – privately – but with Honour!" He didn't seem to have noticed my glove, (I always tried to keep it out of sight in those days.) And by then it was too late to suggest my wounded hand as an excuse for calling the whole thing off. Already he'd be thinking in terms of *Blut und Ehre*, while my old school motto is *Aut Vinceri – Aut Mori* – which you, Young Bill, will remember, translates as *To Conquer, or to Die*, though I very much hoped it would not quite come to that.

Erich advanced slowly, stern faced, crouching, his arms held ready to grapple. Three yards apart we began to circle one another, making several attempts before we did get to grips, and even then, realising that neither had any advantage, he pushed apart to seek a better opening. But I saw my chance and went in fast, taking him down hard, and then it really was like old times. However, there being so much at stake we were both cautious, and much more determined not to submit, than if it had been a normal bout – wrestled just for exercise or enjoyment. We fought on and on; he could have broken my arm if I'd not managed to twist around with him, and at a later stage he was in trouble with a foot forced far back up towards his neck, but by then we had rolled into the edge of the marsh – and my muddy hands couldn't hold him. Our rules said nothing about holding faces in mud, and I didn't intend to find out how my opponent might feel about that. So, as he came on top of me, I got both feet to his thighs, and heaved – sending him hurtling over my head – to land on his back with a terrific splash.

In an instant I was up and running, though only when the grass felt really firm beneath my feet did I begin to understand why. My sudden fear had been – not of Erich – but of those fearsome quags and quicksands ... which have swallowed large animals without trace ... and humans too! In a moment of panic I turned so fast that I almost fell. But my old friend, whilst covered in muck, and still up to his knees in it, was safe – and steadily making his way out of the marsh. When he reached solid ground he dropped on all fours, and began crawling towards me – moaning as he came. (It was apparent that his recent experiences had affected neither his memory, nor his sense of humour.) Then he got up again and came after me, eager to continue our battle. Trying to protect my wounded hand, I kept my left out in front of me. I certainly ought to have known better, because Erich grabbed the wrist in both his hands, turned under it, and in a trice had me stretched along his back, before being thrown high over his shoulder – to land with a bone-jarring thud. Even though I got one of my feet to the ground in time, the fall still knocked most of the wind out of me. Surprisingly Erich didn't follow me down. Instead he just stood there, admiring his handiwork, until he suddenly remembered what we were about – and only then did he begin to count. (Pre-war we never thought seriously in terms of a Knock-out, but occasionally – just for swank – one of us would start the count, but it never got far before the other was 'Up'. Even in those days that throw was Erich's speciality. He'd tried to teach me, and in practice sessions – with his cooperation – I could do it well enough, but whenever I tried it for real he was almost always too quick for me.)

That fall had done my bruised head no good at all ... only dogged determination got me to my feet by *'Acht!'* For a while afterwards I was seeing double, and uncertain which opponent to grapple with. I needed time to gather myself together, and had to get my breath back too. So, shameful though my friend might think it, retreat was the only sensible course open to me. Perhaps it was just foolish pride, or maybe too much trust in our Unarmed Combat Instructors, but I felt a terrible urge to try and catch him out with his own shoulder throw – just this once – When it mattered so much.

Step by step Erich followed me, and it is difficult to be sure who was the more surprised when I got the hold correctly, but unfortunately my grip was weak, and his wrist slimy. Even so he did end up across my hips – and a final heave dumped him over sideways. I'd made such a mess of the move that he had no idea what was going to happen next, so he landed almost as badly as I had done – and on his head too. Certainly the right thing would have been to drop on him there and then, but those quick movements had set my own brain spinning, and again I decided to play for time. He was up at 'Seven' but glad enough to take a rest himself. Then he was advancing again, relentlessly following me up the slope. Had I attacked then, the higher position might have given me a small advantage, but even a few more seconds respite could give me a better chance of winning – so my retreat continued.

Three more steps back ... and something had changed. A brief glance sideways was enough to tell me I'd topped the ridge – and that single moment of inattention was all my opponent needed. He stooped, to grab me behind the knee, and we crashed down together, each frantically striving for any hold that might lead to – or stave off – the one decisive submission. His legs were soon wrapped around mine, but even though he was uppermost, I still had his arm held fast, and well up his back too. I tried to get on top, and managed it – but he rolled on over, taking me with him.

I kept the movement going but couldn't get a leg free to stop myself where I wanted. My head was close to his, as – locked together – we tumbled headlong down the ever steepening slope. At one moment I was looking over his shoulder, up into a dismal sky – and the next – grass and heather would be stabbing into my face. Grimly I tightened my grip, determined to have the advantage of that hold when we did stop. Over and over we went, bumping and thudding, rolling faster, and faster still. Erich shouted something – in German – but it made no sense to me. Then the world that spun so fast around us changed. The grey sky now alternating with darker grey rock ... and I could feel nothing beneath me. We were falling ... falling ... falling ... still helplessly tangled together ....

24. Parting.

I was cold ... and I hurt all over, but the greatest pain was at my shoulder ... and high above me a distant voice was counting unevenly.

"Zwei – Drei, Vier – Funf ..." I had to get up, but the first movement told me my right arm was out of action, and the pain was pretty awful. Even though I finally staggered to my feet at *"Neun!"* I knew at once there was no way I could win, not with an arm like that – not unless Erich had an even more serious injury. Equally there was no way I could yield whilst free and on my feet. Although we were little more than a yard apart, Erich and I seemed to spend a long time staring at each other before he came in to attack me again. In a moment he had my left hand tight up my back, and my head down with his arm locked tightly across my throat. I tried desperately to trip him, but he kept his legs too far back to reach with my feet – and my free hand was quite useless. He was putting on the pressure, it was difficult to know which arm hurt the most ... and my strength was ebbing. I could barely breathe. My vision blurred – there was no option – I had to submit. Erich released, and I crumpled in a heap at his feet.

After a win like that, in earlier days, he'd normally have raised both hands clenched in a 'Boxer's Salute' – a token of pride in his achievement, but now he just stood, breathless, drained, and swaying unsteadily. With his pale blond hair caked and filthy from the marsh, he appeared quite oblivious of the gory patch above his ear, from which a thin trickle of blood ran slowly down through the stubble on his jaw. Even in his moment of triumph he could manage no more than a fleeting hint of a grin.

"Dummkopf Engländer!" He gasped. "This is your countryside. You should have known about that blasted cliff – one of us could have been killed, and what a waste that would be!" Then he became more serious. "Now I must go – and you John – you have to honour your promise, to stay

here for at least thirty minutes. But before I go – for old time's sake." He bent down to give me his hand.

My right arm lay trapped beneath me, and my first attempt to get it free confirmed what I already suspected. The pain made me gasp – and slowly I offered my left hand.

"Your arm, John!" He was kneeling beside me now. "Your right arm? What is wrong with your arm?"

"Only the collar bone gone – but don't worry about that. You must go – I'll be O.K."

"But can you walk? I cannot go – *ich ginge nicht* – not until I know you can walk. Move your legs John – show me!" Only when he was satisfied that I'd be able to get myself off the Moor, did he shake my hand, and reluctantly get to his feet. "This is no way for friends to part ..." There was nothing of the victor about Erich now, and for all that he had just won a degree of freedom, he must know he was still in a hostile land, where every hand save mine would be against him. And now he had to leave me – to lead a life little better than that of a hunted animal.

"Go Erich." I urged him. "Please. Do go now – whilst you still can – and before anybody comes and finds us together. The sooner you go, the safer you will be, and the sooner my arm can get attention." Even as I spoke I was conscious that my words had made my concern for him sound as if I was even more worried for myself. "Good Luck go with you ... my old friend!" It was the best I could think of then.

"Auf wiedersehen." He turned suddenly and hurried off, obviously trying to hide the fact that he was limping. Some twenty yards away a steep and narrow sheep path ran up the face of the cliff, doubling back so it ended almost above my head. Erich paused there, calling down to me. "It was truly *Blut und Ehre* for us, *Mein mutig Kamerad!* But remember to stay there for our agreed thirty minutes – or I may have to shoot you. Just stay there John. And after this wretched war is over – you and I will laugh together about our *härter Kampf.*"

It was certain neither of us had anything to laugh about then, and for my part I could only hope he'd be right about the future. But, in the present circumstances, my sole comfort lay in the knowledge that it would no longer be me who put him into a Prisoner of War camp, for however long the war might last.

* * *

Erich had gone, leaving me with ample time to consider my own situation. Although it had seemed we were falling for ever, that cliff was barely fifteen feet high. Nevertheless we had both been extremely lucky to land on the only patch of grass amidst sharp scree and jumbled boulders, that must surely have caused much more serious injuries had we landed more than a couple of feet in any direction. Gingerly I sat up, easing my arm into a less painful position. There was no doubt, the bone had gone – and with so long to wait I huddled myself into a ball, trying to keep from getting completely chilled. Next there had to be a story that would explain my injury – one that would be plausible enough to be accepted by civilians, the Police, and my Military Masters too.

Whilst I worked on various versions of this, my mind kept on going back to our fight. *'I'll never believe he didn't know about my arm – it was so obvious – he couldn't have missed it, not even in his state. He must surely have known that, but – sportsman that he is – he calculated that last attack would give me the chance of an honourable submission – with minimum risk of further damage to my injured arm.'* Yes. It was indeed *Blut und Ehre* that day, with Erich providing all of the blood and most of the honour too.

* * *

Young Bill now stretched himself, drawing my attention back from the new crack in the ceiling I'd just spotted. Even in the fading firelight I could see a distinctly quizzical – almost doubting – look on his face.

"Yes Bill ... Times have changed, but in those far off days we did think rather more in terms like that. For some of us at least, Friendship was spelt with a very big 'F' – and Honour had an even bigger 'H' ... We were very much brought up to recognise – and to do – 'The Right Thing'. And that usually turned out to be – the Decent Thing. Today, far too many people think only of winning, or putting themselves first every time. And honour; that is something they expect to find in others, and only in themselves if its to their own advantage, or glory. So many youngsters don't know what it is to be unselfish, or the meaning of 'Please' and 'Thank You' either. But, thank goodness – Young Bill – you do! And though you may not realise it – that's one of the reasons why your friends and relations willingly do things for you – and welcome your company too."

I really hadn't intended to go on quite like that, so I cut back quickly to my tale.

* * *

The sky grew steadily darker as I huddled there at the foot of the cliff. Surely half an hour had passed. In such a situation, and without a watch, time passes very slowly – and my promise had to be kept. Finally I too dragged myself to the top of that treacherous path. There I paused, panting hard, whilst scanning the horizon. A mile or more away to the East, I could just discern a solitary figure – dark and lonely. Even as he raised an arm, the mist swirled in, and before I could respond, he had vanished from my sight. *Rather him than me!* I thought, knowing he could never expect anyone's help whilst – at the very worst – three hours would see me warm and comfortable in some hospital.

From a distance it was clear that my clothes had been disturbed. On top now lay a page, ripped from my notebook by muddy fingers. Erich's boldly pencilled message was brief and to the point. '*I.O.U. FOUR POUNDS. E.E. FALKENBERG.*' Below the formal signature, in his normal tidy script, he had added, '*Sorry Mein Freund, but I need this more than you!*' But this time he had signed himself as '*Erich*'. And he had had the sense to return my Webley to its holster – probably realising that the loss of my personal weapon would cause far too many embarrassing questions to be asked. Be that as it may, my old friend hadn't trusted me enough to leave any ammunition in the pouch – and that did hurt me ... *But would I have done any different had our roles been reversed?* And he'd taken my food and chocolate too – though I've never begrudged him any of that.

If you havn't tried to dress yourself with an arm that's newly broken – it hurts like hell. But it was essential that I got mine inside the sleeves of both shirt and battledress blouse, otherwise nobody would believe my carefully concocted tale. My boots posed a real problem too, because tying a bow – single-handed – was quite beyond me, and fumbled reef knots left the laces so slack that both heels were blistered within an hour. First a steady drizzle, then heavy rain began to fall, as I made my way slowly southwards. At one slippery point my feet went from under me. Normally my hand would have saved me but it was held – sling-style – inside my blouse, so the full weight of the fall came on my damaged shoulder.

Quite some time must have passed before I came to – soaked to the skin – and thereafter the pain was doubled. Dartmoor's scenery, which usually gave me such pleasure, was now only hateful distance, stretching darkly, seemingly without end – between myself and safety. At one stage I became aware of the fact that I was lost, and shivering too. Nothing around me was familiar. For a while I blundered around helplessly, until three flashes of lighting showed me the path again. Thankful for that, I decided to sit down and rest, hoping that my mind would clear; but that only made things worse, for my joints began to stiffen up almost at once. So came the realisation that I had to keep moving, otherwise I could die of exposure out on the Moor which I so liked.

There were times when I was conscious of stubbing my toes – on level going – which is a sure sign that the brain no longer has complete control over the feet. Those six miles back to Harford took me almost five hours, and I was in a bad way when three Home Guards found me. What they were doing out there on that filthy night I never asked. It was their dog spotted me first, and the men crossed two fields in semi-darkness to my aid – but I wasn't aware of their presence until one actually touched me.

Being used to 'city folk' wandering the Moor, they showed no surprise at my prepared story. Of being fed up with the war, and spending the day up there to get away from it – and being so engrossed in watching a pair of buzzards soaring and swooping, that I'd tripped, fallen badly, and then rolled down a steep slope. I begged them to get me to a civilian hospital, saying that once the Army got their hands on me, they would be certain to cancel my leave, and heaven only knew when I'd get another.

Somehow they managed to organise a Police Car, and I had to field many more questions whilst I was being driven to hospital. Even so, my story was readily accepted by everyone, except the two young nurses at the Cottage Hospital, who shared the job of cleaning me up. When I realised that they had spotted there was more mud inside my shirt than outside it, I immediately pretended great agony and almost fainted – so they doped me with pain killer, put me to bed and left me in peace. Though, as you may imagine, what with the pain and so much on my mind, I got little sleep that night.

The next morning a sympathetic Doctor strapped my arm in place and signed me off as being fit to travel home. Once there I had little difficulty in persuading our own Doctor to certify that I would need much more than the remainder of my seven days leave, before I'd be fit to return – even for 'Light Duties' – back to Devon.

Nevertheless – being concerned for my men – but not wishing to draw more unwelcome attention to myself, I wrote to Uncle Harry, asking whether they had got their leave, and if there was any more news about the U-boat and her crew. His first reply was oddly worded.

'Your men all went on ten days leave three days after you took up Bird-watching. You'll note that bloody adjutant gave them three days more than he gave you. Your cosy dug-out on the cliff top is now in the sea. As far as I can make out, Jerry sent several bombers over – flying almost at sea level – intending to smash up that U-boat. One of them got it wrong, flew into the cliff – all bombs still on board – and that changed the geography!'

A few days later, Uncle wrote to me a second time. 'Just to bring you up to scratch. The Local Rags are full of the fact that 29 bodies, washed ashore from the U-boat have been buried – with full Naval Honours. Some small-minded folk think 'That was far too good for them.' Remembering what you've told me in the past, I think you'd be not be surprised to know that it appears there are survivors – numbers not given –but they say all the officers except the youngest were amongst those buried. He and some ten more are still 'Missing'. Navy suggest most were probably trapped inside the U-boat when it sank, and then destroyed when she was bombed. Seems Navy have something up their sleeve. So massive is the security that people are talking about it – which rather defeats the object of the exercise.'

P.S. I've been wondering. Would your young friend recognise a Buzzard if he should ever happen to meet one?'

It appeared to me that Uncle's imagination had been working overtime – or was it just intuition. Much as I'd have liked to share my secrets with him, it would have strained our friendship to burden him with the truth, that – as he already suspected – I did indeed meet up with Erich. And of course, that would not have been possible, because I had given my Word to Erich, that I would not tell a soul about our meeting on the Moor, and its outcome.

25. London Cage.

After I had enjoyed a couple of weeks extra leave, the Army got suspicious, and I was ordered to present myself – in three days time – for a medical examination. I had no worries on the medical side, but plenty about the questions that must come at the same time. However, the very next day, I received a conflicting but most explicit order. 'You are to report immediately – without fail – to Number Six, Kensington Palace Gardens, in London.' This address turned out to be a once imposing, and now heavily guarded Georgian Mansion. Inside, after my papers had been carefully checked, I was surprised to learn it was part of the infamous 'London District Cage' – the main Interrogation Centre for the more 'interesting' of newly captured Prisoners of War. And surely that could mean only one thing.

I was introduced to an Interrogation Officer, who told me Erich had been captured a few days previously, and somehow – possibly because he was linked with a U-boat – it had come out that we once knew each other well.

"There are rules here Hardwicke, you must remember at all times that I am 'Charles'. British personnel must only be addressed by their Christian names or 'Cover Names'. No true identities are allowed within the hearing of any prisoner. Now, as you'll know, the Germans are notorious for their respect for superior rank, so I'll give you another blouse, and you'll become 'Major Peter Jackson' whilst you are helping us." This seemed utterly ridiculous – because it was certain Erich would recognise me.

"Certainly not Charles." I told him. "I have no intention of being parted from either my Regimental identity, or my 'little bit of glory'. His eyes slowly followed mine down to the M.C. ribbon on my chest. Although he was much older – being a Base Wallah – he had nothing to show himself. And, to be honest, I still had a boyish urge to be 'one up' on him. Eventually I settled for adding a couple of Major's rank-slides – and that did bring back a whole flood of memories for me. Then, and somewhat resentfully, Charles made it very clear that I had been wished upon him. But, even so, he did want me to talk to Erich, whom he constantly referred to as 'Your Friend' – in a tone that quickly rubbed me up the wrong way.

"Your Friend has been thoroughly difficult – and he's given nothing away."

"What would you expect from a Naval Officer?" I queried. "I have no doubt Erich Falkenberg is just as loyal to his Country as I am to mine – or as you yourself." Charles went on to tell me what I could not say to Erich; what information was most wanted, and what other matters I should introduce into our conversation. That was all fair enough, but when he started telling me how to ask those same questions, I quickly lost patience with him.

"And how long have you known *Leutnant* Falkenberg?" I demanded. "One week – ten days even?" He nodded wisely, though without committing himself. "As long as that! Now I've known him over five years, so you can leave the questions to me, Charles ... even though I don't have a degree in psycho-whatever-it-is." And that didn't go down at all well. (Subsequently I learned he had reported me as being 'Non-cooperating' and – even worse – he suggested my loyalty was somewhat in doubt. So its little wonder I still don't trust psychologists, psychiatrists, and their like.)

I was led along a dark noisy corridor, and got no reply when I asked why what I took to be an officer in Russian uniform, was sitting in a brightly lit alcove. Finally I was shown into the Interrogation Room, which was large but shabby – like the rest of the interior – and now only sparsely furnished. I had the prisoner's chair moved to a corner, and then dismissed my guide. As he left I pulled the peak of my Herbie Johnson cap well down over my face before settling at a table, with my back to the single heavily curtained window. The lights were all positioned to shine from behind me. They were not the harsh lights normally associated with 'Third Degree' questioning; but they served much the same purpose, keeping the interrogator's face in shadow, whilst allowing him to see every reaction of the prisoner.

I pressed a buzzer, and could hear a good deal of shouting and heavy footsteps before the door opened and Erich was brought in, by an armed guard. Instead of his naval uniform, he now had on an ill-fitting, grey chalk-stripe lounge suit. There was a big round red patch sewn into his trouser leg, and – as I saw later – another the size of a large dinner-plate, sewn into the back of his jacket. Somewhat incongruously, he was also wearing a *Kriegsmarine* forage cap with its little Nazi Eagle and round *Kokade*. Beneath this cap, I could just make out the scar he'd picked up all those years ago at Nuremberg. In spite of this unlikely outfit he managed to carry himself smartly, but he was clearly showing signs of strain; and there was no trace of the happy carefree look I remembered so well, nor of the confidence he'd shown up on the Moor.

The guard took a seat by the door whilst Erich strode over and stood to attention in front of me. After checking my rank, he gave me a very correct naval salute. I was toying with Uncle's swagger stick, running my left fingers over its raised nodes, and after a moment's delay, I casually touched the peak of my cap with its thimble.

"G'morning, Lieutenant." I spoke in English, using my very best 'Brigade of Guards' voice. "Few questions I've got to ask you – hope you won't mind." I yawned, and he showed no sign of recognition.

"Falkenberg. Erich. Leutnant zur See. Kriegsmarine. Nummer ... "

"Lieutenant!" I cut in irritably. "We are already very well aware of your name, your number, and your rank. However there are certain other things I do need to know from you." Erich held his head up, even more stiffly. Defiantly he repeated himself – to the curtain above my head. There was a long silence afterwards. I concentrated my gaze on Uncle's cane, in order to avoid looking up at him. It was only too clear – as I had expected – that he would not willingly give us any information whatsoever.

Finally, I put down the cane, and began slowly removing the glove from my right hand. Erich pretended not to be watching, but I saw his reaction when I pulled it off. Then, with difficulty – because my arm should still have been in a sling – I unbuttoned a pocket of my battledress, and drew out a packet of cigarettes, held insecurely between my remaining fingers.

"Do you use these Lieutenant?" I offered them to him, well knowing what answer to expect.

"Certainly not *Herr Major,* I never have used the filthy things!"

"No more do I, Lieutenant. But what about you Corporal? D'you smoke?" The guard nodded eagerly. Airily I flipped the packet across the room at him. He failed to catch it, but managed to drop his weapon in the attempt.

"I think your soldiers should be made to play more cricket *Herr Major."* For just one moment Erich showed a trace of the look I knew so well. I passed no comment, but slowly unbuttoned the other pocket, and even more slowly drew out two bars of chocolate. (They made up nearly half of my ration for the month, but I understood that real chocolate was virtually unknown in Germany by that stage of the war.)

"And what about these Lieutenant Falkenberg?" Placing one of my remaining fingers on each, I slid them across the table, watching him closely as I did so. Almost involuntarily his hand came out to take them, but then he cut it back to his side, and snapped rigidly to attention again.

"Herr Major! I protest! You should not try to insult me this way. A German Naval Officer is not to be treated like a child – is not to be bribed with *Bonbons!"*

"Herr Leutnant" I had changed abruptly into German. "I had a young friend once ... he too was German, and he never used to feel insulted when I offered him such a small gift ... You might even know him. For he too is a Falkenberg ... Erich ... Emil ... Falkenberg." A look of total disbelief flitted across the face in front of me. Then Erich leaned forward, trying to see beneath the peak of my cap.

"Herr Major? Can it be – is it – are you ... John? John Hardwicke?"

"Corporal. A chair for the Lieutenant – and then get these damned lights turned off. I threw my cap on the table before drawing back the curtains with a flourish. "I told them you wouldn't give us any secret information Erich. Now I'll not insult you further by asking for it. And how are you?"

"In better shape than you, I think. But your wound John, if only I had known about that hand when we ..."

"DUNKIRK Erich, it happened at Dunkirk!" I almost shouted that, knowing just three or four words from him could have landed me with a Court Martial. "Yes. It happened at Dunkirk, but I don't know quite how." I could see Erich realised how very close we had come to total disaster, but he was already in full control again.

"Ah – Dunkirk. A Great German Victory! But ... you remember Otto – the boy who boxed like a windmill? He was killed near there with the *Panzers* ... and you have a medal too." Of course he knew that already, but I wasn't able tell him much about how or why I got it.

"I also have a medal John, given to me by Admiral Doenitz himself, on the deck of a U-boat. I must not tell you what it was for, though perhaps you can guess ... but I don't expect I'll ever see my *Eiserne Kreuz* again now."

"No, I don't think so either, Erich – but of course you won't know about the bombing." A new light came into his eyes at this. "The *Luftwaffe* dropped a hell of a lot of bombs into the sea exactly where she sank; but one of the planes crashed into the cliffs – with its bombs still on board. They exploded and brought down the whole of the cliff face. Nobody will ever go to Porthyn Pryva as we used to do Erich – it just isn't there any more." He had nothing to say, so I continued, more confidentially. "It cannot matter now Erich, but why was that booby-trap left at SAFE? We'd have been a lot less worried if it had been left fully armed."

"I'm surprised you need to ask about that my friend. Who else but you would go into that cave? I've never forgotten how you saved me at *Nürnberg* – so I owed you that much at least ... but John, they must never know about that here, or in a camp later. If even one of the other prisoners found out, I'd be Court Martialled for disobeying an order, and so losing the boat – and they'd hang me as a traitor to *Kriegsmarine und Reich.*"

I could fully sympathise with that, because – knowing what we were saying was most probably being recorded – I certainly wasn't able to tell him that I too had disobeyed a direct order – to leave the switch set to LIVE – so that it would kill him, or whoever returned to correct the timing. I would have liked my friend to know about that – and that I wasn't really such a Judas as he must have believed.

There was an embarrassed silence before he mentioned my Grandmother, asking as if he thought she was still alive. It came as a sudden change of topic and one that suited me well enough. (Erich could not have known that I visited the cottage after him; and now – for some unknown reason – he did not want me to know he had been there.) For a while longer we exchanged news of our families. I was alarmed to learn that Dr Falkenberg had been denounced as 'politically unreliable' and was being held in a Concentration Camp. Erich was very worried about this, because so many people never came out of those camps alive.

"And the lads I knew in the H.J.?" I asked, to take his mind off his father. "What of Gerhard, did he become an airman?"

"Yes. A fighter-pilot. He shot down two English planes, and then a Hurricane came out of the sun and caught him. He crashed in flames – and now he is blind."

"I am sorry." It was all I could find to say – and it sounded so trite, but I meant it sincerely. "And what of Kurt?"

"*Ach. Die Spinne!* His father is high up in the Party, so Kurt got a fancy uniform and a job on *Reichsmarschall* Goering's Staff. Can you imagine him standing together with fat Hermann – like a pencil beside an apple! But John," Erich's tone had changed, and he was suddenly serious again, "it was only after we left port, on the U-boat, that I met Kurt's kid brother – a fine lad too. Franzel was on his first operational patrol, and ... I don't know ... if ... if he is amongst the survivors. He might perhaps have been saved by one of the boats. Would it be possible for you to find out, and perhaps to let me know if ... if it was so?"

"I wish to God I'd never taken you to Porthyn Pryva Erich. No wonder they say 'If you have a secret – keep it to yourself.'"

"We had our happy times together John ... before all this, and we did enjoy ourselves then. Now – my old friend – we have to pay for it. You and me both." How right he was; but after that our conversation flagged. I looked at my watch and then rose, holding out the chocolate to him.

"You'll take these now Erich?" Shyly he pocketed them. "For old time's sake?" I asked, looking down at my still out-stretched gloveless hand. He took it without hesitation, relaxing his grip when I winced at the pain he caused me.

"Goodbye John."

"Auf Wiedersehen Erich – Auf Wiedersehen." We exchanged salutes and then he was led away by the guard.

* * *

To my surprise Bill suddenly interrupted me. "Gramps. Did you ever manage to find out what Erich did between leaving you on the Moor – and being captured? Did he do anything awful – wrecking a train or something like that?"

"No. I certainly didn't want to know then, and I don't even want to know now. It would probably only make me feel worse than I already do, about the whole wretched business. Just occasionally Bill, although I don't recommend it as a general rule, there are times when it can be easier to live without knowing the truth." That seemed to have satisfied the lad, so I continued with my tale .

26. Aftermath.

The Interrogation Officer was quite angry with me because I had given what he insisted were 'prohibited articles' to a Prisoner of War. In fact Charles only shut up after I'd asked whether he thought I'd baked a file into one of those small bars of chocolate. However, he did show a little interest when I said that Erich had been relieved to hear about the bombing – and that I felt certain he'd been expecting, or at least hoping, to hear about it.

"Yes. For a time now, we've had suspicions there was some sort of communication between 'The Cage' and Germany. Now we know for sure, so we must either stop it, or make better use of it – as you have just done – by passing false information to the prisoners whilst they are held here." After that Charles did unbend enough to answer my cautious question about Erich's dress. "Ah Yes. He stole that suit somewhere, and because we'll never be able to get it back to the proper owner, your friend can keep it for the time being. But – as is usual – round holes have been cut in the trousers and jacket, and those contrasting patches sewn in, so he'll never go on the run looking like a civilian again! Only when he gets to a normal P.O.W. Camp will he be issued with the blue battledress with red patches appropriate to a Naval Officer who doesn't have his own uniform. But we'll keep him in that grey suit – as long as he's here – because it makes him feel inferior, even ridiculous. So, with a bit of luck, that'll undermine his self-confidence, and maybe – sooner or later – he'll let something slip out."

"And that cap he was wearing, it is German Navy – isn't it?" (I judged it best not to speak of *Kriegsmarine*, nor that I thought Charles would certainly be wasting his time whilst waiting for Erich to weaken. And of course I could not let it slip out, that 'my friend' had been bare-headed – even though in uniform – when last I'd seen him.)

"Yes. He had sense enough to carry that cap hidden. Odd thing about it – that made us very suspicious at first – it is the Other Rank's pattern. But it appears many of the U-boat officers choose to wear that pattern. And he'd had the sense to keep a shoulder-strap and his identity disc too – to prove his rank, and that he really is a serving Naval Officer. Just as well too, because several of his crew were wearing British Battledress, and if we'd caught him wearing that any distance from where he came ashore – we'd most probably have shot him as a spy!" The I.O. sounded as though he somewhat regretted what he saw as a missed opportunity.

*   *   *

After that I got away from The Cage and Kensington – just as quickly as I could. Meeting Erich again, and under those circumstances, had left me with very confused emotions. It had been good to see him alive and well, but he knew who had betrayed him – by setting the trap that so nearly killed him. Up on the Moor, that Affair of Honour had salved both our consciences for the moment. But afterwards – by my silence – I had honoured my word to a friend ... and at the same time, I'd shamefully betrayed the trust placed in me by my King, and my Countrymen.

In an attempt to shake off my black mood, I paid a Spiv the Black Market rate for a ticket to a very popular West End Show. But after what I'd been through that day, I just wasn't in the mood for cheap laughs. At the interval I went to the bar for a drink, and stayed on there – attempting to drown my sorrows – until they threw me out. Of course that solved nothing, giving me only a wretchedly disturbed night; before I set off home – like a bear with a sore head – still feeling more than a little ashamed of myself. And I was wondering what unanswerable questions would be waiting for me when I did finally get back to Devon.

A week, later a Medical Board ordered me to report myself as 'Fit for Light Duties'. It was then I received word that the Powers-that-be had graciously instructed me to send word to Erich – that Franzel had been buried, with Full Naval Honours, beside his Commander and twenty seven more members of the U-boat's crew. Uncle had been correct in assuming that the Navy had something up their sleeve, and they needed their cover story spreading. Maybe that explained why I was permitted to communicate with Erich. Being so much involved, I had been let into the secret, though the real truth had to be kept from my old friend – and from as many other people as possible. Franzel's body, together with the nine others buried on that day, had been found inside U-330, after she was pumped out, in the floating dock, to which she was towed, after being raised to the surface. And this only a matter of a few hours before five *Luftwaffe* bombers arrived over Porthyn Pryva, with the specific intention of destroying her where she lay on the bottom.

I was questioned at length about my report, in which I'd told how the crew were trying to force the deflated dinghy through an open hatch. Then I was told the fore hatch into the hull been closed at the time, and was only slightly damaged by gun fire. The dinghy was actually being replaced in its normal water and pressure resistant storage between the pressure hull and the wooden upper deck. Just why they hadn't abandoned the dinghy, and so possibly avoided having to scuttle the U-boat, remained something of a mystery. A further mystery was the failure of explosive scuttling charges attached to vital parts of the machinery and torpedoes, which together should have ensured the total destruction of the vessel. As it was, the Dockyard took just over three months to refit that U-boat. Then she was commissioned into the Royal Navy– though not as H.M. Submarine Judas, as had been suggested. She was used successfully as a decoy, and sank a U-boat, but was nearly lost at the second attempt. Somehow the Germans had learned she was in our hands and they were waiting for her. After that she went into ordinary service, but eventually failed to return. It is thought she must have struck a mine, because there is no record of the enemy claiming to have sunk any of our submarines at that time.

* * *

'Uncle' Hanson had only been with us for a little over six months when he became ill. Then his old wound broke open, and he had to be hospitalised. I was called to his room before the ambulance arrived. There, and in private, he handed the Malacca Cane to me.

"Here John, I don't think I'm going to need this again. You take it, and if that bloody fool of an Adjutant should object, you'll know exactly where to stick it – and you'll have my blessing if and when you do that!"

Two weeks later, I was called to the C.O.'s office.

"Bad news Hardwicke. I've just been notified that Harry Hanson died an hour ago. He was a good man, and I know you were close to him, so I want you to take charge of his funeral – full Military Honours, as far as is possible. I'll notify his last lot; the Shiny Silvers have their depot at ... Crediton ... is it?" I could only nod, because the news of Uncle's death had hit me hard. "That's close enough, so I expect they will want to be represented on the day. Harry was a deal more important when he was with The Silvers, but he died one of us. And so I shall be relying on you to put on a Good

Show for the old man ... and for our own reputation too." I knew that the Colonel had had to deal with many casualties in his time, so his rather brusque off-hand manner could be forgiven.

I contacted the nearest Gunner unit. They offered a Quad armoured tractor and limber, saying the coffin would easily fit on that. I had to 'pull rank' by reminding them we had to bury a Colonel, and that tradition demanded a 'Gun-carriage' and not a mere 'ammunition wagon'. From somewhere they obtained a suitable attachment to mount on the barrel of their 25 pounder, and they also suggested that wreaths could be carried on the limber, 'so adding to the spectacle.' It was clear enough what they meant, though I hardly liked their choice of words; and anyway, it being wartime, suitable flowers would be hard to come by.

I held a long rehearsal with the Bearers, using a borrowed, and ballasted, coffin. As a result of what I'd seen then, I had complete confidence in the six N.C.O.s and Privates, and was equally certain the Staff Sergeant could be left to control their somewhat complex movements, and also those of the Firing Party, with no more than a few softly spoken orders. I was particularly pleased that all these men, and several more, had volunteered for those duties, in a touching demonstration of their respect for 'Uncle'.

Nevertheless, on the day, I found myself pounding the thimble of his cane firmly into my palm, because the Adjutant butted in and confused the Bearer Party, by giving loud, unexpected, unnecessary and conflicting orders. All that, when he must have known about our rehearsal, and would certainly know that I had been appointed to supervise the whole affair. During the service we learned more about Uncle's past, and how he came to be twice 'Mentioned in Despatches'. The Padre also told us that Uncle's Death Certificate recorded that he 'Died from a wound sustained on Active Service, in November 1918'.

The following evening my Batman gleefully reported to me that the Adjutant had been up on the mat before the Commanding Officer, who had told him – in no uncertain terms – that he had 'let the side down very badly.' The Colonel had closed his dressing down with:-

'And finally, Captain Ward, I would ask you to remember that Lieutenant Hanson was commanding a battalion, in front line action, at a time when you yourself were a mere civilian – and barely out of safety pins at that! You May Go!' I did not of course enquire, but I had very little doubt this pleasing information came direct from the C.O's clerk; there being only a head high partition between his office and that of the Colonel next door. For the next two or three days I took a wicked pleasure in complaining loudly – in Ward's hearing – about the considerable difficulties my wife was having in obtaining any large sized safety-pins.

I continued to carry that cane and – so far as I know – nobody ever heard the Adjutant complain; nor indeed even comment on the fact that I did so. Maybe he had an inkling of what Uncle and I had planned I would do, if he did.

* * *

Although I had been returned to Full Duty, my right arm was still not right. Our Medical Officer – who had been a rising Gynaecologist before he volunteered – did try to reassure me.

"Give it time John, that's all it needs. Its only what – twelve weeks now? Just give it time." A month later our C.O. had a big purge on fitness, and we all had to go on a series of long runs. Then he found a Royal Marines' Assault Course for us to use, and this included a sprint up a ramp followed by a leap out towards a large-mesh scrambling net. That was something I'd have enjoyed a lot more when I was sixteen or seventeen, and still had my full quota of fingers and toes. As it was my left hand went through the netting, and all my weight came onto my right. Perhaps unfortunately, my remaining fingers were strong enough to take my weight. But this proved my collar bone was not as well healed as everyone thought – and it parted.

A series of X-rays, and the subsequent operation to re-set my collarbone showed that the original break was much worse than at first thought. It must have been that second fall, as I was making my way off the Moor, that did the real damage. One M.O. did murmur about a Medical Discharge, but anybody could see the war had a long time to run, and officers with battle experience were still in demand. So my arm was strapped firmly in place, and I was granted extended Sick Leave instead. Travelling home with an empty sleeve, I received pitying looks, and had the odd experience of returning salutes with my left hand. That leave ran on into Christmas; and I was able to spend much of the time with Anna, who had wangled a whole week off too. It was almost a second honeymoon – even though our activities were somewhat curtailed by my strapped up arm.

* * *

Early in March a small group of Moundshire officers and senior N.C.O.s were rushed to Cornwall where we joined others for a whole week of worsening weather 'exercising' on an Earl's Estate. Although on 'Light Duties', I was included in an Admin: role. There we spent our time fighting

– in every sense of the words – through Rhododendrons that had been allowed to run amok, growing to twelve or fifteen feet, and even higher. To show willing, I joined in, but left the heavy work of wielding machetes to the others. On the last day large dollops of ice and snow were dropping onto us each time we pushed a stem aside. Despite this, those who claimed to be 'in the know', persisted in the belief we were engaged in 'Jungle Training' which meant it was certain we'd soon be taking a very long voyage to India, and then be moved on into Burma, to fight the Japs. But after that exhausting week, we went back to watching, waiting and wondering – when and where – we'd next be sent, to get involved in some sort of active soldiering.

27. Falkenberg as PoW.

After further interrogation at the London Cage, during which he gave nothing away, Falkenberg is moved to join other officers in Prisoner of War Camp Number One, at Grizedale Hall in the Lake District. He would have found the accommodation there far better than on any U-boat. So expensive was it to run this former stately home, that a Member of Parliament asked – in the House of Commons – 'Would it not be cheaper to hold these Prisoners in the Ritz Hotel here in London?' Whilst at Grizedale, Falkenberg is closely interrogated about the loss of U-330, and how it was that he came to arrive at the Hall so many weeks after she was lost. Amongst his questioners is *Korvettenkapitän* Otto Kretschmer, the most successful U-boat commander of all time.

After several months in the splendour of Grizedale Hall, Falkenberg, together with a number of U-boat officers, is shipped to Canada on board the Canadian Pacific steamship *Duchess of York*. There being considerable anxiety expressed by the prisoners, that the ship might be torpedoed – without any warning – by one of their own U-boats. This was not the case, but there was much discomfort amongst the other PoW and Royal Air Force Flight Cadets on board, because of the uneasy motion of the ship, which led to her being widely known as '*The Rolling Duchess*'. But she did arrive safely in Quebec, and from there the Grizedale group moved on by train to Camp Number 30 at Bowmanville, on the north shore of Lake Ontario.

This Officer's Camp was based on a former Home for Delinquent Boys, with its gymnasium, indoor swimming pool and several large two storey accommodation blocks. On clear nights, the prisoners would look longingly across the lake, to the glow of lights reflected on clouds above towns and cities of the still neutral United States of America. In later months, additional wooden huts have to be built to accommodate the increasing number of Officer prisoners, who come from all three Services. The camp perimeter wire – with its nine high Watch Towers – did finally enclose some 14 acres.

The Veterans' Guard of Canada – men aged between 40 and 65 – provide most of the guards at Camp 30. Many of the prisoners had been brought up on the stories written by Karl May (whose numerous books about the Wild West were much admired by Adolf Hitler too) and they are disappointed that none of the Indians serving with the Veterans' Guard were wearing any feathers, let alone war paint. There is, however, the fear that their much vaunted tracking skills will be called upon, if any prisoners do try an escape.

Soon after his arrival at Bowmanville, Falkenberg and others receive a gift parcel from Gottfried Gruber, a member of the German-American Bund, who enclosed his address at Yaphank on Long Island, New York State. And this reminds Erich of 'Yank' Schrulle, who often bragged about his days in the USA, and time spent with the Bund, regularly attending their Camp Siegfried, at Yaphank. Erich sends a letter of thanks through a couple of teenage girls outside the camp wire. These youngsters were flattered by the attentions of handsome young German Officers, who had little difficulty persuading them to post several unauthorised – and so uncensored – letters to the U.S.A. and elsewhere. This eventually becomes known to the Camp Authorities, and firm steps are taken to prevent any repetitions.

In addition to the Officers, there are a number of *Kriegsmarine* Other Ranks at Bowmanville, serving as Batmen, or doing menial tasks around the camp. One these has charge of the furnace that provided hot water, and disposed of much of the camp's refuse – which included the contents of the waste-paper baskets in the Censor's office. He was ordered – by the Senior German Officer – to check through this paper for any useful information before feeding it into the furnace. Amongst other 'finds', he hands over two letters, both in envelopes addressed to Erich Falkenberg, and marked as coming from Gottfried Gruber at Yaphank. The first had been opened; it ended '*Hope we might meet up after the war is over*'. The second envelope had been torn almost in half – without even being opened. This letter was altogether more suggestive. '*Will be pleased to see you any time you are passing.*' Both letters were passed on to Falkenberg.

*　　*　　*

It is early December, there has been snow on the ground for days and more is expected. A loaded Laundry truck is about to leave the wired enclosure at Bowmanville, but it stalls several times. Canadian heads under the hood are joined by four 'helpful' Prisoners. Falkenberg and three others seize the opportunity to scramble over the tailgate, and hide under the bags. This is not spotted by any of the guards; but a number of PoW did see, and they now insist on giving a helpful push-start, so preventing any Guard getting near the back of the vehicle. The engine fires – uncertainly – but they continue pushing, shouting, in English, 'Do Not Stop! You Must Keep The Motor Going!' The Guard are immediately alarmed by this, thinking that the Germans may be attempting a mass break out as they continue pushing the truck. Whistles are blown, and all available Guards rush to prevent this; concentrating on getting the gates closed behind the truck – and so preventing any of the prisoners following it out. Because of this the truck is allowed to go spluttering on its way unchecked.

Five miles from camp, the escaping prisoners get the attention of the civilian driver, who gets out of the cab to investigate, and is overpowered. The escape being totally unplanned, the four have nothing with them, but what they stand up in. After a brief discussion, two of the prisoners decide they will drive on, taking the driver with them. But *Ober-Leutnant zur See* Hans Älpmann agrees with Falkenberg that the truck could too easily be recognised, and – despite his poor health – he decides that it will be wiser to continue on foot. For warmth, they both take extra clothing from the laundry bags.

Älpmann has numerous relatives in Milwaukee and he insists on heading West, aiming to cross the border at Niagara, believing that to be the quickest route into neutral U.S.A. where he would be safe from Canadian arrest. Falkenberg considers this – being the nearest border crossing point – will always be the most closely watched, and so should be avoided. Although a longer distance is involved, he favours heading East, and finding a bridge over the St Lawrence River. His intention being then to head south for Long Island, there to contact Gottfried Gruber; hoping that he – through the German-American Bund – would get in touch with German Consular Officials in New York, who might be able to arrange repatriation for 'a German national', without disclosing his PoW status.

Falkenberg and Älpmann cannot agree, and so go their separate ways. Later that same day, the truck is stopped by Royal Canadian Mounted Police near Toronto, and both Prisoners are returned to Bowmanville. There they are sentenced to 14 days Detention for escaping. For the next three days, two dummy 'officers' are carried onto parade during Roll Calls, and so both Falkenberg and Älpmann are able to 'answer' their names, loud and clear. Only on the fourth morning are the Guard allowed to discover they are two prisoners short.

More snow falls and the cold intensifies as Erich makes his way Eastwards, aiming for Montreal, with its bridges. Near Brockville he finds the river is frozen over, and he makes a risky crossing – walking on the ice – into New York State, narrowly avoiding being caught by the U.S. Border Patrol as he does so. Now in stolen civilian clothes, he boards a freight train heading South, to Utica.

* * *

It is early morning on the twelfth of December 1941, at Yaphank on Long Island, New York State. After repeated knockings, the house door is finally opened a few inches, revealing the worried and uncomprehending face of a middle-aged man.

"Herr Gruber? ich heisse Erich Falkenberg, von Bowmanville Lager, Canada."

"Mein Gott! Come in. Quickly! But no more German, and let me shut the door. Do you not know that Germany yesterday declared war on America? You did well to get here at all. But your timing is bad, very very bad! Things are now so different to when I wrote you. And you cannot stay here with me. But in one way you could not have come to a better friend. I am the Janitor of the Youth House at D.A.B. Camp Siegfried, not half a mile from here. There is nobody there now. We will go there together tonight. You will have to be very careful. No light must show, but there is a small room with no windows. And no fires either, because smoke from the chimney might be seen, but there is an electric cooking stove. I will switch the power back on and you can leave the oven door open."

* * *

Camp Siegfried, being now legally 'Enemy Property ' is considered suitable for use as an internment camp. Prior to requisitioning it, Immigration officials force an entry. They find signs somebody is living there. After a search, Falkenberg is caught hiding in the innermost room. Being unshaven, he offers the explanation that he is a hobo – and being such – has of course no papers, nor is he able to offer any other proof of identity. Police are called, and when Erich is searched his *Kriegsmarine* identity discs are found.

'I never saw no hobo a'wearin' dawg tags!' Commented the Officer. For once Officialdom does not hesitate, and Falkenberg is handed straight back to the Canadian authorities at Niagara.

On his return to Bowmanville, Falkenberg is sentenced to the routine 28 days Detention, on reduced rations, as punishment for a successful escape. When released back into the camp, he is treated as something of a hero, and is closely questioned for any information that would be useful to future escapees. But before long, new arrivals at the camp tell of rumours circulating in U-boat circles, about the circumstances surrounding the loss of U-330. Later on, other prisoners bring definite news of her being raised and used by the Royal Navy.

Then – making matters even worse – Kretschmer, as Senior Naval Officer, is notified that the body of Älpmann has been found in a farmer's shed. He had got well beyond Niagara, although still on the Canadian side of Lake Eire The cause of his death was certified as 'Uncertain – probably exposure.'

General opinion in the camp holds that Falkenberg ought to have stayed with the sick man, and so his life might have been saved. Erich's position gets steadily more perilous, and there is talk of a Council of Honour. With Kretschmer at its head, an adverse decision by such a Council would be serious indeed. There had already been beatings, and even hangings of prisoners at several other PoW camps in Canada.)

Nevertheless, despite general distrust, Falkenberg is allowed to continue his active part in digging the three escape tunnels. Two of these tunnels are only dummies, being less well concealed than the third, which they intend to complete, and use for the actual escape. The hope being that if one, or both of the dummy tunnels be discovered, the Guard – working on the assumption that the whole escape has been prevented – will be less vigilant, at least until the escape has taken place.

Kriegsmarine Officer's Quarters.
Bowmanville Prisoner of War Camp.
Ontario, Canada.

28. Erich's Second Escape.

A group of *Kriegsmarine* Officers are being addressed by *Hauptmann* Engelhardt, the Escape Officer at Bowmanville PoW Camp.

"On orders from Admiral Doenitz himself! You eight have been selected to escape, through one of the three tunnels we are now digging. Once out of this camp, you will make your own way to the East coast; there to board a U-boat for return to the Fatherland. You will travel in pairs, to an as yet Undecided location, probably the Gaspé Peninsular at the mouth of the St Lawrence River. Old Dähnhard is needed because of his highly specialised technical knowledge of Radar and its avoidance – a fact which is still not yet known to our captors. Because of his limited English and very pronounced Saxon accent, it has been agreed that he will practice being older, blind, and a little deaf. He will travel with a white stick, and on the arm of Falkenberg, who takes on the role of his son or nephew, and will always speak for him. This, because of the general misconception that anyone physically handicapped must also be mentally handicapped. Although junior in rank, and not a U-boat officer, Falkenberg is included in this escape, primarily because of helping Dähnhard, but he does have experience of escaping; both in England, and here in Canada, partly along the route you must take, where his excellent English has already proved so useful. He also has experience with beach landings. This escape will also give him a chance to redeem his doubtful reputation.

The remainder of you already know why you have been selected to return to Active Service. You will pair up together as you wish." Engelhardt then looked around, as if expecting questions. "Start practising your escape roles now. You will each be given a strict priority for boarding the U-boat; naturally Falkenberg has the lowest priority. Documents and clothing for your escape are now being prepared. The date is not yet set, but you will go before the darker nights arrive. Nobody would expect an escape attempt before then – and the weather will be better. Also, the longer the delay, the greater chance all three tunnels will be discovered. I wish you Good Luck Gentlemen! That is all for the present."

Engelhardt then stands, comes to Attention, and raises his arm stiffly to *Grüss*.

" *Heil Hitler!*" He almost shouts. Then looks around him, and shakes his head sadly. "Oh. Gentlemen! It should not be necessary for me to have to remind you of something that Falkenberg here has just shown he fully understands. No Canadian would so smartly return my *Gruss*, as most of you have just done. You must learn not to respond – in any way – to anything said in German, because that will immediately give you away."

* * *

Falkenberg knows he and Dähnhard will have to travel through Quebec Province – and possibly the City itself. So he begins to cultivate friendly relations with French-Canadians in the Veteran Guard, quite openly learning – and more subtly practising – words and phrases that will help convert his German-English into something more like French-Canadian English. However, Dähnhard can only rehearse his 'blindness' when indoors, whilst hidden from any of the more observant Guards.

Lots have been drawn to determine the order in which escapee-pairs are to leave the tunnel – after the exit has been opened for them by one of the tunnellers. It fell to Dähnhard and Falkenberg to be the first pair to go. Dähnhard, as first out, to make straight for distant cover. Falkenberg would follow, taking a cord to the nearest bushes, and lie there – waiting and watching – signalling 'Safe' or 'Stop' until the next head appears above ground, only then will he be free to join Dähnhard.

* * *

On the night, all being quiet behind them, the pair break cover and go off immediately, on their planned walk to the nearest Railway station. They have Travel Warrants – stolen only that morning from the Camp Administration Office – and these will save breaking into their meagre stock of Canadian Dollars. Ten minutes before the early morning stopping-train is due, Falkenberg exchanges the warrants for tickets to St Hyacinthe, which was as far as the warrants would take them. But, according to plan, they get off one station before that, believing it unlikely they would be expected there – even if the escape had been discovered, and a general alarm broadcast.

When they alight, they are alarmed to see Provost Corps police checking the papers of all males – civilian and military – but it is too late to re-board the train. To Falkenberg's alarm, Dähnhard becomes most difficult, clumsily bumping into people, and almost tripping up an old woman with his stick – acting as though he is trying to draw attention to them both. Erich begins to scold him, attempting to minimise the commotion as they near the barrier. But all was well, and the Provosts stood aside, considerately waving the couple through.

Afterwards, when he can speak freely, Dähnhard comments on their good fortune.

'If they were looking for us, they paid a great compliment to the *Kriegsmarine!* They knew no German Officer could ever behave like I did. But Falkenberg, when you got so angry with me, you addressed me as' *Vati'* – not as '*Papa*' And that could have been a very serious mistake!"

* * *

Falkenberg and Dähnhard, footsore and weary, having travelled almost 800 miles, have reached *Crique Charlotte,* the isolated cove some 40 miles West of *Cap Gaspé, w*here they expected to board the U-boat. There was no sign of any other escapees, but the two of them are in good time for the first scheduled pick-up, though they are alarmed to see a moderate sea running. Taking it in turn to watch all night, they even risk flashing Dash Dot Dot as the agreed recognition letter, 'D' – for *Deutschländ.* However, no answering signal comes from seaward.

The couple spent a cold wet day hiding in sparse woodland, from which they watch Catalina flying-boats patrolling the area, passing close inshore in an Easterly direction, and returning a mile and a half further out. That evening they make their way back to *Crique Charlotte,* finding themselves still alone, and the sea is now even rougher. Shortly after midnight, they spot a green light flashing Dot Dot Dash, the long awaited letter 'U' – for *U-boot.* Dähnhard replies, repeating 'D' 'D'. Again comes 'U', after which he keeps his green lit, whilst sending Falkenberg down onto the shingle, to await events.

Suddenly a rocket screeches overhead, and a thin line falls close to Falkenberg. He begins to pull on this, and by the time Dähnhard joins him, a thicker rope has appeared, tailed on the end of it. When they see 'U' again, they both haul hard on the rope, and eventually an inflatable dinghy comes in sight – bucking wildly on the waves.

Two men in civilian clothes wade ashore, cursing, as each staggers under the weight of a large suitcase. They are followed by a young *Fähnrich*, carrying a wooden box which he hands to the larger man. He then peers around in the murk, and salutes Dähnhard.

"Are there only two of you, Sir? I was expecting more. Will you please go to the U-boat now Sir? We four will remain here to unload the 'packages." Dähnhard hands the torch to Falkenberg before clambering aboard the dinghy. After 'D' it begins moving away, with Falkenberg and the *Fähnrich* keeping some tension on the rope in an attempt to control it.

"What's your rank?" asks the *Fähnrich*.

"Leutnant zur See," replies Falkenberg, "but you know what's happening. So I am at your disposal, *Herr Fähnrich*."

"We have to set up an automatic weather reporting station, on high ground further inland They've code-named it Klara, and packed most of it into ten one hundred kilo cannisters; and there are several more longer bits besides. Its going to be difficult getting that lot ashore with this sea running. Ah. Now there's 'U', so everybody pulls." He turns around. "Now where have those *verdammt* civilians gone?"

"Looks like they've bolted. Both of their cases, and the box have gone too."

"Just what you'd expect from the *Abwher!* They were meant to stay and help with the heavy stuff, but that's too much like hard work for clever sneaky spies. If they do get themselves caught before we've done, we'll be enjoying a Canadian holiday too. So, come on, *Leutnant* – Heave!"

For the first two minutes they have a hard struggle, then it is suddenly much easier. To their dismay, it soon becomes apparent something is wrong with the dinghy, though a *Matrose* could be seen clinging to it.

"Alles Kaputt!" he calls as he drags himself ashore. "That's an end of it! One of those two canisters contained the clever bits, the weather recording gear. The other was just batteries. *Herr Kapitän* will want my guts for garters. But a big wave almost turned this *Verdammt Slauchboot* over. The canisters moved and then the bottom ripped apart. Nothing at all I could do! These things should never be used at sea. Only fit for a kid's paddling pool!"

"That will do, Seaman!"' The *Fähnrich* interrupts him. "You heard what he said, Falkenberg? You go now to the U-boat. Report to *Herr Kapitän*, and say that I await his orders."

After nearly being capsized as he sat astride the tube, Falkenberg reaches the U-boat, where a Petty Officer insists he catch a rope and bowline it around his chest before attempting to leave the dinghy. Even so, he has difficulty clambering up to the deck. His report as to how both canisters were lost was not well received by the *Kapitän.*

"*Gott Himmel, Katastrophe!* And how many more of you escapees are there ashore? I've not got another dinghy. They'll have to get wet like you – whatever their rank." He seems almost relieved when told none of the other six had yet arrived. "Well you go below Falkenberg, and keep out of the way! Now Schmidt. You go ashore, tell *Fähnrich* Sebald to remove all traces of our action, and to bring all three of you back aboard – *Möglichst eilig!* Let's get away from this accursed coast fast! Go man – *Go!*"

Down below, Falkenberg looks around, and then asks for Dähnhard.

"Lost!" comes the grim reply. "He slipped, and was swept away by a wave when getting aboard. A seaman went after him. They're both lost. Can't just up anchor in this situation, and couldn't use a light to look for them either. *Für Führer und Vaterland.* " Erich's informant gives a derisive salute, and turns away. Shaken by this news, Falkenberg stands listening to the orders being given on the bridge above him.

"Stand by motors. Prepare to raise anchor. When the dinghy returns, get them all aboard, then puncture it and let the damn thing float away, but for God's sake make sure the ropes don't get around our screws!" Ten minutes later there was a warning of distant propeller noise, and Falkenberg could hear faint Asdic pings too. Men are soon sliding down the ladder into the control room. The hatch above is slammed shut, and the Captain lands beside him.

"Motors Slow ahead. Up Anchor. Steer 120. Stand by to dive!" He then turns to Erich. "Well *Leutnant,* I do hope Admiral Doenitz thinks you are of sufficient importance. You are all we've got to show for everything we've risked tonight. Who was it that we lost? The old man who went overboard? I suppose I'll have to recommend our *Matrose* for some award, though the fool must have known he'd not got a chance of getting that old man back on board, nor that we could go chasing after them both."

* * *

Two nights later U-781 returns, and for the next five nights she lies surfaced off *Crique Charlotte,* staying there from midnight until first light. But no response comes to her cautious signals. On the last night she again leaves hurriedly, pursued by Asdic pings and several uncomfortably close depth charges.

*　　　*　　　*

Toronto Star. 30/10/42.

News has just been released that last month 2 German spies were arrested, after coming ashore from a submarine near Cap Gaspé. They had with them a watertight box holding $ 20,000 in genuine Canadian notes, and forged English £5 notes totalling £1500.

In addition they had a variety of explosives some even disguised as lumps of coal. Also timing devices, fuse and detonators.

In the following days an inflatable rubber dinghy was recovered. Two bodies were found on the shore. One, in the uniform of a German seaman. The other, in civilian clothes, has been identified as a German Naval officer, one of eight who escaped from the Bowmanville (Ontario) Prisoner of War camp on August 30th. Six are already back in the camp. But one is still not yet accounted for.

Depth charges were dropped, but it is thought the U-boat got away.

It will be remembered Bowmanville camp was the scene of serious rioting by the Officer Prisoners early in the month.

The following messages were encoded on board U-boats, using their Enigma machine, and then transmitted by radio to U-boat Headquarters, on the Avenue Maréchal Maunoury in Paris.

These were intercepted, and then decoded at Bletchley Park using 'Ultra':-

1942.

September 17. Klara lost overboard. Only Falkenberg on board.
To patrol CA.* U781

September 23. 2 sunk 3780 tons. Depth-charged. Damaged.
Fuel Low. U781.

September 28. Supplied Fuel, Torpedoes & Stores to U781 – U463.

October 14. Depth-charged. Damaged. All torpedoes expended.
Returning to base. U781.

November 3. Sighted Large Convoy. CE 16 . Heading WSW
10 knots. No Torpedoes. Shadowing. U781.

* Square CA was the sea area off the coast of U.S.A. between Boston and Norfolk, Virginia.

Square CE 16 being almost mid-atlantic.

29. John In North Africa.

Having been neglected for so long, we Moundshires were amongst the first to be given a demonstration of a very new – and at that time very secret – weapon. This being the 'Projector, Infantry, Anti-Tank', thankfully shortened to 'Piat'. With its bomb-shaped and very scientific hollow charge projectile, this was – so we were assured – going to be most effective against even well armoured tanks, at a range of up to 100 yards. And that would certainly be a vast improvement on the cumbersome and discredited 1937 Boys A/T rifle. I quickly realised that if we had had a Piat, when I was with the North Ridings, I would have dragged it forward, and – taking full advantage of its having a much longer range than any hand thrown grenade – I'd have destroyed our own tank well before that all-too English expletive could be uttered to save it.

Even when one was lying prone behind the Piat, it was a force to be reckoned with. It did not so much 'Kick' like a rifle, rather it gave one's shoulder an almighty 'Shove' that could slide a grown man back several inches. Six of us officers were allowed to fire a practice round, and afterwards I made much of the fact that I alone had been man enough not to lose my side cap, when thrust backwards so suddenly. To be honest, I was last to go, and having seen the others disgrace themselves – to the undisguised amusement of the watching N.C.O.s – I jammed my cap very firmly in place, and so came through triumphant. In fact I had caused consternation by settling down to fire that Piat left-handed.

"Wrong way round, Sir," hissed the exasperated Sergeant-Instructor. "You can't see the sights if yer tries to fire it left-'anded."

"With this damn great trigger, Sergeant, I'll need all four fingers." At that I held up my right hand to him. (And that must be a rare case of an Officer and a Gentleman being correct when giving 'Two Fingers' to an

N.C.O.) "And what you cannot see, is that I have a dodgy right collar bone that just wouldn't take the strain. So – taken all in all – I think you'll have to agree, that for me at least, my way is best, Sergeant." It was suggested later that I should have opted out of that firing, but I certainly wasn't going to miss a chance of playing with the Infantry's newest 'toy'.

Quite suddenly the Moundshire's training took on a new focus. It was apparent that somebody knew what lay ahead of us – but naturally that was Top Secret. We spent our time 'Exercising' on Dartmoor, under strange Training Officers. They kept us endlessly moving position, meeting only tiny pockets of 'resistance' which surrendered quite happily. It was noticeable that we almost never launched a serious attack on anybody – certainly there was no suggestion of an organised enemy to our immediate front. The Colonel eventually worked out that we were to have the unglamorous role of Support Troops, mopping up behind the main advance. He cheerfully summarised the possibilities.

"As long as that lasts, none of you are likely to get a proper gong, but more will live to collect one of those nice Campaign Stars that are being rumoured."

After the first day on the Moor, it was apparent that most of our younger men – those who had joined us after Dunkirk – had no idea how to handle Prisoners of War. Afterwards I gave them a brief talk on how to behave in this respect, and – to enliven matters – I had them all reciting *"Handy Hock!"* and *"Fuere zee Fritz, der kreeeg tsu endy isst!"* ... as I had written it on the blackboard for them. After all, it was well known that every German could say *"For you Tommi, ze war iss ofer!"* And I thought our lads should do be able to do at least as well. Though it came as a nasty afterthought – that maybe the average Japanese would not be acquainted with either version.

* * *

Dusk on October 28th 1942 saw me still with the 5th battalion Moundshires, on board a camouflage-painted Hired Transport, slipping down the Firth of Clyde from Gourock. In company with many other ships, we were bound for some unknown destination. All we did know was that our newly issued clothing was suitable for a warm climate. In anticipation of a long voyage through the Tropics, I managed to get myself appointed in charge of men who had volunteered as extra Gun Crew on the elderly 4 inch, and two 20 mm Oerlikons we carried as 'Defensive Armament'. I had quickly realised that this duty would get me out on deck every time there was an alarm. And – so it was rumoured – when it got hot, we would be allowed to sleep at the guns. Whereas, others, sweltering down below – some even below the waterline – would have little possibility of even reaching the open deck, let alone boats or rafts, if the ship was torpedoed.

We skirted the north coast of Ireland, and only then were we told that we were engaged in Operation Torch, and would head out into the Atlantic, firstly to mislead the enemy about our intentions, and secondly in the hope of avoiding U-boats. Then, as part of the newly formed First Army, consisting of American, Free French and British troops, we would be landed in North Africa, to attack the rear of Rommel's *Afrika Korps*.

Our Hired Transport was an ageing Cargo-Passenger liner, whose holds had been hurriedly converted into troop space. We soon re-christened her *Dilatory Dora*, from her habit of slowing or stopping, due to recurrent engine troubles. When temporary repairs had been effected, she'd go at full speed to catch up with the convoy. Five days out, when *Dora* was lagging far behind as usual, the alarm was sounded, and at first it seemed this was yet another false panic. Then, well after midnight, I saw star-shells bursting perhaps a couple of miles to starboard. Our two escorts dashed off to assist – leaving us feeling very much alone. There was gunfire and depth charges, which even at that distance, really hammered our hull.

"Sounds like somebody's having Guy Fawkes night early." Quipped our Joker. "But I could never buy bangers like those. Pity the poor sods who are on the receiving end." In the morning, after we had re-joined the convoy, the Tannoy announced that it was considered 'probable' that a U-boat had been sunk close by. Shortly afterwards the whole convoy wheeled around and headed for Africa.

With only two more false alarms, we passed through the Straits of Gibraltar and reached Algiers on the eighth of November. We could consider ourselves fortunate to be in The Reserve, and so it was not until evening that *Dora* was brought alongside in Algiers harbour, amidst signs of earlier fierce resistance by Vichy French troops. The landings generally had gone well, despite difficulties over negotiations with the Vichy Government authorities and some of their troops. However, the Germans were taken by surprise and Allied forces advanced rapidly, seizing Bougie and Bone, but Jerry moved quickly enough to prevent us from taking Tunis.

Despite our 'Reserve' tag, the Moundshires were all too soon in front line action and so our 'Support' training on Dartmoor was of little use. Nevertheless when our first German Prisoner was brought to me, his captor proudly announced.

"I told him 'Handy Hock' and the rest, and then the blighter started jabbering on, expecting I'd understand all that too." The prisoner was a former school teacher, and old enough to be my father. It was clear he had no wish to be in the army, let alone in Africa, and he was glad enough to be captured. Fritz was surprised at my German, even complimented me on it. With very little encouragement he talked freely, giving me some useful information. I sent him back – kept separate from other prisoners – with a note strongly recommending that he be interrogated further, and urging that should happen before he was allowed to mix with any other Germans. There were, I knew, many *Waffen SS* men already 'in the bag' and some of them would almost certainly 'persuade' him not to talk.

During the next month we Moundshires were heavily engaged, and took casualties at all ranks, so I was once again Acting Major. Replacements from the home Depot were expected at Bougie, and I was sent back to meet them. En route, needing fuel for the Jeep, and food for my driver and myself, I followed signs to an American Supply Depot. Even before we had come to a stop at the barrier, a white-helmeted gum-chewing Military Policeman was bawling at us.

"Why ain't you guys a'wearin' yu're goddam helmets. You know the goddam orders." In response I spoke slowly, and softly.

"Corporal. Will you please tell me why I should be wearing my helmet? We are at least twenty five miles from the nearest enemy artillery. And I cannot see a single aeroplane in the sky." My enunciation had been perfect, and very very 'English.' But neither that, nor my rank, made any impression on the 'Snowdrop.'

"Doesn't matter bud. Its General's goddam Orders. Any one who doesn't wear his goddam helmet does K.P. Or even worse "

"Tell me please, Corporal. Does your General wear one of those nicely polished helmets, with the bright stars on the front?"

"Yep. He sure does!"

"And does he get any nearer the Front than this?"

"Yep. He sure does. Th'ol Mans a real fire-eater!"

"Well Corporal. You take my good advice. Don't you go with him. The sun glinting on that helmet would bring down fire from every battery within a five mile radius ... and your own smart white-painted helmet, will make you yourself a perfect target for every half-awake sniper."

* * *

At Bougie docks I was far from pleased to be greeted by Captain Ward, who 'forgot' to give me the salute due to my new rank. (During Embarkation Leave prior to our sailing for 'Torch', Ward had gone sick – very conveniently – or so many thought it.) Now our Adjutant was in charge of the newcomers. Having got them into trucks, Ward was most insistent that he should drive my Jeep, because he'd never had the chance to drive one before. My Driver looked at me questioningly. I nodded, he shrugged his shoulders, and climbed into the back seat.

Some twenty miles, and several very noisy gear changes later, we were well ahead of the trucks. (Ward prided himself on being a good, fast driver – though only the latter half of that was in any way true.) The area had been fought over twice and was heavily mined. The roads and verges had been swept clear, and broad white 'Tapes Tracing' marked the limit of that clearing. Beyond them the usual battlefield litter blew about in a gusting wind.

Suddenly – and without any warning – Ward jammed on the brakes, nearly putting my head into the windscreen; and behind me the Driver swore audibly.

"Did you see that?" Demanded Ward, crashing the gears into reverse. Thirty yards back we jerked to a standstill, Ward pointing excitedly. "I saw a bit of paper or something move clear of that Luger. I'm going to have it. I've always wanted one of those!"

"Leave it man." I told him. "Its too far beyond the tape."

"No. I can get it easily." He jumped out and ran around the Jeep, shouting to me. "They always lay the tape well inside the cleared area. I know – because I went on a Course once.".

"Don't be a bloody fool!" I yelled. "Its not worth it – and it could be booby-trapped!" Ward was never one to take advice, nor even orders, from a 'Mere Amateur'. He put one foot well over the tape. As he did so I turned my back on him; behind me the driver flattened himself, muttering. 'Bloody Fool Officers!' Even at full stretch Ward could not reach that pistol. His next step was his last, and I was blown sideways from the Jeep, almost taking the steering column with me.

I had been peppered with fragments, and my left arm was smashed 'Beyond Economical Repair' – as our storekeeper would have described it. The Driver was luckier, receiving only one large fragment in his backside, which probably caused him rather more embarrassment than pain.

I never did shed any tears over the demise of Captain Ward. Maybe the stupid Bastard had managed to get his own back on me in the end. It still irks me that his name will have an honoured place on some War Memorial, alongside those of men who were worth at least three of him.

*   *   *

One month later I was in England again, and contemplating life as a civilian, having been advised that this time I would definitely get a Medical Discharge, and that just as soon as they judged I was fit enough to leave hospital. But at least it meant I would be able to resume uninterrupted married life, with Anna – and the baby we were both eagerly expecting.

John Hardwicke's medals.

Epilogue.

Now that my story was ended, I sat watching the boy, waiting for his reaction. At first he didn't move, and I thought he might have fallen asleep.

"That baby turned out to be your father." I had spoken rather louder than necessary, but he seemed to ignore that when he turned to me.

"Gramps. Is that why I was christened Eric – and Dad too?"

"That's right." I told the boy. "We named your father Eric, for my friend, and William for his Grandfather Van Dieman. And then you, only the other way round. Erich was a very good friend to me, and a brave one too. You should be proud to bear his name, Bill. Its a thousand pities that we had to be on opposite sides – to become enemies; and that he should die in that U-boat as I was on my way to North Africa. I do wish you could have met him, for had he lived, he'd have been a sort of honorary Great Uncle to you. I'm sure Erich would have liked you – he'd probably describe you as *Flink – Zäh – und Hart.*"

Young Bill looked up at that, with just a hint of the look that reminded me so much of Erich.

"Vlink? Tsaey?" He murmured – almost to himself – knowing the remark was complementary, but pretending he was too modest to ask for a full translation.

"SWIFT – as a Greyhound," I told him, "TOUGH – as leather. And HARD – as Krupp steel, like Erich's *Fahrtenmesser* ... which I know he'd like you to have. It's lain hidden away in my desk all these years – but its your's now. You should treasure it Bill, because it is a little bit of England's history, and an important part of your own family history too. If I had been foolish and tried to deal with the Porthyn Pryva transmitter on my own, that could easily have been the end of me. Then nobody would ever have found that knife – and you, Young Bill, would never even have been so much as a twinkle in your Daddy's eye." Bill gave me a broad wink and a nod at this. (When the lad was younger, neither of his parents would ever give him a straight answer when he asked about the facts of life, and eventually he'd come to me. I told him as much as he needed to know then, and more later on, but it had to be our secret. Had Maureen got to know that her son had 'gone behind her back', and that I'd been 'meddling' in such a matter, there would certainly have been trouble – for Young Bill – if not for the both of us.)

Even though he must have realised I had nothing more to tell, the boy sat staring silently into the flames. I didn't want to break into his thoughts, but I did want him to tell me what he'd made of my tale – before I handed over Erich's *Fahrtenmesser,* and packed him off home. Stiffly he got up and stood in front of me.

"Although you wouldn't set that bomb to kill him, you knew you had to do it, Gramps – to put your Country first – even at the risk of your friend's life." He spoke softly, and yet with an understanding beyond his years. "It was the right thing to do, the only thing you ought to have done. And that last time, up on the Moor, that was honourable too – just as Erich told you – and it was right too. Though I do hope I'll never be faced with such terrible choices. But, even I have learned, that you can't always be friends with your best friend – not all the time anyway." He gave me a wry smile, and gingerly rubbed his swollen eye. "But Gramps ... you should have seen the blood on Graham's shirt! And I'll beat him next time – if there has to be a next time. But don't you worry – we'll be friends till then – and real friends too ... like you and Uncle Erich."

And how my old *Kamarad* would have liked to hear the boy say that.

An der Atlantischer Ozean, am 3. November 1942
unser sonniger Junge, unser einziger lieber Sohn,
Neffe und Vetter.

Erich Emil Falkenberg

Leutnant zur See, in einem U-boot.

Inhaber des E.K.11.

Ein Kriegsgefangener flucht zurück ins Vaterland.

Kurz nach Vollendung des 21. Lebensjahr nach
treuester Pflichterfüllung für Führer und Vaterland,
den Seemannstod starb. Unsere ganze Hoffnung
und Lebensfreude ist dahin, seine und unsere
Wünsche blieben unerfüllt.

In tiefstem Schmerz:
Frau Helga Falkenberg, geb Hoffer
und die übrigen Anverwandten.

Fürth, den 18. Oktober 1944.
Lantstrasse 15.

Whilst researching for this story, the author accumulated a collection of Hitler Youth items, documents, and historical facts. The knowledge so gained – together with some 950 illustrations, 100 of them in full colour – are published in the three volumes of Youth Led By Youth, Vilmor Publications.

Included are personal accounts, told to him, in Germany, by those who spent months or years in the Hitler Youth, in both peace and wartime. They ranged from the lowest boys and girls, to very high ranking officers.

About the Author.

Although slightly younger, the author lived through the same stirring times as his characters. He well remembers some of the activities, events, emotions and places mentioned in this story. He has also incorporated a few of his own personal experiences, in and out of uniform.

In the Royal Air Force, he encountered the often-questionable wisdom of Rules, Regulations and Higher Ranks. These he frequently circumvented or frustrated, as does 'John Hardwicke', the principle character, and narrator, of **'Not Quite A Judas'.**

Whilst researching for this book, the author visited Germany, and there met former members of the Hitler Youth, with widely varying ranks. Their experiences, and attitudes, are included. At the same time, he built up a collection of uniforms, badges, documents etc; and the accumulated knowledge of these has been worked into 'Not Quite A Judas', and into the three volumes of his **'Youth Led By Youth',** Vilmor Publications.

Lightning Source UK Ltd.
Milton Keynes UK
171644UK00002B/34/P